Hannah Emery writes women's fiction and studied an MA in Creative Writing at Manchester Metropolitan University. She has worked in higher education on student achievement and outcomes for over fifteen years. She works at the University of Lancashire and lives with her husband and two children.

Also by Hannah Emery

Secrets in the Shadows
The Secrets of Castle Du Rêve
The Start of Us
The New Year's Eve Party

EVERYONE HAS SOMETHING TO HIDE

HANNAH EMERY

One More Chapter
a division of HarperCollins*Publishers* Ltd
1 London Bridge Street
London SE1 9GF
www.harpercollins.co.uk
HarperCollins*Publishers*
Macken House, 39/40 Mayor Street Upper,
Dublin 1, D01 C9W8, Ireland

This paperback edition 2025
1
First published in Great Britain in ebook format
by HarperCollins*Publishers* 2025
Copyright © Hannah Emery 2025
Hannah Emery asserts the moral right to be identified
as the author of this work

A catalogue record of this book is available from the British Library
ISBN: 978-0-00-879492-7

This novel is entirely a work of fiction. The names, characters and incidents portrayed in it are the work of the author's imagination. Any resemblance to actual persons, living or dead, events or localities is entirely coincidental.
Printed and bound in the UK using 100% Renewable Electricity
by CPI Group (UK) Ltd
All rights reserved. No part of this publication may be reproduced, stored in a retrieval system, or transmitted, in any form or by any means, electronic, mechanical, photocopying, recording or otherwise, without the prior permission of the publishers.
Without limiting the exclusive rights of any author, contributor or the publisher of this publication, any unauthorised use of this publication to train generative artificial intelligence (AI) technologies is expressly prohibited. HarperCollins also exercise their rights under Article 4(3) of the Digital Single Market Directive 2019/790 and expressly reserve this publication from the text and data mining exception.

To Lindsey and Lee (who definitely make life more bearable).

ONE

Sadie

'I asked you not to do it,' Sadie said as she arranged Blake's roses.

Her daughter had been presented with the flowers an hour earlier at her final school performance of *Into the Woods*. They were yellow, strongly perfumed and doomed to die a horrible death in this brutal July heat. For days, Kings Hill West had been burning and luminous, the sun blazing on and on. It was impossible to sleep, to walk anywhere, eat anything hot or *do* anything. Tonight, as she'd watched Blake on the stage and fanned herself with the thin paper programme, Sadie had thought she might pass out.

The flowers would last a few days at best.

'You were great in the play, Blake,' Rob said. 'I loved it.' He moved over to the French doors and flung them open. 'This weather. It's unbearable.'

'I loved you in the play, too. Watching you was incredible.' Sadie meant it. She really had loved it, in a way.

For a few moments, Sadie had enjoyed watching Blake on the school stage more than anything she'd done in years: tall, caramel-limbed, hair the same blonde as Sadie's, a voice as high and clear as a bright blue sky. Curves that promised a body more feminine than Sadie had ever had. Rob's sharp cheekbones and subtly angled face. Sadie's whole world. 'But, Blake, making yourself so *available* online is asking for trouble, and that's why I asked you not to do it. Mrs Brayer told me she'd seen your story, that you'd probably go viral.' That word said it all. Unseen spores contaminating everything, impossible to clean away. Thomas, the head of music, had even gone on stage and named Blake, thanking her and some of the other leads. Sadie's stomach swirled at the memory of it. Hundreds of people watching, hearing Blake's name, finding her on Instagram probably, and knowing way too much in just the click of a button.

Blake let out an exasperated puff of air. 'I barely even posted anything.' She threw her words at Sadie casually, not even looking up from her phone.

That *phone*.

Rob sighed too and stepped outside, even though it was probably even hotter out there than in the kitchen. Something shifted in the garden as he did, a flicker of a shadow, a movement of light. Sadie's chest tightened but she kept quiet, feeling the tightrope below her, the huge black drop beneath.

When Sadie got home from her job teaching music at Kings Hill High the next day, the last day of the summer term, the house was empty.

Rob was on a late ambulance shift and he wouldn't be home until the early hours, but Sadie had expected signs of Blake being back from school: biscuit crumbs, a Diet Coke can, pop music, the scent of vanilla perfume so sweet it almost smelled toxic. Things that her colleagues with teenage girls moaned about in the staffroom, but that Sadie held close.

Today, there was nothing but silence and heat. It was as though Blake hadn't been there in days.

The gleaming double doors to the kitchen diner were not flung open.

The magazines on the oak coffee table in the lounge were still meticulously fanned out, the cushions plumped.

Blake's bedroom, from the doorway, appeared surface-tidy. Her double bed was made, complete with a faux-fur throw and mint-green scatter cushions. Blake's books and laptop were stacked neatly on the desk. Musical theatre posters lined the wall, perfectly spaced and aligned: *West Side Story*; *Grease*; *Wicked*. A single sock on the floor was the only blemish. Having said that, Sadie knew if she went digging (which she would *not*) there would be clothes stuffed into the wardrobe and loose pages of paper wedged into drawers. There would be things Sadie didn't know about. The thought of it made the back of her neck prickle, and she reached up and pushed her short blonde hair away from her hot skin.

Sadie went back downstairs and unlocked the French

doors, stepping outside into the scalding afternoon. The air smelled of charred meat and scorched grass. There had been various garden parties on Radley Drive over the last week, and Sadie had heard the repeated clink of wine bottles and the tinkle of thoughtful music and conversations through her open windows. Nobody ever partied late into the night, though: the short row of houses in one of the nicest parts of Sussex belonged to people who knew how to control themselves.

The neighbours never bothered inviting Sadie and Rob to their garden parties because they knew Sadie wouldn't go anywhere to socialise, even sedate gatherings. The invitations had stopped years ago. Rob had battled Sadie's refusals at first. Now, he didn't even bother. They'd moved to Kings Hill West about sixteen years ago when Sadie was pregnant with Blake. The houses were within walking distance of the lower end of the town which had good baby groups and people with expensive changing bags and bang-on-trend prams to push along the tree-lined streets.

Sadie had made loads of friends at first. And then she'd made the one who had changed everything, the one she should have avoided.

Sadie stepped back inside, pulled her phone from her black leather handbag and called Blake.

Voicemail.

She checked WhatsApp: Blake last seen 4.23pm.

Sadie exhaled, the noise louder than she expected in the empty kitchen. It was 4.55pm now. The walk from where Kings Hill High sat, at the very middle point between Kings Hill East and Kings Hill West, was only a half hour walk from their house, and the school day had ended at 3pm. One hour and fifty-five minutes ago. That was a lot of minutes for things to go wrong.

She pressed call again, but when the ringing went unanswered she clicked on the tracking app she shared with Rob and Blake.

Location not found.

It was after another two hours, the terrible heat and worry making it almost impossible to breathe, that Sadie messaged Rob. He called her a few minutes later. Rob used to call Sadie about plans for their evening all the time, sometimes just to say hi. She couldn't remember the last time he'd done that.

'Maybe she's at the beach?' Rob offered after she'd told him that she was worried. Sadie closed her eyes for just a moment and saw a winding road leading to cliffs and screaming gulls. Her eyes flew open again.

'She knows we don't like her going there.'

'Exactly. So she wouldn't tell us if she did. I'm just trying to think like a fifteen-year-old girl. She's probably just with some boy. Kissing.' Rob groaned. 'Or worse.'

'I just wish…'

'She's not going to tell you everything about herself and what she's been up to. She's a normal teenager.'

Sadie thought about when she was a teenager. Smoke, bottles, strangers she wanted nothing to do with. Rough hands on her skin. Her mother's laughter belting out from another room. 'I suppose.'

'It's not going to be like you and your mum,' Rob said, reading her mind and injecting a little sharpness into his voice. He knew so much – too much – about Sadie's mother. He'd been one of the paramedics who knew her by name, which meant that Sadie saw him often, mostly when Sadie was at her worst. He had been the one there nineteen years ago, when Sadie's mum had put herself into her final alcohol blackout and her poor organs had given in. After he'd taken her mother's body away, Sadie had thought that she'd never see Rob again. But then he had come back for her. He'd gone to every single one of Sadie's concerts back when she played as a pianist, and he'd kept every one of her programmes. That was the kind of thing that Sadie might have thought was a bit much before she met Rob. She'd always imagined being with someone a bit stand-offish. But then Rob had come along with his strength and kindness, and he'd made her imaginary stand-offish man seem like a horrible choice in comparison.

Rob had spent his early inheritance on a house with Sadie and built a home and a family with her. He'd been careful and funny, and he'd helped her glue herself back together. But Rob had lost his parents too, he sometimes reminded her. And he didn't behave like this, he'd added once, although he'd looked immediately guilty, as though he wanted to scoop up the words and pop them back in his mouth.

'I didn't hear anything at school about anyone going to the beach,' Sadie said. 'And I was on rota duty at break and lunch today.' There was a short silence. Sadie did this too much: listened to the children's plans and sprang them on Blake like magic tricks. *I know the year tens are heading to Sam Taylor's house for a party tonight. And I know his parents are away. Ta-daa!* It was such an annoying thing to do but she couldn't help it for some reason. Blake definitely found it annoying. Rob probably did too.

'Anyway,' Sadie said, pressing on. 'I've messaged Evie's mum. Evie hasn't seen Blake since they left school, although apparently Blake has plans to stay over at Evie's house tonight.'

'Okay. Well, let's just both keep trying to call her. And if she's not been in touch in another couple of hours, then maybe we—'

'Yep. Got it.' Sadie knew what Rob was going to say, but she couldn't even begin to consider the police and all their questions. Panic flickered inside her. If it would protect Blake, she would simply have to tell them everything. If she wanted the anxiety gone, she'd have to pick it up and carry it away herself.

But then what?

And why, they would all ask, are you only just telling us all this now, ten years later?

Sadie would say that she didn't know for sure what happened. That she'd believed Maddy.

But she hadn't believed her really, had she? She'd just wanted to believe her, and there was a whole, frightening world of difference between the two.

At first, when those hideous images had arrived in the post, Sadie had been so frightened of losing all the tangible things she valued. She'd worried about what Rob would think, and about their jobs. She'd thought about their house in Kings Hill West with its double front and nice, big garden. The fear was at its sharpest when she thought of

Blake and the risk of not being able to touch her daughter's clean golden curls or achingly soft cheeks. But now, after all this time, it had become obvious that there was so much more than all that to lose.

If Sadie had told the truth about what she'd suspected all that time ago, when the newspeople were asking for anyone to come forward with information, when she had known that the police had been led down a path that might be the wrong one, those things might have all come back to her, eventually.

Now, it all felt too late. It also felt like she was close to losing a lot of it anyway.

'Look, I've got to go,' Rob said. Sadie heard noise beyond: sirens and movement. She didn't know how he could stand it. All the blood he saw, all the broken lives and mess and horror.

Maybe it was easier when it wasn't your own fault.

Sadie hung up and stared out of her wide lounge window. Radley Drive and the surrounding areas were not the old money, rambling houses of Kings Hill East, but it was still a very desirable area. Close enough to London to visit in a day. Sadie and Rob had only managed to afford to buy their house because of Rob's parents and their fortunate combination of being careful with money and also dead (what an awful thing to think). But anyway, Sadie and Blake lived in a place that should be *safe*. The streets of Kings Hill West were not the kinds of streets where Sadie might be worried that Blake had been mugged in an alley or persuaded by hooded boys to hang out in a park and smoke joints and do inconceivable things. From her window, Sadie saw perfectly spaced trees, rich with glossy leaves: spacious lawns; a gleaming Range Rover reversing gently onto a wide driveway across the road. And then a figure coming into focus from around the corner: a hot pink cropped top, little denim shorts, long brown legs.

Sadie rushed outside. The burning tarmac scalded her bare feet.

'Blake!' She grabbed her daughter and hugged her tightly, even though she could feel Blake pulling away like an irritated cat. There was a scent tangled in Blake's smooth golden hair other than her usual vanilla. It was salt and something deeper, like old expensive leather. It made Sadie feel nauseous, and she stepped back.

'Where have you been? I've been so worried!'

'I know. I have about a million missed calls. I'm fifteen years old. It's literally been a couple of hours.'

'Why didn't you answer?'

'Because I've been doing stuff.'

What stuff, and where, and who were you with? Sadie wanted to grab Blake's hand and never let it go, so that she could never lose her or let her get broken or hurt.

'You should have told me where you were, Blake.'

'It's not really something I can talk about yet,' Blake said as they went into the house, the wide hallway lit golden by the evening sun. She flung her school bag down: she must have gone out straight from school, and taken a change of clothes with her. 'But it's good,' Blake added hurriedly, throwing a quick smile in Sadie's direction. Maybe it was something about college, where Blake wanted to study performing arts, be famous, launch herself into the public eye. Or maybe she'd been performing something that would be shared online, duplicated and passed from person to person. It was like trying to stop an express train.

'Look, I know you think I'm on you like this just to be annoying...' Sadie began. Blake stared back at her, her pretty face becoming defiant. *Yeah. I do think that.* 'But I need to know where you are, and what you're doing. I need to check out your plans first, before you go ahead with them.'

'So every single thing I do this summer, I need to ask you first?' Blake looked in the huge round feature mirror beside her and puffed her hair up. It fell across her eyes and she squinted at her flawless reflection, then smoothed it down again.

Sadie thought of her own mother, oblivious to day and night. What she'd have given for her to ask where Sadie was going or who with. To even be conscious for most of the time. 'Well, yes.'

Blake carried on staring at her reflection, fiddling with strands of blonde hair. 'You're meant to be giving me more freedom, Mum. This is the first night of the summer holidays. Everyone else's parents are letting them have fun and you're basically acting like I'm twelve.'

'Yes, because it's dangerous when nobody knows where you are.'

'Oh my *God*, Mum. Life around here is boring. It is *not* dangerous.' Blake turned back to Sadie, her blue eyes cool.

Had it really been so long ago that Blake had gobbled up everything that Sadie said, with her big earnest eyes; that she'd crawled into Sadie's lap, chubby arms tight around Sadie's neck, so close to her that their warm breaths were mingled together, straight from Blake's lungs to Sadie's? So long ago that Sadie felt she could protect her child from anything because she knew where she was every single second of every single day? It was so *hard* to not be able to protect her now, like she'd been able to then. Sadie didn't care about Blake any less now that she was older. If anything, she loved her more because she knew who Blake was now. She knew how much there was to lose. And she knew how she'd feel if someone hurt her.

She'd hunt them down, and she'd kill them.

TWO

Maddy

Maddy Archer, alone in the orangery with an ice-cold glass of Sancerre, stared down at the text message that had arrived that morning. Gregory had been upstairs for ages doing God knew what. Maddy's new blue diamond Piaget watch told her that Eliot should have been home by now: pink-cheeked and sweaty and smelling of the other pink-cheeked and sweaty year-six children in his class. She'd not put up much of a fight when Eliot had asked if he could walk home from school alone. He was tall and looked much older than the other children in his year. He got his height from Gregory, and Maddy was glad for him. Nobody wanted to inherit Maddy's squatness. She was lucky she had good hair (glass-shiny and almost black), good boobs and clear skin, otherwise it would have been game over for her from the very start, even when she'd been young.

Maddy locked her phone so that the message disappeared. Her screen went black but her body was still tight with tension.

What a game changer. Ten years of silence. And now this. Things were suddenly different and Maddy couldn't work out what had changed. Somehow Sadie was braving it (or faking it?) and actually wanting to spend time together again. It was a gear change that Maddy had not expected after so long. There had to be more to it.

Maddy took a sip of wine, and as her glass slid down to empty, Gregory finally wandered in, his loafers tapping on the Georgian oak floorboards. He was wearing his blue suit – one of his favourites – and smelled of the Gucci aftershave she'd bought him for his birthday the month before.

Maddy looked over at him. 'I'll come with you to the Masquerade Ball tomorrow.' She tried to make her words even. Maybe the message from Sadie meant nothing. Or maybe it wasn't really even from Sadie. The thought made it feel like a drip of icy Sancerre was travelling down Maddy's spine.

Maddy had been disappointed with Sadie's silence at first. Their growing friendship had been so important to her, but it'd all seemed to go so wrong on that awful night.

Yet another thing Pearl had tried to take from her.

Sadie obviously wanted nothing more to do with Maddy, even after Maddy had sent on those awful photos. And that hurt. She hadn't been able to stop wondering how she might become close to Sadie again, to reinstate what had been increasingly regular meet-ups at The Cellar for wine and coffee. But then Gregory and Maddy's life had begun to glitter with more money and a bigger house. There had been no mention of Pearl, from either of them. Their marriage, which Maddy had thought might be drowning, had risen and taken a gulp of breath. Gregory's book sales had skyrocketed and so it had reached the point where there had been more and more to lose. Maddy had started to think that leaving her friendship with Sadie behind, and everything that bound them together, might be for the best after all. Sadie probably did miss Maddy, but she was sensible and knew that being friends might drag things up that needed to stay buried. Gregory's book launches, trending posts and interviews had continued, and the public eye, suspended above them, watched everything Maddy and Gregory did. Then there had been prizes, and advertising and all the things that had made them richer than the thing Gregory had started out doing, which had been writing thrillers he never even thought would be published. *Who* magazine had done a feature on Maddy and Gregory and there had been a podcast where they had chatted together about the meaning of success.

Returning to a friendship with Sadie and even *mentioning* that night, the lie Maddy had told, would be like a soldier dismounting his horse in the midst of winning a battle.

It made no sense. So why was Sadie back, now of all times?

'Maddy?' Gregory was looking down his square Prada glasses at her, his hands deep in the pockets of his pale blue linen trousers, jangling money, keys, whatever else he had in there. 'Did you hear me? I think it's fantastic that you're coming. White Feather is such an excellent cause, and we both need to support it. Plus, you know that it's sponsored by Vibe, don't you?'

'Yes, I know.' Vibe was Maddy's enormous, glass-fronted gym where she took classes and bought smoothies that promised eternal youth and happiness and tasted of grass. And of course, Maddy and Gregory had already been to a Vibe-sponsored ball ten years ago. That night.

It had been the first Vibe ball, and its theme had been *Gatsby*. It hadn't been a particularly impressive event, from what Maddy could remember – they'd become bigger and better over time – and probably hadn't even raised much money for whatever its cause had been. Even if it had, the whole night had been eclipsed by what had happened afterwards.

Maddy glanced down at her phone again and opened it, hot fear pooling in her stomach. Her reply to the message from Sadie (*See you there x*) hung on the screen giving nothing away.

'I'll regret it if I miss it,' she told Gregory.

'Good girl. I think you're absolutely right.' Gregory seemed distracted as he spoke. He glanced towards the door and pulled at the collar of his shirt. It was way too hot for a suit. This heatwave seemed to be lasting for all of eternity. Maddy wanted to pass out at the thought of a mask pressed against her face tomorrow night.

She gestured to the wine bottle which was lying on ice, lucky thing. She felt like she couldn't quite breathe, like she might lose her mind if it didn't cool down soon. If only she could lie in a bucket of ice too. 'Want one?'

'No. I'm going to London shortly to discuss my launch.' Gregory's next book was out in a couple of months. There would be a small explosion of reviews, of more contracts and money.

'Tonight? But by the time you get there and back, you'll have missed Candice's dinner party.' The thought of going to her sister's later on, alone, made something shrivel up and die inside Maddy.

'Yes, I should have said. I've told her I won't be there. I'm catching the four thirty-two and meeting Tim in London for drinks.' Tim was Gregory's agent: a neat, small man with a neat, small smile and a sharp white beard that made him look slightly devilish. Maddy had been the one to find him. She'd met him at a publisher's event back in her marketing days. Maybe both Tim and Gregory had forgotten that Maddy had been the one to approach Tim, to sell *Watched* to him in one sentence at a work event she'd organised in London. Gregory hadn't even been interested in finding an agent in those early days. It had always been Maddy. She'd believed in him. She'd thought he was talented and deserved to be recognised. It seemed strange to think about that now: the simplicity of it all.

'I'll perhaps stay in London for the night,' Gregory continued, not meeting Maddy's eye. 'There's a little shop in Primrose Hill that wants me to pop in and sign some books, which I'll do tomorrow morning.'

'Then be back here for us to go to the ball together?'

'No. I think I'll go straight to the ball from London and

meet you there.' Gregory put his hands back in his pocket, coins quietly jangling again. 'I've messaged Candice to have Eliot over at theirs for the night tomorrow. I knew you wouldn't want to miss the ball, in the end.'

A message to Candice. Never to Candice's husband, Aiden.

But how could Gregory have a problem with Aiden, really? If Maddy's latest lot of suspicions were founded, Gregory was actually being quite hypocritical by having a problem with Aiden. In the last few months, Gregory had disappeared more, sending Maddy hurtling back into the past. More 'London'. More nights away. More days where he said vague things about playing squash with unnamed friends. It made her thoughts jerk in reflex and she wondered if he really was going to spend his evening with Tim, in some moneyed bar full of brown leather booths and compliments and whiskey glasses so thick that they wouldn't break if you dropped them.

'It's a shame we can't go together.' It was more than a shame. It was a horrible echo of last time, a ghostly reflection in the mirror of the past: Gregory arriving late at Falcon Castle, Maddy left alone with her dark suspicions until he arrived.

But Gregory didn't answer. He wandered over to the huge cabinet and fingered the petals of the rather garish flowers that had been delivered for Maddy that morning. 'How beautiful. Are they from a client?' His words were clipped and on edge, as though he didn't want to be in the room anymore.

'Yes.' Maddy nodded. 'They came this morning.' She'd

taken the card with Aiden's name off as soon as the bouquet had arrived, and immediately torn it into pieces. The card had said nothing more. Just *Aiden*, and one single *X*.

Why?

The story Maddy had told in an interview about meeting Gregory had grown legs over time, as all good white lies did. It walked by itself now and nobody ever thought to challenge it. But the truth was, Maddy had first met her husband at a drunken party about fifteen years ago. Gregory had been a friend of a friend and everyone had said how attractive he was so that his name preceded him. Something had spread inside Maddy that night, so soon after Maddy's sister, Candice, and Maddy's best friend, Aiden, had announced their engagement. Gregory Archer was a chance to get something that other people wanted. Maybe Aiden would realise what a mistake he'd made if Maddy was someone who could get Gregory. But whilst she'd been waiting for Aiden to have his epiphany, she'd actually fallen for Gregory, and he, at least at first, had fallen for Maddy.

'Very nice.' Gregory released the petal and moved over to Maddy, then leaned down and kissed her. What would he have done if he had seen the card, signed by Maddy's brother-in-law, her first love? Gregory always swore on his own faithfulness. She had eventually confronted him – without specifically mentioning Pearl, but about infidelities in general – when enough time had passed for it to seem as though the question was innocent. She had hoped, in a way, for Gregory to admit his affair with Pearl. Because if he admitted it then Maddy would have a reason for her madness.

I have never, ever strayed, Maddy. And I never intend to.

She'd believed him for a time, and still did some days. Of course he hadn't done it! There had been no reason to doubt him after the Gatsby Ball. Their marriage had carried on. Stunning holidays. Stunning house. Eliot got a bit older, a bit more predictable and a bit less frightening to handle. So they were fine. Pearl had just been a silly young girl with a crush. She'd been part of the reason Gregory had wanted to escape teaching: she hadn't been the first or the last to fall hard for her teacher. Something to do with all those female hormones crashing around in their brand-new, almost-adult bodies. But then the story would suddenly shift in Maddy's mind. She'd be drifting off to sleep in their huge, comfortable bed, or she'd be yawning her way through an intelligent film in their cinema room and a sharp realisation would pierce her heart suddenly and cruelly. Of *course* he did it! You saw him holding her hand.

And now he was doing it again, going to London for questionable amounts or time, absent for hours that spanned into days. Meeting her at balls she didn't really want to go to. Did Aiden know what Gregory was up to? Did he feel sorry for Maddy, a part of his heart lit bright by her vulnerability?

It was either that, or something worse. The conversation she always tried to bury stirred in the ground of her memory, lifting its hand from the soil.

Come on, Maddy. Be honest. Aiden's eyes hadn't looked like his own. They'd been desperate, unblinking.

'Right then.' Gregory pulled away from her and the present was back, the past dead and buried again.

And then as Gregory left the room, there was banging: the front door closing. All the heat of the day suddenly left Maddy's body as she imagined Aiden, Sadie or Pearl or someone else who knew too much appearing in their gorgeous hallway, dripping blood and secrets on their beautiful, polished oak floor. She sprung from her chair, hearing footsteps, a voice.

But the voice was Eliot's. There was nobody to fear in her home. It was just her child, home from school, and today was just the same as any other.

THREE

Sadie

It had only been about half an hour since she arrived home and Blake was about to vanish from the house again. Sadie watched as her daughter swiped her favourite designer skin products from the bathroom shelf and threw them into a giant white make-up bag.

'I'm staying at Evie's for the weekend,' Blake said, her eyes lowered, avoiding Sadie, who loitered behind her in the bathroom mirror.

'All weekend?'

'Yeah.' She looked up at Sadie for a moment and hesitated, about to say more. Then she zipped up the make-up bag and gave Sadie a quick kiss on the cheek before disappearing into her bedroom to get the rest of her things together.

'By the way,' Sadie said, following Blake, 'have you seen my black dress anywhere?'

'No.' Blake was pulling things out of a drawer. Tangled

bras and socks tumbled onto the floor and she stuffed them back in impatiently. A rogue sweet wrapper floated down to the carpet like a feather.

'It's just that it's disappeared from my wardrobe. I wouldn't mind you borrowing it, you know.' Sadie would love it if Blake borrowed her things, if she'd asked to wear the dress so that Sadie could smell her daughter's skin and perfume when she got it back, so that she could see a better version of herself in it. But Blake hadn't asked to borrow anything at all and then the dress had disappeared from its place in Sadie's wardrobe. The only possible explanation that Sadie could bear to consider was that Blake had taken it without asking and spilled nail polish or salsa or something irresponsible on it and stuffed it away somewhere with odd socks and sweet wrappers.

Blake rolled her eyes. She rolled her eyes so much these days that it sometimes felt like they might roll right out of their sockets and fall onto the floor like soft marbles. 'I just told you. I don't have it.'

'Maybe you took it and forgot?' Sadie was desperate. She wanted this to be a Blake problem, not something that made her wake up screaming in the night. Not something that made her feel like someone had been inside her bedroom, their silent fingers opening her wardrobe doors and touching her clothes while she slept.

'Stop accusing me!' Blake's voice was close to a shout. She sighed and put her bag on her shoulder. 'I don't have it. And I'm late for Evie's. See you on Sunday.'

Sadie checked her phone as she climbed into bed at nine forty: no messages or calls. She was probably the only teacher from the school who wasn't out on the end-of-term drinks night. She pictured her colleagues getting louder, red-faced and clumsy as their after-work drinks wore on. *Just a few*, they always said, but it never was just a few; it was always what seemed like hundreds to Sadie. They used to send her messages about what they were getting up to, to try and include her and make her change her mind and join them, but they didn't even bother doing that anymore. Nobody wanted a sober person there mopping up the spills with clean napkins and remembering everything.

Sadie had been sent to Kings Hill High School for a teacher training placement before Blake had even started there. After the placement was over, Sadie had applied for a permanent job. Teaching music had offered a pleasing sense of control: timetables, schemes of work, reports. She'd been able to help some of the teenagers too. Not many of them wanted to talk about their problems with a music teacher. But some did. And when girls in her form cried to Sadie about their friendships or parents or boyfriends, and she managed to stop their tears and make them smile before they went back out into the brutal high school corridors, she felt like she had, in a miniscule way, tried to make right what had gone so wrong. Then Blake had eventually started at the school and made Sadie wonder how on earth she could work anywhere else, somewhere where she didn't know exactly where Blake was and what she was doing every moment of the day.

But now, it was the end of term, and when they weren't both at school it was a lot harder to feel in control.

Sadie closed her eyes and tried to think of the soft mattress underneath her, the feel of cotton against her skin. She tried not to think of her last couple of conversations with Blake, how she'd accused her and pushed her away. She tried not to pull at the thread of what it meant if Blake was telling the truth and didn't have Sadie's dress. If Sadie tried to forget all that, then sleep would come, eventually. If she just breathed evenly, and ignored the heat and the feeling of uneasiness that was snaking around her stomach, it would happen. And eventually, a pleasant drowsiness did move closer. She saw half-dreamed images of Blake dressed as Cinderella. A wasp flying lazily towards Sadie. Sunlight. School, the classrooms empty and hot. All the memories of the day were filtered through her mind, pulling her into sleep. Rob on his bike, holding dead, black flowers and smiling and then falling off his bike, smashing against a ground that was made of glass.

Sadie's eyes were suddenly wide open. She sat bolt upright up in bed, her nightie sticking to her sweating back. The smash had been real and had woken her up. She was sure of it. And now, there was a noise from downstairs. A soft, clicking noise, like the closing of a door.

She looked at her phone: just after midnight. Rob wasn't due home from his shift for another hour or so. He never came home early. She tensed, waiting for the familiar noises of him locking up, taking off his shoes, coming up the stairs with a sigh of quiet relief.

Nothing.

Because there's nobody there, Rob would say on autopilot if he was in bed with Sadie now. *You were just dreaming. The noises weren't real.*

Go back to sleep, he always told her, barely conscious. It was one of the multiple reasons they were cracking into pieces. Sadie, her eyes bright with panic in the darkness, insisting she'd heard something or seen something or *felt* something. Rob telling her she was paranoid, falling back into bed and sighing heavily after checking the house and finding it was all in order, *again*. Sadie had gone downstairs by herself a lot, too. But she'd never found anything either and then had often lay awake for hours, remembering when her mother used to scream blue murder about a hallucinated intruder or enemy.

Sadie had no idea how Rob could be so calm after losing both his parents so suddenly in the car accident that had happened when he was only in his early twenties. Surely, surely, he should be wracked with a cold fear even sharper than Sadie's, slicing through him like ice every time he started to drift off? Surely he should lie awake waiting for his life to go wrong somehow, wondering about his escape routes if it did?

Perhaps fear and guilt were very different creatures.

She took a deep breath and got out of bed. At the window, she saw that Rob's car wasn't on the drive, so it definitely hadn't been him waking her up. But there was the sound again. A click, gone before she could work out where it was coming from or what it might be.

At the top of the stairs, Sadie paused. The hallway was bathed in the buttery light of the lamp that she always left on, but it might as well have been pitch black for all the panic that was spreading through her.

She forced herself downstairs quickly. When she reached the front lounge, she peered inside. Nobody was there. Nothing was moved. The cream sofas were immaculate: the throw expertly draped over one side. The timed lamp on the sideboard hadn't turned on yet, but would ping into action in about fifteen minutes. Sadie stole a glance out of the window. There was no movement outside, nothing going on in the street that she could attribute the noises to. After checking the kitchen, she returned to the hall and froze. The feature mirror on the wall by the front door was smashed, as though someone had thrown something at it. Sadie thought of the smashing noise that she'd thought had been part of a dream and felt horror unfurl inside her.

Someone had been in her house, whilst she'd been asleep.

She forced herself to take a breath and stepped a little closer to the mirror, tiny shards of glass prickling the bare skin of her feet. Her hand reached out to the front door handle.

Locked.

She backed away from the mirror, seeing her frightened face over and over again in the jagged glass. Maybe she hadn't locked the French doors at the back of the house when she'd come in from the garden earlier? She went into the kitchen again, her eyes scanning the garden, her heart bashing against her ribs.

What was worse: someone breaking in, or someone

who'd managed to be inside even though all the doors were still locked?

She reached for the handle of the French door, and it didn't budge. Her hand shook as she pulled it away. The garden, when she flipped open the fitted blinds, seemed empty – although who really knew what might be lurking in the shadows?

Sadie never, ever felt completely safe. Terror walked beside her like a faithful dog, and had done for ten years. But lately, in the last few weeks, it had intensified. Tonight, the thought that someone had been inside – perhaps still here, breathing in the shadows, wanting to jump out at her – made the terror run at her and almost knock her over with its strength.

She snapped the blinds shut, turned from the window and edged towards the larder door, breathing a sigh of relief as soon as it swung open.

Of course there was nobody in there. A person wouldn't fit in there, between her perfectly stacked shelves and wicker baskets of cleaning products. And there was nowhere else down here where somebody could hide.

She stepped towards the hall again and stared up the staircase, taking deep breaths. She would surely have heard someone go upstairs, towards her bedroom, or – the thought made her feel faint – passed them on the stairs.

Was there any chance that the heat of the day had cracked the glass of the mirror? Maybe Sadie should turn up at the Craven wine bar now, in her pale blue nightie covered in miniature pandas, and ask Gerard, the head of science, if this disgusting weather might be able to crack a mirror all by itself.

No, Gerard would say. Absolutely no chance.

She moved upwards, one step at a time, her eyes fixed on Blake's bedroom, which was at the top. Maybe Blake had sneaked back in?

But no, Blake's room was empty just as Sadie knew it would be. She turned on the bedroom light and stood in the doorway for a moment, breathing in the perfumed air. She eyed the wardrobe. It was a walk-in wardrobe, one that Blake had posted on Instagram, much to Sadie's horror. There were rows of Converse, tops on pastel hangers and boxes of earrings and claw clips. It was small in there, but a room in itself. Once, about a year ago, Blake had hidden in there with two of her friends and made Sadie feel like she might pass out with fear until they fell from the glossy white door, all giggles, long hair and innocence.

She forced herself towards the door of the wardrobe and pulled it open slowly, so that it dragged along the thick carpet. She walked into the little room, where the vanilla scent of Blake was even stronger. And then she saw it: a small white bear holding a heart. The initials *B & G* were stitched on the red heart in sparkly thread that glinted in the yellow light from the bedroom. Sadie picked it up, thinking about Rob's worries about teenage boys. The bear hadn't been there a couple of days ago. She placed it back on the shelf and closed the door. As she pushed herself to check all the rooms and all the cupboards, even the tiny ones, her heart still thudding in her chest, the boys from school whose name began with G circled around her mind like crows: Grayson, George, Gabriel.

They circled and circled. Sadie knew how some of the boys performed in their classes; if they were well-equipped for lessons and stayed on task. She knew some of their parents and roughly where some of them lived in Kings Hill or in the sprawl of nearby towns. But that was all. She didn't know enough to protect Blake from them, from who and what they might know.

Sadie went downstairs and sat on the edge of the sofa as she checked the footage from the video doorbell.

Nothing.

Nobody had been near the front door during the time she'd been in bed. So perhaps it had been through the back door, through the kitchen? But no, because the doors had been locked. She put her phone on the coffee table and lay back on the sofa, unable to relax, listening to every single sound. The glug of the American fridge as it made ice. A car outside, the neat thudding of a door and hushed voices. The tapping of something near her house outside – footsteps? No, not footsteps, the sound of something from within the walls of the house. Pipes, or mice, or something else, something hidden that was impossible to see.

She turned on the television and flicked through reality shows, old sitcoms, cooking programmes, and tried to settle on something to calm her down. Eventually, after what felt like a lifetime, she heard the crunch of Rob's SUV on the driveway.

'What happened?' he asked as he took in the smashed

mirror in the hall, Sadie's wide-awake face. She caught herself in the shards of glass, crazed, horrified and pale.

'I was upstairs and I heard something. So I came down and found it like this. I think someone came in and did it. I heard it happen.'

Rob frowned. 'Were all the doors locked?'

'Yes. I checked them all. The windows too. Nobody was on the camera at the front.'

'So how do you think someone got in? And then got back out, and locked up again?'

Sadie stared at him. Once again they were here. Round and round they went like this: him thinking she was paranoid, Sadie *knowing* that she wasn't.

'Look, there'll be an explanation. Maybe you caught it with the vacuum or something by accident.' He was taking off his shoes methodically, slowly, untying the laces patiently. It sometimes felt like he was trying to drown out Sadie's noise and panic with a calm silence of his own.

But that was because he didn't know, and couldn't know, because then the space between them would become an ocean. She had put them all at risk, for all these years. She was desperate to tell him and desperate for him to never know: someone was trying to frighten her.

Sadie moved towards Rob, pressing her head against his chest. He put his arms around her and she felt, for a moment, as though they were plummeting back to how things used to be. If only she could unravel time, soft as a ball of wool, and try it all again.

'Maybe it was Blake.' Sadie tried not to let panic flutter into her words. It hadn't been Blake, because Sadie had heard it happen and Blake hadn't been there then. But she needed to believe that the mirror might have been broken earlier, that there was a reason for it that wouldn't make her heart jump from her chest and splatter onto the hallway floor.

Rob pulled away. 'Wouldn't she have told us?'

Sadie nodded, her heart ready to leap. Blake would have told Rob, even if she hadn't wanted to tell Sadie. He knew it, and she knew it.

Rob thought for a moment, scratched his head. 'Maybe we should sort out the CCTV cameras at the back.'

'No.'

'But then we could go to the police if things like this were bothering you.'

Sadie shook her head. 'Let's try to forget it. How was your shift?' she asked, even though she couldn't think of anything other than the broken glass, someone creeping beside her as she slept.

'It was difficult. A toddler... You don't want to know.' He used to tell her stories about work all the time. But now, he didn't want to do anything to add to Sadie's anxiety, to her ever-precarious tower of things that could go wrong. He touched her waist softly. Pull then push: the way it always was. 'We should get some sleep otherwise we won't be able to stay awake for our date tomorrow.'

Sadie stared at Rob. His features had lifted when he said the word *date*. And now, they fell again.

'You forgot?'

'No. I didn't.'

'Come on, Sadie. At least pretend you're excited.'

Rob was trying to remove the space between them, pull them back together straight through the pool of broken glass and the secrets, while Sadie was trying her hardest to keep them both at the edge. 'When was the last time we went somewhere together? Just us?'

That was the problem, though. Sadie glanced at the remains of the broken mirror again and caught her own eye. *You never know if it is just us. You never know who might be watching.*

FOUR

Maddy

Maddy stood at Candice's double front door with Eliot for a moment longer than she needed to before ringing the bell. She looked behind her onto the stretch of trees and enormous houses. Leaves fluttered softly, making shadows dance around on the ground beneath.

There were a lot of places to hide around here.

Eliot followed Maddy's gaze, his face puckered against the burning sun. 'Who are you looking for?'

'Oh, nobody.' Maddy leaned forwards and forced herself to ring the bell, even though she wanted to bolt, speed back to her own home and lock all the doors behind her. The message from Sadie, Gregory vanishing again, the flowers with the card from Aiden and the thought of returning to Falcon Castle tomorrow were all making Maddy feel as though she might walk into a net or fall into a trapdoor or be stabbed in the back at any moment.

'Did you bring the salad?' Candice asked in greeting.

'I forgot,' said Maddy as she forced herself through the

threshold and into the enormous kitchen where the rest of her tiny family stood around the sprawling marble worktops: Candice, willowy and blonde like their dead father, arranging crystal glasses on a tray; Aiden, in a short-sleeved shirt the colour of raw salmon, chopping lemons. Their sour scent lingered in the air: soft and sharp all at once.

'Honestly, Maddy,' Candice shook her head and her green earrings jangled. 'I gave you one job.'

Maddy swallowed down her irritation and it landed in her stomach with a bump. What would it be like to have a sister who just ordered pizza on a Friday night?

'I can go and buy one.'

'Ready-prepared salad? Really?' Candice looked like Maddy had suggested they gnaw on each other's legs. 'Absolutely not. We'll do without. Go and sit at the table in the garden. It's all ready.'

Maddy and Eliot followed Candice through to the garden, where outdoor furniture was lined up. Maddy sat down and took the glass of Pimm's that Aiden was holding out. She could really do with something stronger, but that was Candice all over. The sun came out and she thought she was hosting Wimbledon.

'No Gregory tonight?' asked Aiden. He sank into a wicker chair, long legs splayed out in front of him. His legs had been hairless for so many years, until one summer when they were suddenly a man's legs, covered in fine black hairs that Maddy always used to have to stop herself from reaching out and touching.

She held her hand over her eyes to block out the hostile

sunlight that was piercing her vision. 'He's in London again.' Her voice raised itself slightly at the end of her sentence and made it sound like a question, to see if Aiden had some kind of answer.

'Nice.'

Maddy sat down on the chair next to Aiden's, the scorched wicker jabbing into her thighs, beads of sweat springing up on her back beneath her clothes.

'So,' Aiden said, a frown on his face. He cleared his throat loudly, angrily.

'So?'

'I want to talk to you.' He reached out and swept something from her arm: a small insect that had landed on her, emerald-green and glinting.

'And I need to talk to you,' she said, her words coming out in a rush. 'Aiden, those—'

'No. Don't, Maddy. Don't interrupt. This is important. You're going back to Falcon Castle tomorrow.'

Maddy felt fear lace through her blood and bones as the past hurtled closer. 'And?'

Aiden watched her. She swallowed, swatted a fruit fly from her face so that it collided with her palm. A tiny little death, because of her. She looked back at Aiden, trying to look casual, wondering what the best arrangement of facial features to do that was, wondering what he was going to say.

'The hit and run?'

Maddy thought she might be sick. The evening took on a dream-like quality, as though she were floating above it, watching it from a cloud. 'I don't know.'

'You *do* know, Maddy.' Aiden spat his words out and didn't meet her eye.

He was pushing it further than last time.

They had been at Maddy's mother's house a few weeks after the Gatsby Ball. Maddy had used the downstairs bathroom, and when she had come out, Aiden had been there at the door, making her jump and bang her elbow against the doorframe.

'You need to tell the truth,' he'd said.

She had known what he meant straight away but she had flashed him a smile. 'That my mother is terrible at cooking beef?'

It was then that his eyes had changed, become wide with desperation. 'Maddy, you know exactly what I mean. The accident. That night.'

Maddy had rubbed her elbow, wincing at the tenderness. 'The hit and run after the ball? They're still looking for a red car, Aiden.' It was cruel of her, and she knew that. But she also knew that Aiden's red car was parked on her mother's sweeping gravel driveway at that very moment, and that if anyone did decide to inspect it, they would not find a mark on it. They would have simply zero evidence. Aiden would be okay. Maddy would be okay.

He had stared at her and they'd heard a hoot of laughter from Gregory, a wail from Eliot and the crashing of something falling to the floor. Normal sounds, a normal day that Maddy would *not* permit to fly off its rails.

'Come on, Maddy. Be honest,' he'd said.

Maddy had looked at her call log the morning after the

Gatsby Ball. She'd apparently called Aiden at one minute past ten the night before. It would have taken him about forty minutes to reach the castle. The newspapers had said that the accident had happened at about ten forty-six. Maddy had swiped the call from her phone, from reality, with a shaking finger.

Outside her mother's downstairs bathroom, Maddy had shaken her head. 'I don't know what you're talking about.' She'd moved past him, back to the dining room which smelled of roasted flesh and rosemary.

Her elbow had bruised a few days later, a burst of violet on her skin.

Aiden had never brought it up again. He'd obviously decided to let it go. Nobody had ever inspected his car. He hadn't even had that car for years. He must have cared about Maddy, to not push her again. She'd always felt quite reassured about that. But now? Flowers and more snatched conversations? She felt a wave of fear.

'I know you, Maddy.' Aiden stopped speaking and stood up abruptly. Maddy saw that Candice was arriving at the table, armed with dishes that gleamed white in the sun. If Aiden had said a few more words, Candice might have heard him. And then what? And what had he been going to say? Maddy downed her Pimm's and chewed on a soggy strawberry that had been lodged at the bottom of the glass.

'What's up with you?' Maddy's mother sat down next to Maddy. She was wearing a ridiculous straw hat and smelled faintly of cucumber. 'You're in one of your moods.'

Maddy shook her head, the strawberry sticking in her

throat. 'I'm not. Nothing is the matter. I'm absolutely fine, except I don't really like Pimm's.'

'Well, be nice tonight, Maddison. It costs nothing.'

'I'm always nice,' retorted Maddy. She glanced at Candice and her mind whirred on and on, its tracks rusted and jarring. The flowers had arrived at almost exactly the same time as the message from Sadie had done. That felt significant although Maddy couldn't work out how. The heat and the confusion and the thought that Aiden wanted the truth out in the open was making her feel like she might collapse on Candice's flawless lawn.

'Some flowers arrived for me this morning,' she said.

Aiden was sitting opposite her now and squeezing lemon over his food. He didn't look up, or change his expression.

Candice raised her eyebrows. 'From?'

Maddy shrugged. 'I don't know. There was no card.' Lies upon lies. She pictured the card with Aiden's name written on it, and she wondered how many times she'd ripped into it before the pieces had fluttered down from her fingers into the bin, in case the letters might still make sense to Gregory should he come across it.

She should have been more careful.

'A client?' Aiden was looking straight at Maddy now, wiping his lemony fingers on a white linen napkin. His voice was even.

'Maybe.'

'They look like maggots,' Eliot said, wrinkling his nose and holding up a pale pink prawn.

'Are you busy these days, Maddison? With clients?' Maddy's mother paused, her silver fork glinting in the sun.

Eliot dropped the prawn and it tumbled down onto the ground. 'Can we get Burger King on the way home?'

Aiden smirked. 'Maybe you have an admirer.'

Her mother set her fork down. 'The problem with freelancing is, you never really know what's around the corner.'

'Prawns are good for you. Try one.' Candice's voice this time, merging into the others and making Maddy's head spin.

She stood up, the heat making her dizzier by the second. Visions of Sadie, ten years older, Pearl's scarred face, the road stretching out to the castle and the bright burst of flowers in the orangery jolted against each other in her mind. Tomorrow would be even worse than this. But Maddy had to go. She had to see if Sadie was there. She had to be at Gregory's side, gripping tightly on to her version of events, keeping those horrible secrets at bay. 'I'm going to find some wine.'

The dinner party was finally over.

Maddy was outside with Aiden and Eliot, all three assigned by Candice to put the garden furniture away. She was aware of her mother and Candice buzzing around efficiently together in the kitchen-diner that overlooked the garden.

She unwrapped a blueberry muffin she'd taken from

Candice's ostentatious cake selection after their meal. She'd barely eaten any paella and needed something sweet to try and dull the nausea that she'd had all night.

'Can I have some?' Eliot asked.

'You can go inside and get one of your own.' She didn't know if she wanted Eliot there or not. If he did go inside, she'd be left on her own with Aiden.

I know you.

'I don't want to. There are only lemon ones left now. They taste weird. Like old ladies. Blueberry ones are nicer.'

Maddy gave Eliot a piece then popped the last bit into her mouth. 'They really are.' She chewed and forced it down.

'I have a "would you rather",' Aiden said, collecting the cushions from the chairs. 'Death or no blueberry muffins?'

'Death, obviously.' Maddy glanced at Eliot as she spoke but he seemed unaware of her words, chewing with his mouth open, staring out at the enormous garden, silvery blue in the moonlight. What was Aiden trying to get at? She fanned her face with her hand.

'You go,' Aiden said. Aiden and Maddy had played thousands of games of 'would you rather' when they were young: their endless days laced together by an equally endless string of questions. *Would you rather have one eye and your own sweet shop, or both eyes and no sweets? Would you rather have no head or no body? No cake or no bed? A million pounds or a million houses? Would you rather he'd protected you all this time or knew nothing at all?*

Sometimes it was impossible to choose.

Maybe Aiden was trying to pull Maddy back into a

world they'd both left, where they were best friends and the future was rolled out so far that they couldn't see the end. Maybe he was trying to tell her she had nothing to worry about.

She shook her head. 'I can't think of one.'

There was a shout from inside then: Maddy's mother.

'Come on, you three. Time to go. It's way past Eliot's bed time!'

Maddy reached out to touch Eliot's cheek and he dodged her, quick as a pro-boxer, and scowled. 'I don't want to go home.'

'You'll be back tomorrow. I'm going to a party with Daddy.' She wished she hadn't eaten the muffin. A violent wave of nausea washed over her.

'She's going to a castle,' Aiden told Eliot.

Maddy stared at him for a moment but he didn't look up or meet her eye. Sometimes she felt like everything could unravel at any moment. Or maybe it already had, and she just didn't know it yet.

'Maddy!' Candice was still shouting from the kitchen-diner. 'Come and get some of Mum's meringue to take home for Gregory.'

Maddy ignored her and continued looking at Aiden. His nose was pink on the bridge. He'd never tanned, always burned. One summer when they were about fourteen, he'd burned his back so badly that Maddy had helped him to rub calamine lotion onto his skin. She still remembered it now: the strange, hot sensation that travelled down her stomach to places she hadn't known she had before as she touched his warm skin. That feeling, of being new and excited, seemed like it had been felt by someone else now, someone on a different planet to Maddy.

She leaned over and kissed Aiden lightly on the cheek. She did this sometimes just to see how she felt. But it was the same as it had been for a long time now. There was no jolt, no electric longing from deep inside. Just fear and a sense of Aiden pushing her towards a place she didn't want to go.

Perhaps it wasn't only Aiden who knew. Perhaps other people knew too. Perhaps a whole army of people were aware of what Maddy was really capable of. Perhaps they'd all been waiting in a line for Maddy to come clean and tell the truth.

Aiden stepped back.

Candice watched them from the kitchen.

They moved towards the soft yellow lights of the house. As they did, Maddy heard something in the darkness behind her, beyond the garden, outside the high stone walls. It could have been anything: a bird or a squirrel or someone walking a dog or a hundred other things that would make sense in the nicest, safest street at the top of Kings Hill East.

FIVE

Sadie

When Sadie woke up the next day, the heat still hadn't broken. She had a cold shower, the noise of the water closing in on her and making her feel like her house was full of intruders that she couldn't hear, smashing things to match the broken mirror and smiling as they did it. The day felt foggy. Her head pounded.

She forced herself downstairs. Rob was bending down in the hallway, sweeping glass from the floor. They thought they'd cleaned it all up the night before, but now Sadie could see that tiny shards had been left behind. Rob had removed the mirror altogether now too, and the paint beneath where it had hung was brighter, untouched.

'Blake messaged me.' His words were quiet and Sadie had to strain to hear them.

'Is she okay?' Anxiety prickled at Sadie: knives from the inside.

'She said you think she's stolen your dress.'

Blake had been doing this more and more lately:

confiding in Rob, sometimes complaining about Sadie. Part of her felt relieved that Blake confided in one of them. The other part felt the tug of sadness that it wasn't her.

'I didn't say *stolen*.'

'Well, taken then. What's the difference?'

'I just don't know where else it could be.' Sadie had worn the dress during her last concert about nine years ago. It had been expensive, from a designer department store that she would never usually go in. Rob had pushed her to buy it. *Treat yourself.*

Like she deserved a treat.

Rob stood up for a moment and wiped his head with the back of his hand. His gold wedding ring glinted in the early morning sun and yanked at Sadie's heart. She imagined it taken off, set down somewhere, the feeling of a door being closed. 'Blake wouldn't just take it. She'd ask you if she wanted to borrow it.'

'I wouldn't have minded her borrowing it. But I want to believe that she would ask me, that she wouldn't just help herself to it.'

'Then believe it.'

'But then I still have no dress, and Blake's saying she doesn't have it. And it's usually in my wardrobe, but now it's not.'

'The dress section?' Rob gave Sadie a small smile that was affectionate and said, *you organise your clothes in a ridiculously over-the-top way and I love you for it*, and she felt a small puff of relaxation. They could be okay. For fragments of seconds, they could work.

She opened the front door for him so he could take out

the glass, her fingers reluctant to touch the handle after last night. She imagined police here, dusting powder over their surfaces, asking questions. 'I don't care about the actual dress. I'm just feeling weird that it's disappeared.'

'Blake said she doesn't have it,' Rob said as he came back inside, hot air following him. 'That should probably be enough. We have to trust her and believe what she tells us.'

'Okay. I get it. I'll keep looking for it.' The relief Sadie had felt only seconds earlier evaporated. 'So what time are we leaving today? And can you tell me where we're going yet?' It wasn't like Rob to plan a surprise. Surprise parties, surprise presents, anything that she hadn't scoured the internet for and created multiple spreadsheets about, made Sadie feel like she might hyperventilate. People were obsessed with surprises: with jumping out and appearing when you weren't expecting them to, with throwing your careful plans off course. As if life itself didn't jump up in your face often enough to smack you with something you didn't expect.

'I know you hate surprises. But this one's good. Hang on, I'll show you.' Rob pulled his phone from his pocket and tapped away, humming as though this was all average, as though they always went out on dates he'd planned. Actually, Sadie couldn't remember the last time they'd done something together that wasn't shopping for chicken and vegetables or going to the dentist or to give blood. 'Here we go. Look at this. They messaged me on Instagram about some prize draw for NHS workers and said I'd won two tickets. I thought it was a scam at first but I've checked it out with the company who run it and it's all totally legit.

We get food, drinks and a luxury room for a night. It's good timing. We need it. And it's such a brilliant cause. They're raising money for White Feather.'

Sadie looked down at the e-ticket on Rob's screen and felt acid rise up from her stomach. She put her hand out to the banister to steady herself and took a deep breath as the hallway swirled around her.

'You've been to the venue before, haven't you? Years ago. Sadie?'

'Yeah.' She forced a smile and it felt like her skull might crack with tension. 'I think I have.' Did he *know*? Was Rob playing some game with her? Had he known all this time? Was any of this true, about the prize draw and the tickets? Her mind raced.

'Try to not look too horrified at the prospect of a weekend away with me.' Rob put his phone back in his pocket and sighed. 'Come on, Sadie. I honestly don't know what to do anymore.'

'I just don't know if it's…' The sentence trailed off. She couldn't possibly finish it. White Feather was a charity for bereaved children. Although Sadie hadn't been a child when she'd lost her mother, she felt like she might as well have been. She'd become an orphan at twenty when her mother had died. At least that's how she'd seen it, because she'd never even met her father. And there had been so many times when she could have lost her mother as a child. The thought of helping to make money for children like Sadie bloomed inside her, making her feel strangely light, as though she might take off through the window and float like a balloon over the trees until the houses on Radley

Drive looked like toys. She knew White Feather meant a lot to Rob too. He'd even donated to them in the past.

But Falcon Castle? She didn't think she could do it.

'I'm not going to force you.' Rob stalked past her, into the kitchen. She stood frozen in the hallway, bare without its feature mirror. From the kitchen, she heard the coffee machine click into action. The bitter smell of espresso filled the air. She forced herself towards it, heaving her body forwards. Rob had turned the radio to Classic FM and notes floated out into the room. He still wouldn't accept that Sadie couldn't bear classical music anymore. And she obviously couldn't tell him why Chopin and Mozart and Debussy made her feel as though she couldn't breathe, why any music made her feel as though she was enjoying her life more than she deserved to. She'd always told him that it was because the music was everywhere now, too mainstream to enjoy in the same way.

'Rob, I'm sorry. I—' Sadie stopped as she saw Blake's yellow roses from the other night. Her blood ran cold.

Rob followed her gaze to the vase. 'Why did you chop their heads off?'

Sadie stared in horror at the headless roses, trying desperately to remember if she'd looked at the flowers last night when she'd assessed the house and found the broken mirror. Sweat broke out all over her body, as though tiny insects were burrowing into her skin.

'I didn't do that.'

Rob shrugged and went back to his coffee.

'Rob, what's happened to the flowers? Why are they like that?'

Rob stirred his coffee slowly and tapped his teaspoon against his mug. The serene stream of piano notes unfolded gently from the radio.

'Rob?'

'I don't know what to say. You seem to be looking for things to freak you out. But things like this can have logical explanations.'

Oh, but how logical it would be. Sadie bit her lip. She'd been waiting for this, for someone to sneak in and threaten her, to write *I know what you did* on her walls in blood-red lipstick.

'This one probably *was* Blake, actually. Hacks,' Rob was saying. 'I bet she's put the petals in ice. She's always showing me people restocking their ice trays, putting flowers and fruit in it. It's what cool people do these days. It's a thing.'

Sadie took a breath and tried to block out the images in her mind: Blake accepting the flowers on the stage the other night. Falcon Castle all those years ago. Blake revelling in the attention and the applause. Blake's Instagram posts; the photographs that would float along the seabed of the internet for all time, threatening to pull Blake down with them at any moment. Blood. A puckered line along a once-perfect face.

It's not Blake, she wanted to tell Rob. It's someone else doing all these things: someone who knows more about me than you do.

Rob came closer, put his coffee down and put his arms around Sadie. His touch was cautious, ready to spring back at any moment. 'I really don't want to force you to go this weekend. But I do think you need to relax. I thought I was doing something good, accepting the tickets.' There was so much more he could have said. *We're hanging by a thread. I don't understand what's happened to you. I don't like who you are anymore.*

They were still for a minute, and Sadie put her head against Rob and felt the pulse of his heart beneath his warm chest. Rob had always made her feel safe. But nothing made her feel safe now. Her own heart fluttered higher and higher with the notes of the music.

She pulled away from Rob and gazed over at the flowers. What had happened that night near Falcon Castle – what Sadie had been a part of, or thought she might have been a part of – had always threatened to dismantle all she had. And now, the threat seemed to be getting closer to her – in her home, watching her, waking her from her own bed, breaking and taking things whilst she slept – just as she'd known it would. It was a dire choice: going back to the place of all her nightmares, or staying at home, where she was meant to be safe, but where life was becoming just as frightening.

If she went to the place of her nightmares, at least she would be with Rob. She would be doing something for him, for them.

'Okay,' she said. She forced herself to look away from the flowers and at Rob: his face that was so beautiful to her, that was echoed in Blake's. 'Let's go.'

SIX

Pearl

I shouldn't have been back in Kings Hill East. It was only an hour and a half from London, but it felt like another world.

I should have been moving in with Trafford in his Soho townhouse full of parquet floors and stacks of huge photography books, and I should have been busy with bookings. I'd waited long enough. Endless nights in my empty flat while London buzzed around me like a nest of wasps. And then everyone had let me down all at once.

It had been such a cliché but I'd really believed that Trafford would leave Samantha. I'd thought that it might be after his trip to Thailand or after Christmas. And then, the worst one of all, the jack-in-the-box news that had showed me the dead-end road I'd been on: after the baby had been born. (Apart from all the heartbreak of realising Trafford and Samantha were stronger than I had given them credit for, there was the image of those exquisite floors covered in gaudy plastic toys. Horrendous.)

I never did get copies of the photos Trafford took of me

when we first met last year. 'Black and white would be perfect,' he'd said. My long blonde hair had been artfully arranged around my face, my breasts and waist. I'd loved that camera nearly as much as I loved him. The way it made me almost feel like myself again. The way Trafford's huge hands moved on it, pressing buttons, adjusting lenses and making things seem possible. I'd spent hours curled up on his grey felt sofa flicking through the images in his coffee table books. I'd pored over close-ups of perfect people who looked like I used to look. Symmetrical. Beautiful. There were no images of people who looked like I did now.

'Not yet there aren't,' Trafford had said.

'You're beautiful,' he'd told me.

And I'd believed him time and time again. Whenever he said it, the way I used to feel, that confidence that I should have bottled, would seep into my blood, just for a few moments. Before, I'd used my looks like money. My face had got me places, and it had been going to get me even further, before it all went so wrong. After, Trafford had made me think for a time that it still might, just in a different way. The inclusive modelling agency I'd signed up with never got me much work, but that would all change, he was sure. He'd show them our photos and he'd get them to add them to my page on their site, and that would be it. Everything would change for me. It would make his name even bigger too.

But he obviously hadn't meant it. Not a word.

And then, the week I found out about his baby, RAW Talent modelling agency released me. I'd noticed that my profile had been taken off their website. Nobody had even had the guts to tell me why. I asked them and got three lines back which scored over my ego like blades. Something about not booking enough work and a cool confirmation I'd been released from my contract.

And so, after eight years in London waiting and waiting for my big break, and a year after I'd first met Trafford at an agency party, I finally admitted defeat and came back home in the spring. Luckily, there was a spare flat at my parents', separate from the rest of the house.

'You might be in the flat but you'll have your own life, won't you?' My mother, Blanche, had said this on my first evening back. It wasn't such a bad thing to say, for her. She had said worse to me over the years.

'Let's put you in your bedroom for the day, shall we?'

'A D in English? Oh, Pearl. I always got straight As. What will I tell people if you fail?'

She'd been nervous when I had come back. She'd liked me tucked away in London, away from her perfect life and the shining Goldman Estates that rained money down on her. All those times when she'd ignored me completely or left me alone for full evenings while she 'networked' at events had, it seemed, paid off. In some ways, at least.

My dad had stuck up for me. He always had done, when he'd been there. I would never have come back if it hadn't been for him. 'Of course she'll have her own life.' He was the one who suggested that I move away from it all, back to him and my mother.

Have a fresh start. Come home.

A fresh start in the place where beauty had turned to dust. My dad had been so relieved when I'd finally agreed to leave London. Most people probably thought he was hard: a classic businessman out for himself and his bank account. But he was always out for me too. Only this morning, he'd presented me with a huge gift box when I went over to their house to get some coffee. Inside had been a cashmere bathrobe the colour of candyfloss.

Welcome home. Love from Dad.

I didn't particularly like the colour pink but I wouldn't have ever told him. Blanche had done, obviously. Couldn't miss an opportunity to be a cow.

'Pink? Honestly, she's not a child, Warwick. She's twenty-seven years old.'

I'd gone back to my flat with the huge box, the ribbon trailing on the floor, and burst into tears. I hadn't cried in years up until now. I'd always presumed that I couldn't: that something in my brain had been broken when they'd messed with my face and tried to glue it back together. But in the couple of months I'd been back, I cried all the time.

I'd put the robe on with nothing underneath and then picked up my phone and video-called Trafford. I couldn't remember how many times I tried him. No more than a normal person would have done. I forgot for a moment that I wasn't in London, waiting for him to finish a shoot so I could meet him. I blinked and saw the white wall of the bedroom in the flat at my parents', felt my soft new robe on my skin, and the sense of who I had become slid into focus again.

A giddy relief flooded through me when Trafford finally

returned my call. He turned his camera off almost straight away but not before I'd seen him: black hair and dark eyebrows and a stare that ripped open my body. I had him back. He would come and see me. My mother would see that I wasn't a loser, that some people saw through the surface to what actually mattered.

But then he'd started speaking.

'Fucking leave me alone, Pearl. Hear me? I'm blocking you. And if you try it again, I'm going back to the police. I'll make them take it seriously this time. They'll do something.'

I'd laughed. It was a joke, surely. 'As if! You love it.' He *loved* it. He loved me.

As I laughed, I thought of the first time he'd taken photographs of me and my chest pulsed with sadness.

'I'm serious. I gave you a chance because I felt sorry for you. But this is enough. Carry on like this and I'll do it. I'll tell the papers too. And people are easily put off.' Trafford was ranting like a madman. He was a madman; I just hadn't realised in time. 'Doesn't take much, and your family's precious Goldman businesses will be cancelled.'

My mum would obviously be horrified if her empire was ever touched. She lived for money, for her name to be uttered by stuck-up people at the stuck-up parties that her company organised. But it was my dad's face that flitted through my mind. He'd put so many years into his property business and my mother's events business. Success and reputation were like water and food to him. I knew how easily things could be cancelled these days. I couldn't be the one to start a procession of trolls stamping over what he'd so carefully built up.

I listened mutely to Trafford's threats, his anger that streamed through the phone and I thought of Dad ordering the bathrobe, choosing the colour, asking for it to be gift-wrapped. All for me.

I didn't think Trafford's rants about him having the power to ruin two of the most successful businesses in the country were true. But I couldn't risk it. I couldn't bear the thought of my mother's disapproval, my dad's disappointment. And Trafford was the type of person people would believe. I wasn't stupid, and I'd believed him.

I had to let him go.

'Fine,' I'd said to Trafford, and hung up. As I did, something had snapped inside me, willpower or whatever it was, pinged apart like a rubber band stretched too far.

And now, here I was: in Maddy and Gregory Archer's enormous bedroom whilst Maddy sat, oblivious, in the orangery at the back of the house.

SEVEN

Maddy

Ten years earlier

Maddy had never been to the playgroup before. Someone had posted a leaflet through the door a week or so ago.

STAY AND PLAY EVERY TUESDAY. TOYS, JUICE, MAKE FRIENDS, BISCUITS. ANY AGE WELCOME.

Gregory had sniggered at the strange order of words and Maddy had joined in. A little part of her heart had broken at the sound of their shared laughter. Her heart had been brittle since the envelope had arrived a few weeks before, bits snapping off here and there and making it smaller and smaller each day.

How had she let him slip away? She'd thought it would never happen to her, to them. She'd found life so easy. But then Eliot had come along, and life had become a little more complex, her thighs a little wobblier, her days more unpredictable. Then the Manilla envelope had arrived. It had been addressed to Maddy and there had been a simple smiley face on a sticky note attached to the tie inside. The face had been drawn with a glittery pink pen. Maddy had taken the tie, put it back in Gregory's wardrobe and torn up the note. But it had made Maddy feel more on edge than she'd ever been: as though something was going to trip her up and she might end up losing everything she had, money and success and her marriage, everything rolling away from her like apples from a dropped shopping bag.

'I might go to the play group, though.' Maddy needed something to occupy her days, terrible syntax or not. She had decided whilst she was on maternity leave to leave her full-time position in marketing and go freelance. It was exciting and – she'd thought – daring. She had a baby *and* her own, flexible career. She was living the dream; doing it all; having it all. But it didn't quite seem to be working out. Freelance work hadn't fallen into her lap like she'd expected it to. Gregory's success, his bestselling books alongside his English teaching job, was paying plenty. But now everything seemed to be changing, and she was having the sinking realisation that depending on Gregory – for anything – might not be such a good idea. Should she have really given up her job, her pencil skirts and her calendar full of important meetings?

There wasn't much time to think about it: Eliot began to wail and point at something that he wanted, although it was anyone's guess what it might be. Maddy followed the line of his chubby finger helplessly, offering him a banana, holding up his blue toy truck, unstrapping him from his highchair. Nothing worked. She wondered for the millionth time that week if it was normal to not know instinctively what he needed, or if she was a particularly inept mother.

Gregory pulled his face so that his perfect features contorted for a second. He tossed a little red bunny at Eliot, who stopped crying and gave a toothy, dribbly grin to his father. 'To a play group? It doesn't seem very you.'

'The company might be nice.' She hadn't worked out what to do yet, how to confront him. Because what if she confronted him and he said *yes, I've fallen for someone else. It's over with us.* What then?

'Then ignore me. You should go. I'm sure Eliot would like it.'

It was a few hours later when Gregory had already left for work at Kings Hill High that Maddy saw his diary lying on the kitchen worktop. She flicked through it, his illegible scribbles standing out like spiders on the bright-white pages. He loved his diary. He loved writing by hand. It was one of the things that made him who he was. *Oh, Gregory and his paper diary!* He always transferred all of the appointments that popped into his digital calendar to this leather-bound diary that was the colour of summer leaves. Kings Hill High was finally finishing for summer in a couple of days and plans for the new academic year would be being made. So really, he needed it with him. Nobody respected Gregory's attachment for his diary and it irritated him. But Maddy did. She understood how Gregory worked and she needed to remind him of that. She swiped the diary from the worktop, the leather warm and smooth underneath her fingers.

It was a hot, blue day and Maddy strapped Eliot in his new pushchair and set off for Kings Hill High. There was plenty of time for her to walk to the school and give the diary to Gregory before lunch (Maddy sighed: lunch used to be clients and sharp martinis. Now it was smeared yoghurt and endless baby wipes) then Stay and Play.

She pushed Eliot further and further up the hill, stopping every now and again to retrieve his small purple dog, which he regularly launched to an indeterminate side and then wailed about furiously as though someone else had done it. Sweat sprung out from her skin. Eventually, she was on the school grounds, moving through the tangle of red brick buildings and climbing ivy. It was third period and Gregory was free. She moved closer and closer to the small flat building where his office was. Purple Dog was launched straight ahead, and Maddy stopped abruptly to avoid wheeling over him. She picked him up and gave him to Eliot. If only she could staple the thing to him somehow.

When Maddy looked up from Eliot and his dog, she felt as though she'd looked up into another world, and her insides shrivelled with stone-cold horror and fear.

There was Gregory, leaving the building. And there was a girl, holding his hand. She had long, long blonde hair that glistened in the sunlight. Long legs too, barely covered by her little black skirt. Maddy's brain screamed. The girl was obviously a sixth-former. Skinny, and coltish, and *young*.

Maddy thought of how much she'd, stupidly, trusted

Gregory. How she'd taken it for granted that he would continue to choose Maddy over everyone else. Then she thought of her walk-in wardrobe, Eliot's playroom, Gabriella who cleaned for them each week and their pantry full of hand-selected wines from France and jars of artichokes and olives.

She almost smiled to herself.

Here she was, watching her life crumble into dust, and one of her first thoughts was artichokes.

But the jar of artichokes – she could see it now, with gold string tied around its lid, sitting on the top shelf of the pantry, the shiny lid dusted every Thursday – represented so much. It told Maddy that she'd made it. That even though Aiden hadn't wanted her and had chosen her sister instead because they had a *connection*, and even though Maddy didn't have much of a career anymore, she didn't need to worry because she was a woman who went travelling with her husband and had a pantry full of nice things they had chosen together. She had happiness and success.

Did have, a voice said in her head.

Maddy turned around and left.

'Sorry,' Maddy said to another baby's mother. She'd been at Stay and Play for about seven minutes and already wanted to go home, put her pillow over her head to drown out the world and everything in it. 'He's going through a grumpy phase.' She peeled Eliot's furious hand from the other baby's leg and he wailed, his cheeks an embarrassing fuchsia.

The awkward words hung in the air as the other mother, all messy bun and pretty dangly earrings, gave a frosty smile and then swung around so that her back was to Maddy.

Another woman, one with an older little girl: beautiful, blonde, about five, grinned at Maddy and gave a subtle shrug of the shoulders. *Screw her*, the shrug seemed to say. This woman was younger than Maddy too. Did nobody past thirty have babies anymore?

'I'm Maddy,' she told the woman, waiting to realise that she'd got it all wrong and that the woman hadn't been smiling at her.

But the woman smiled again. 'Sadie Summer.' She held out her hand and gave Maddy a surprisingly strong handshake for her slim frame, as though they were at a business meeting, not a village hall that smelled of baby sick. 'I was late today,' she told Maddy conspiratorially. 'Blake spilled blackcurrant down her white dress so we had to start all over again. She only finished school on Friday. I still have six weeks to go. That's a lot of outfit changes.'

Maddy glanced at Blake. She didn't look like she'd ever spilled anything in her life. She sat calmly playing with a naked doll, nursing it and gazing at it adoringly.

'She's beautiful,' Maddy told Sadie. Sadie Summer. What a perfect name.

Sadie ruffled Blake's silky golden hair. 'Thanks. What's your little boy called?'

'Eliot.'

'As in E.T?'

Maddy blushed. 'As in T.S.'

'Sorry.' Sadie laughed.

Maddy waved the apology away. If Gregory and their couple friends could see her now, they'd scoff themselves to death. *She didn't know T. S. Eliot? Oh, Maddy, you can't be going there again. We're staging an intervention!* 'He's a poet.'

'I know. Honestly!' Sadie burst out laughing. 'I'm such an idiot.'

Maddy laughed too and shook her head. 'It's my fault.' They'd thought they were so clever. They'd decided on it one night just before Maddy's due date. Maddy had been soaking in their free-standing bathtub and Gregory had been sitting next to her feeling Eliot kick, her huge baby bump slimy with bathwater and crudely expensive bubbles. It was the perfect name, they'd agreed. But now, naming her child after a dead poet suddenly seemed to border on the obscene. Who actually did that? A nightmarish feeling, a bit like realising she was on the wrong flight to somewhere she really didn't want to go, shot through her. But Sadie grinned as though Maddy could have said any name in the world and it wouldn't have mattered.

The smile took Maddy by surprise: a sudden gift in her lap that she hadn't known she'd wanted. It wasn't just a smile. It was an acknowledgement that Sadie knew who Maddy was, and even more spectacularly, was fine with it: with Maddy not being a natural mother; with Eliot not being angelic; with Maddy stamping him with a pretentious literary name. Maddy had read about people who stripped away your top layer to reveal the real you in novels, and heard about them in songs, and she'd never found the concept particularly appealing. She'd never felt as though Gregory stripped a layer away from her, or revealed a truth that Maddy was less than perfect. That couldn't possibly be a good thing, she'd thought up until this moment.

After the playgroup, Sadie and Maddy went to The Cellar, Maddy's favourite wine and coffee bar at the bottom of Kings Hill East, where all the nicest places were. It was crowded, but they were lucky enough to find a table near the door. They had two glasses of Miraval, and then a cappuccino each to sober up before driving home. Blake was perfection, colouring quietly and licking a bright yellow lollipop that the waiter had given her. Even Eliot was quite good. There wasn't any of the tension Maddy had always assumed was part and parcel of friendship. She listened to Sadie say interesting things about her friends and her life as a pianist: concerts and applause and the thrill of performing. Sadie was one of those people who sparkled and smiled and made the world seem a little bit brighter. She didn't mention money or home refurbs or Blake's vocabulary. She laughed at Maddy's little quips. She made Maddy feel as though she'd been plucked from an exam hall or maths lesson and dropped into a fairground full of sugar and fun instead.

But then as soon as Maddy got home and looked up at the enormous black-and-white print of her in her wedding dress in the hallway, the memory of Gregory and that *girl* holding hands blazed its way through her mind. She'd already had this feeling when she was young: when Aiden had chosen Candice even though it was Maddy who had always loved him. Maddy had felt this desolateness then, a feeling of being the only person left in the world.

She stared at the print: at her custom wedding gown and tiara; at the way Gregory's eyes crinkled around the edges as he smiled at his brand-new bride; at her own pleasantly sharp clavicle that had since disappeared under curves of flesh. Perhaps Gregory didn't care about his teaching job now that he was almost at the point where he could write for a living. The prospect of writing instead of teaching had probably been the final straw for him caring about his future at the school. Or perhaps he'd thought he could get out on a loophole. Maybe the girl had finished her exams and wasn't technically a student anymore. She might not even be a sixth former at Kings Hill High. If she was at a different school, her summer might have started last week – Kings Hill always dragged out the summer term. But regardless of all that, it was more than his job at stake, wasn't it? Famous writers can't have affairs with girls that much younger than them either, Maddy wanted to warn him. It wasn't only teachers who couldn't and shouldn't. It was all husbands, wasn't it? All men. Or at least it should be.

Would people buy books from a man who had affairs with his students, or other people's students?

Would another man ever want Maddy?

Could she raise Eliot alone?

She put her hand on her chest and felt her heart running away with itself, or perhaps running *from* itself, frightened of its own shadow.

The week dragged on. Maddy went to seven gym classes at Vibe and then, feeling guilty after every single one for leaving Eliot in Vibe's creche, took him to the park, a farm, an oh-so-loud soft play centre and out for a cookie at Kendall's. She told herself she was enjoying endlessly strapping and unstrapping him into highchairs and prams and car seats, showing him pictures of fat cartoon animals in his picture books and wiping his beautiful little cherry lips when they were covered in organic chocolate.

Years ago, Maddy had been out of the house day and night, powering her way through meetings in glassy board rooms, laughing at clients' jokes and attending functions. She'd been the one to fund exquisite décor; weekends away in spa hotels and Caribbean holidays whilst Gregory reduced his teaching hours to part time so that he could spend time tearing his hair out over this line or that character. She'd pushed him to send his first book, *Watched*, out to agents. She had pored over that year's Writers' and Artists' Yearbook and talked about Gregory and his debut to selected strangers over free wine and canapés until Tim had signed him. She'd seen a potential in him, a glitter that she wanted to polish and polish until it shone so brightly it would blind people.

And now, here they were. Gregory had an agent who thought he was just *brilliant*. *Watched* had sold extremely well, and he'd just signed a hefty contract for three more novels. There were even emails floating about that mentioned a celebrity book club.

'And what are you doing today?' Gregory asked Eliot on Saturday. He did that a lot, these days. Asked Eliot questions instead of addressing Maddy. Eliot couldn't even talk yet, so Maddy was sure this said something about their relationship, although it hurt her head to try and decipher what that might be.

Maddy hadn't said anything about the girl to him yet. She had put his diary back where she'd found it on the worktop the other day. And she had zipped her mouth shut because all her questions were just too big and would open up a world of horror that she wasn't ready for. Why would he be so reckless now, when he was just making a name for himself? What was the *matter* with him? And why had he gone for somebody so *young*? Maddy felt a flutter in her chest: a feeling that all her hard work was uncoiling, ready to spring and fly apart into a hundred broken pieces.

'I'm seeing my new friend. I met her at the Stay and Play. We've been messaging a lot.'

'Nice, nice.' Gregory straightened his collar. He wasn't wearing a tie. Maddy wondered if all his ties were in his wardrobe, or if one might be strewn over someone's bed or a desk at school or the seat of a car or somewhere equally illicit. He downed his espresso. 'Right. I should get going. Edits call. I think I'm going to find a café and work there.' He looked at Eliot again. 'Family day tomorrow, I promise.'

I saw you, Maddy imagined saying to him now. He'd swipe off his navy glasses and look at her as though she'd lost the plot. *I saw you with a blonde girl near your office last week. You were holding her hand.*

Gregory liked a blonde, even though he was with

Maddy. Maddy had always known that. And she would bleach her hair, if that was what she needed to do. But she couldn't turn back time and be seventeen, eighteen, nineteen again. The girl hadn't left Maddy's mind for a whole week. She was like a child, for God's sake. So young that the thought of Gregory being seen with her by anybody else took Maddy by the shoulders and shook her so violently that her mind whacked against the sides of her skull.

Maddy might not work in marketing in the truest sense anymore but she still worked harder on herself than anyone would realise. She used £140 bottles of serum on her face and décolletage every single night, even when she was so tired that she wanted to forget she even had a face. She went to those torturous gym classes and picked at salads; had Botox and brow, leg and bikini waxes; she listened to podcasts about being emotionally balanced and having healthy relationships.

People thought that those amusing 1950s *How to be a Good Wife* manuals were so kitsch, so far out, so remote. But really, life was no fucking different from how it had been then. *Do the lion's share of all the hard work that nobody else even notices and look good too. Then watch and weep as he tosses it all away: see the beautiful world you spent years building burn to the ground.*

No. It wasn't going to happen.

'Daddy's going now, little E,' Gregory said.

Eliot erupted into howls and threw a plastic dinosaur across the kitchen so that it bounced across the tiles, landing at Maddy's feet. She picked it up calmly and squeezed it in her hand so that its claws pierced her skin.

'We'll have a good day, won't we, Eliot? We'll go and see your new friend, Blake.'

'Sounds wonderful,' Gregory shouted over Eliot's wails, and put his tiny cup into their enormous dishwasher before he disappeared for another day.

EIGHT

Pearl

Gregory lived with Maddy and their ten-year-old son in Kings Hill East. They'd moved further uphill, closer to the peak where the school stood like a castle, about five years ago. That's when I knew Gregory's writing career had really started to take off because I'd seen their new home featured in a magazine at the time. I'd spent hours studying the photographs of the enormous kitchen diner, lit with so many spotlights it sparkled like a room full of cut diamonds; the lounge full of luxury faux fur blankets and Eliot's room, where a whole wall was painted to look just like an aquarium.

Gregory had just showered. He came out from the en-suite bathroom wearing his blue suit and those glasses that still drove me a little bit wild when he looked over them at me. Like a male version of a hot secretary, I thought, but he seemed distant, and not in the mood to laugh, so I didn't say it. Maybe later.

He was still acting like he was surprised I was back. But

he couldn't be that surprised; surely he'd known it was all going to happen again at some point? There was too much unfinished business between us. How else could it have gone, in the end? I studied his face. A few more lines than last time but still gorgeous, even up this close. No stubble: clean cut like a crystal glass. He looked surprised, but glad.

I pulled him towards me with his tie and laughed at the cheesiness of it. Heat radiated from him.

'Do you know I took your tie from your office when you first started to give me those English tutorials?' I grinned at him, running my fingers up and down the deep blue silk. It was insensitive of me, really, but it felt so good to be with him again that I was overcome by a kind of euphoria, and words kept spilling out of me as though I was drunk. 'I sent it to your house.' I closed my eyes briefly and remembered it all. My mother making me have extra English tutorials, one-to-ones. *You need to work a bit harder than everyone else, Pearl.* Asking at the school reception for an envelope as wild butterflies chased their way through my stomach. Choosing my nicest pen to draw a smiley face.

My time in Gregory's office had been where it had all started. I could see his little room now, even after all those years: messier than I would keep it if I worked at the school, but pretty nice in its own way. It had stayed in my memory when so many other things had drifted away. Warm and cosy and full of books. I'd been transferred into Gregory's A-Level English Literature class just before my eighteenth birthday when our other teacher, some boring old woman, had gone on long-term sick leave. I'd been restless before he started to teach me. I hadn't wanted to be sitting at a desk; I'd been desperate to get to London, to the modelling career I'd been obsessed with for years. Lights, angles, solving the mathematical problem of beauty with my body and face. Nobody would ask me to write essays there; nobody would circle my ideas with big red pens. Everyone would take notice of me. I'd been starved of attention and was drooping. I needed its warmth and water before I shrivelled up completely. It didn't take much to work that out.

I'd been doodling in my notebook, thinking about my catwalk. The last time I'd filmed myself practising, I'd dropped my left shoulder slightly without realising I was doing it. I raised my shoulder now and put my hand up to it. Gregory had appeared at my table at that moment and looked down at me. Before then, I'd always thought he was quite good-looking whenever I'd seen him in passing in the corridors, but at that moment something inside me shifted.

He asked me a question about Othello, I sometimes fantasised about telling guests at our wedding, *and the rest was history!*

'I had a feeling you took things,' he said now. 'But I didn't know about a tie.'

'I sent it to Maddy.'

'I hope you're joking.' Gregory's voice was much sharper than I wanted it to be. How could he be annoyed about that now, after ten long years? It obviously hadn't ruined his perfect life: I was surrounded by it all right now, up so close it felt like it might choke me.

'I thought you'd have known. I thought Maddy might be angry.' Anger was exactly what I'd wanted. I'd imagined hurled words, maybe something thrown. Shards of glass, beads of wine crawling down their gorgeous walls.

Gregory glanced quickly at my face. 'Maddy trusted me.'

'Past tense?' I teased, hearing horrible uncertainty in my voice. 'She doesn't trust you now?'

'Maddy is my wife. You have to understand that.' His voice had become gentler. He knew how hard it was for me.

I inhaled deeply. There was a deep, musky smell in their bedroom that lay underneath the scent of the White Company diffuser and the lingering, grapefruit fragrance of Maddy's perfume. It was the kind of smell I'd catch on my clothes when I was back in the flat later on. Alone.

'So, I'll wait for you to leave her. I'll wait until you're ready to do it.' He had always intended to leave Maddy. I leaned forwards as we kissed, Gregory's lips warm as coffee under mine. I moved again so that our bodies pressed together and for a moment, things were perfect. I was living as Maddy must live every single day. But then there was a noise from downstairs, a glass or a bottle, perhaps.

'You should go,' Gregory whispered. 'Maddison can't find out you're here. Nobody can.' Even with panic written all over it, Gregory's face was as beautiful as it has been all those years ago, and I was grateful for that. His perfection was making it so much easier to continue to rip Trafford from the follicle of my life and to ignore my own enormous flaws. It was making it easier to wait for him to change things. 'I'm going downstairs. I will make sure Maddy stays in the orangery, at the back. You can go out the front door.'

Hurt pulled at my insides, its fingers sharp.

He shook himself from me.

'Go,' he said.

It had been a bit of a stupid fantasy to tell people at the wedding about Gregory being my teacher, I realised as I sat on Maddy and Gregory's luxurious bed and pulled my hair back into a bun – Maddy had some of those nice satin hair ties and I'd helped myself to a grey one after Gregory had disappeared downstairs. I suddenly realised that it would have been tasteless to refer to him being my teacher on our wedding day. Even though I'd been pretty much an adult, about to leave sixth form, people wouldn't like it. That had been the problem all along. The point I wanted to make was that we'd had this thing going on for a long time, longer than my imaginary wedding guests would probably give us credit for.

Imaginary, because who would actually come to watch if I got married?

I lay back on the cool, soft bed for a moment and stared at the ceiling. The ceiling in the flat I was staying at in my parents' grounds was as flawlessly white as a professionally iced cake. Maddy and Gregory's ceiling – because the house was older with decades of money and success trapped in its walls – had spidery cracks in it if I looked closely enough.

Did Maddy notice those when she was lying here, too?

I sprang up and wandered over to the gigantic dressing table, taking care to avoid the mirror towering over it.

The house was so massive that Gregory was worrying

over nothing. I was a million miles from Maddy. He seemed even more nervous about being caught this time, probably because now, on top of everything else, he thought he had his fame to lose. Gregory Archer, drop-dead gorgeous author. But he needed to listen to me and relax. Maddy, all the way downstairs, had absolutely no chance of knowing I was here – unless, of course, she came into the bedroom. That meant I had a little time to look around and move a few things so that the certainty that Maddy took for granted would disappear, just like mine had.

Maddy's jewellery glinted in the afternoon sun that poured through the window. Row upon row of necklaces and earrings and bracelets. A few carefully selected bottles of perfume arranged on a gold tray. Hundreds of matching cosmetics in glass dividers waiting to be used. God, this woman used a lot of shit on her skin. I had always avoided make-up. I'd always wanted to be a blank canvas, ready to be anyone for the camera.

I finally glanced up into the mirror, unable to help myself. I saw the jagged pull on the left side of my lips. The scar creeping down my cheek. My slightly receded hairline at my left temple.

Now I could never be anyone else but myself: the last person in the world I wanted to be.

I heard a noise from downstairs, a door closing perhaps or the thud of a cupboard. Maybe it wouldn't be the worst thing if Maddy came up here. Something had to change the way things were, otherwise I'd end up the other woman forever. It would feel like Trafford all over again.

Maddy didn't come upstairs, in the end.

I made the most of my time in the bedroom, luxuriating in the scent of Gregory and Maddy, running my fingertips along Gregory's clothes and smoothing Maddy's creams and serums into my skin. Eventually, Gregory appeared upstairs again, hissing my name from the vast landing. He'd kept Maddy talking downstairs for quite some time, probably to give me time to leave. But a part of me just hadn't been able to. Why leave this exquisite home to go back to the flat all on my own?

'Get out,' Gregory said when he got to the bedroom, and a part of me chipped off and was lost somewhere, a little piece of pain absorbed into my body. He had never spoken to me like this years ago, when I'd looked perfect. And now, because I didn't look like that anymore – because I wasn't parading around with a symmetrical face and perfect breasts and a glossy life like Maddy did, he wasn't treating me like he needed to. It stung badly, even more than the agony of flesh being ripped apart.

He pulled my arm harder than he meant to as he helped me downstairs to guide me out of the house, and pain bloomed on my skin.

'I'll be on your cameras. What if she—'

'I'll wipe them.' His words were rushed and panicked now that we were downstairs, so close to Maddy. What would it be like for us to have all the time and freedom in the world?

'Gregory?' Maddy's voice came from the back of the

house. 'Are you sure you don't want one glass of wine before you go? I'm having another one.'

'No, thanks,' Gregory shouted back to Maddy. 'I'm fine.' His voice dropped to a sharp whisper as he spoke to me. 'Go.'

The air outside was suffocating after the cool interior of the house. I made a show of walking quickly down the wide, tree-lined street, past a couple of other huge houses crawling with money. When I glanced back, I saw with satisfaction that Gregory was watching me from the doorway. I turned away again.

Let him watch.

It was around an hour after Gregory had told me to leave, when he'd watched me from his doorway as I'd disappeared around the corner of their enormous street, that I returned. I stood silently in Maddy and Gregory's front garden, shaded from the aggressive heat behind one of the enormous oak trees in the dappled shade. Gregory's car was gone now, but Maddy's was still up the gargantuan drive: a big white SUV. She obviously didn't want a black one.

Bad memories, Maddy?

I waited a while and then opened Instagram, scrolling through until I found Maddy's latest post from just a few minutes ago. There she was, posing in a white, low-cut playsuit.

#dinnerparty#family#friday

So she was going to Candice's house, like she sometimes did on a Friday night. I shifted to make sure that I wasn't visible from the house, and then stared down at the photo. Gregory had always kept quiet about his thoughts about my body, but I'd always worried that I was too boy-like compared to Maddy, who was all curves and femininity, like a designer vase.

I glanced up when I saw movement at the edge of my vision. Maddy. She came out of her front door with her son quickly, giving me no opportunity to squint and see behind it. Even before I'd been inside the house today, I'd known it all so well from the photos I'd seen Maddy post and the floorplan and photos from Rightmove. One day, when I'd been particularly bored, I'd printed the floorplan and added on drawings of their furniture, piecing together every room I'd ever seen glimpses of in photos. I'd kept the copy of the magazine that had featured Maddy and Gregory, so that had helped too. There was a silver lamp on a white cabinet in the left-hand corner of the hallway and an obscure metal ornament that was the kind of thing I would never put in the flat but that worked in Gregory's house as careful evidence of his creativity and style. There was an enormous black-and-white canvas of Maddy and Gregory on their wedding day on the opposite wall. I would have something much more subtle, but that was Maddy all over, pushing everything she had in people's faces. A staircase ran down into the middle of the hall with a cream carpet runner and polished dark wood either side.

And then there was Maddy, who was meters away from me now for the first time in so long. She looked the same, as though time hadn't touched her. Still perfectly groomed: the woman who had absolutely everything. Her tight white outfit shone in the sun, and her dark hair was pulled into a bun with gigantic sunglasses perched on her head. I touched my own hair and pulled out the silk tie I'd taken from Maddy's bedside table. I never usually wore my hair up, for obvious reasons. But maybe being in Maddy's bedroom had given me some kind of temporary liberation.

I watched as Maddy gestured for Eliot to get in the car, then hopped in herself and pulled out of the driveway smoothly. I'd seen Eliot a few times when I first met Gregory. Eliot had been a baby then, and had looked like all other babies. He was lanky now, not petite like Maddy, the kind of boy that looked awkward and a bit sorry about the fact he existed.

Maddy had said something to Gregory about having wine before she'd left, hadn't she? I strained to remember the words but they wouldn't come. It didn't matter. The point was that by tonight there would definitely be more than one pretty glass bottle in the recycling bin. And now Maddy was *driving*? With her son in the car?

I moved quickly through the thick, hot air to my own car, the Audi convertible that my dad had bought me a couple of weeks ago to give me some more independence. I followed Maddy as she drove towards Candice's house, which was at the pinnacle of Kings Hill, just near the school. Maddy was driving fast, and adrenaline buzzed through my blood as I pressed my foot on the accelerator too and felt the Audi zip beneath me.

The need to drive full speed at Maddy, to rush at that

white car with all the hurt and fury of the last ten years, was sudden and overtook me. I imagined broken bones, Maddy's flesh ripped apart, Maddy having to press stop on her life and spend endless days in airless hospital rooms. My breaths became uneven with the images in my mind and I forced myself to slow them down, take one gulp of air at a time.

NINE

Maddy

Ten years earlier

The Gatsby Ball happened a few months after Maddy's life had been poisoned by the tie in the envelope and the sight of Gregory with the girl. The air was thick with summer thunder, the sky a dirty, threatening yellow.

Maddy straightened out her red flapper dress and put on another coat of mascara. Standing back from the mirror, she tilted her head to the left. Time was a dirty sneak. She was due more Botox. She should have worked her timings out better because tonight was a big deal. It was the first of a series of charity balls sponsored by her gym, Vibe, that Gregory had been given complimentary tickets to because of his standing as a local author. Whenever Gregory attended events like those, Maddy attended with him. Maddy had soon realised that she even needed to invent a little story about how she'd met him.

'Most people think we met at a party,' she'd said to an

interviewer at one charity function a while ago. 'But we've actually known each other for a lot longer. We were childhood friends. We used to play in the park together sometimes. Not many people know that although he was slightly older than me and we were at different schools, I had the biggest crush on him for years. Eventually he told me he felt the same, in the best way that a twelve-year-old boy can.' She'd let out a laugh here as she pushed away her real memories of being twelve, of a longing for Aiden so strong it felt like it might kill her. 'There's actually a tree with our initials carved into it in East Park.' Gregory had gone along with it all, smooth as a show pony with his nodding in agreement and his small additions to the story. And when Maddy had gone to the park in the dark later that night to carve their initials into a tree, fairly low down, so inconspicuous nobody would have ever noticed whether they'd been there before or not, Gregory had laughed and squeezed her hand. 'This is just what madness looks like,' he'd told her, his tone affectionate. 'Sneaking around an old creaking oak tree in the middle of the night!' But he understood that people needed a brand, that they liked to see a rosy past placed next to the present, a nice shiny end to follow childhood. *Who is this cute couple*, people would think. *How can I make my life closer to the perfection of theirs so that their magic might trickle into my mundanity? Ah look, he has a book out! I'll read it! I'll get inside his mind!*

Maddy had been starting to wonder before the girl if she should bring out a book on marketing, instead of actually doing marketing. She could be one of those wonder mothers who wrote at four in the morning while the baby slept, and when it was published it would stand out on the shelf, Maddy's name holding its own near Gregory's, the cover a glossy yellow against his hues of moody deep greens and blues.

Her phone buzzed next to her. Gregory was due home from a book signing any minute now. She put down the mascara and pulled her forehead taut with her free hand as she answered the call. Much better.

'I got stuck talking to a few people.' The line crackled and Gregory's voice broke. '…longer than I thought. I think I'll head straight to the ball.'

Maddy let go of her forehead and stared at herself in the mirror, her eyes boring through the glass. 'What about your outfit?'

There was a crackle, something incomprehensible at the other end. Maddy swallowed down frustration.

'Gregory? Are you there?'

His voice returned, tinny and fractured. 'Just in case,' he was saying. The line went dead and Maddy threw her phone onto the bed. It missed and cracked against the wall. She'd probably smashed the screen. She marched over to their enormous wardrobes and yanked at the hangers. His inky scent floated out like a ghost. She had seen his *Gatsby* outfit in there the other day, and now it was gone. So he'd taken it with him to the book signing.

Just in case.

Yeah, right. Did he think she'd been born yesterday?

Maybe there hadn't even been a book signing. Or maybe she would get to the ball and Gregory wouldn't even be there. Perhaps it had all been a pretence: his black waistcoat and braces and the invitation he'd told her about. Maybe Falcon Castle would be in darkness when she arrived, and it had all been a huge trick to get her out of the way.

Maddy reminded herself to breathe. She was being ridiculous and losing her grip on reality. She'd seen huge promotional posters for the ball that very morning at Vibe. She'd even seen the tickets. Of course – the tickets! Maddy rushed out of their bedroom and across the landing to Gregory's study. She pulled open his top drawer and took out both tickets for the Gatsby Ball.

So there was definitely going to be a ball.

She just didn't know if Gregory would be at it.

Maybe he would be waiting for her outside the castle when she arrived, although with the looming storm, it didn't seem like the best idea.

Or maybe he'd managed to talk his way around not being there tonight because that's what Gregory always did.

Maybe, maybe, maybe.

Clutching both tickets, Maddy went back to her bedroom and took out the black velvet box from her vanity unit. She wanted to wear her limited-edition necklace tonight, the one that Gregory had bought her just after they were married. Never in a million years had she imagined all these assets might need to be split. She fastened her necklace, feeling the cool weight of the diamonds and emeralds at her throat.

Maybe what she needed was some company tonight.

She scrolled through her contacts. Luckily, her phone, when she'd retrieved it from where it had bashed against the wall, just had a hairline crack down the screen. You wouldn't even see it unless you looked closely.

Maddy pressed on Sadie's name and imagined her at home, probably in a loungewear set, soft grey maybe, or a deep blue: a cup of herbal tea beside her and little Blake asleep upstairs in a bedroom full of smiling toys. There was something about Sadie's life that made Maddy want to climb inside it. It made her feel uneasy and reassured all at once. They'd formed quite a habit of going for a drink at The Cellar, or meeting at the nearby park with the children. She thought about her other friends. Lucie and Harper would be merrily appalled at Gregory not being there with Maddy at the start of the ball. They'd side-eye each other and bask in the warmth of Maddy's disappointment.

Sadie didn't answer, which was frustrating. Maddy hit *call* again, and again. Something – a small voice somewhere inside her – tried to stop her, tried to tell her that this was too much, too smothering, but then – joy! – Sadie answered. She had been putting Blake to bed, she explained, a little breathless as though she'd run to her phone. Maddy imagined Sadie kissing Blake's soft little forehead, smoothing her covers and turning on a night light.

Sweet dreams.

'Okay,' Sadie said eventually, when Maddy had explained about Gregory going AWOL and asked Sadie if she might want the spare ticket. 'And you're sure Gregory isn't going?'

'Oh no,' Maddy answered brightly. 'Definitely not. He's tied up for the rest of the evening with work.' The more time had passed, the more Maddy had faced up to it.

Of course Gregory wouldn't be there. He'd be with the girl, his tie, his weird, perverted fantasies. 'This year's theme is *Gatsby*.' She paused. Gregory had clapped his hands together in that drama club way he had about him when he'd discovered that. *Ah! The American dream! Rags to riches to dust. Excellent!* 'Do you have something to wear? I have a few flapper dresses if not. I bought a couple because I couldn't choose.' Maddy hesitated as she spoke, unsure if her dresses would swamp the willowy Sadie.

'It's fine,' Sadie said. 'I've played at a Twenties-themed party before so I have a dress I can dig out.'

When Sadie arrived at the house, Maddy waited for her to gawp at the huge, congratulatory images of Gregory's book cover that hung on the wall. Most people who came to the house knew who Gregory was and brought with them a kind of iridescent hope that his success might rub off on them.

'I've got a novel inside me somewhere too', some of them said, as though Gregory might whip a three-book contract and a ghostwriter out of a drawer just for them.

It was only every so often that someone would arrive at the house who didn't know that Gregory Archer, the writer of *Watched*, lived there. And then it would come all at once. Surprise at the cover on the wall. Awe. Glances at the photographs and Maddy and Gregory's belongings as though the house were a gallery. Sometimes she felt as though they should tack on a gift shop on to their orangery.

But Sadie was different. Maddy waited for a gush of questions about Gregory, but instead Sadie looked straight at

Maddy and said how nice she looked. She talked happily about Blake's bedtime and how quickly her cab had arrived, about finding a pair of silver shoes to match her dress. Something about the way she spoke, the way she was suddenly, wonderfully *there*, made Maddy hug her impulsively. Maddy had never been someone to hug her friends. But this felt like a movie-teenage friendship, almost like a crush: contagious laughs and impromptu sleepovers and forbidden junk food at midnight. She'd never had a friendship like it before, and hadn't thought she needed one. Friends were just brought out like cardboard cut-outs for nice brunches and the ongoing game of whose house was the biggest, who had been promoted, whose child had the widest vocab. But things had changed. None of that cat-and-mouse stuff would be much fun now that there was a monster chasing Maddy.

As Sadie followed her into the kitchen, Maddy felt another version of herself – one who hugged people and shared her secrets – glimmer in the distance. Words fizzed inside her, truthful words about her shame and horror at what Gregory had done. She felt like a shaken bottle of champagne, her truths ready to burst from her in a messy froth.

'Can I tell you something?' she asked Sadie, to bide time. Sadie looked at Maddy with her clear, open face and wide blue eyes. The other version of Maddy beckoned: a Maddy who was honest, who had friendships that helped her bob up above the murky water of life, who looked after her friends in return. She felt like she was about to try on an outfit she'd never usually wear. But sometimes, wasn't that just what you needed when you were sick of the same old clothes?

'Gregory's having an affair with one of his students,' she said quietly.

Sadie's eyes widened. 'Oh, Maddy. Since when?'

'I'm not sure.' Maddy thought of the note, the tie. 'A few months, at least.'

'Does he know that you know? Have you spoken to him?'

'He has no idea. He's wrapped up in his own little world. That's probably why he's not going to be at the ball tonight.'

Sadie reached out and touched Maddy on the wrist. Her fingers were warm on Maddy's skin.

'Please don't tell anyone else. You're the only person I've told.'

Sadie squeezed Maddy's wrist then, gently, as though Maddy were a child. Something unfamiliar swelled inside her. A feeling that she wasn't completely alone.

'We have so much!' This was the next thing to burst from her now that she had somehow become uncorked. She was unable to stop herself gesturing wildly to her custom-made kitchen cabinets and huge prints of Maddy in her wedding dress and pieces of ridiculously beautiful abstract art. 'There's all this. And there's Eliot. Our marriage. Our whole life.' Their memories, and their future that had always all seemed so safe. Gregory couldn't just ditch all that now, on a stupid whim. 'I'm not going to let some little girl take it from us. And he won't. He won't leave all this. He's clearly just having a moment of madness.' And didn't everyone have those: give in to their other self sometimes, the stark raving mad version who was trying to escape the attic of their mind?

'You know him better than anyone, Maddy.' Sadie nodded in willing agreement and Maddy wanted to hug her again for it. 'How did you find out?'

'I saw them together a while ago. He'd forgotten his diary, so I went to his office at the school to give it to him. It was the day I first met you at Stay and Play. I had Eliot with me, and I saw him leaving his office with a girl. They were holding hands. The girl posted his tie here before that, too. He'd probably left it at one of their dirty little get-togethers. She addressed it to me. She obviously wanted me to know. Which makes me think it must be a big thing?' Maddy gestured to the bottle of Sauvignon on the worktop. 'Quick drink before we go?'

For the last few years, Maddy had tried to drink a little less (all those empty calories!). The girl and Gregory were undoing all that though, she realised as she uncorked the wine a little too quickly. One glass was often turning into another these days. Even Harper and Lucie had commented on Maddy's drinking. They had both stopped with the alcohol and were doing dry summers. Every time they met for dinner, they sat and sipped at mineral water, hydrating themselves, visibly glowing with health whilst Maddy threw poison down her own throat.

Thankfully, Sadie smiled and took the glass from Maddy. 'Go on, then. So what are you going to do? Will you tell him you know?'

'I haven't said anything to him yet. I'm trying to work

out how to play it.' As though it were a game. It was though, wasn't it? All of life was, really. Making the best moves you could with the number you'd landed, and trying not to bump into any dragons that might eat you and spit you back out. Trying not to lose all your points with one unfortunate move.

Maddy downed her drink, and noticed that Sadie had barely touched hers after all. They sat in silence for a moment and Maddy felt a vague sense of disappointment. Now would be a good time for Sadie to share something too, to reassure Maddy that her life with her nice paramedic husband and her child plucked straight from a nursery rhyme wasn't quite as it seemed. But Sadie was quiet, making Maddy feel like the new self she'd tried might not be a good fit after all. She wondered what Sadie was thinking about, and the rising balloon of joy she'd had just moments before drifted back down, deflated.

Maddy and Sadie took a cab to the Gatsby Ball. Maddy had grabbed her car keys but Sadie had frowned and then glanced towards the kitchen, where Maddy knew her empty wine glass and the almost-empty bottle were both standing by the sink.

'Oh! I'm not driving! I'm going to just get something from the car,' she'd said, feeling her face burn.

The ball was being held at Falcon Castle, which stood on the edge of dramatic cliffs overlooking Falcon beach, to the south of Kings Hill and about a forty-minute drive away.

The cab cost a fortune and Maddy paid, feeling her nerves spring up, electric, now that they had arrived.

'I hope he isn't here,' she said faintly, more to herself, but she felt Sadie's eyes on her as they walked to the enormous entrance flanked by huge flaming torches.

'I thought you said he definitely wasn't coming?' Sadie sounded uncertain and Maddy took a deep breath.

'I'm sure he isn't. He doesn't have a ticket, does he?' She whipped the tickets from her bag and fluttered them around with her best smile, but Sadie didn't look convinced. Maddy felt a flicker of fury at Gregory. Why would he do this to her: make her look so stupid in front of her new friend, make her tell her too much and be someone she shouldn't need to be?

They moved on in a growing crowd of guests in full tuxedos and glittering dresses. Maddy showed their tickets at the door, feeling herself calm a little as she did so. If Gregory did arrive later, he'd have to ask for Maddy because he wouldn't be able to get in. She'd have to save him. It would be up to her whether or not she let him in.

Sadie and Maddy were jostled through the enormous stone entrance and handed coupes of champagne with stems so thin they felt like they might snap. Jazz music floated from what was obviously the main hall and the scents of parties – sweet alcohol and perfume with a hint of cigarette smoke – were heavy in the air.

'It's strange to be a guest,' Sadie was saying. 'I've played the piano at things like this before but I never get to be on the other side.' She had put her still-full glass of champagne down on an elaborately carved table beside her, and her slim arms hung by her side as she swayed ever so slightly to the music. She smiled at Maddy: clean white teeth in a pleasant row. It was then that Maddy saw Gregory, a few metres away. He was pulling at his collar as though it was strangling him. His face was a little flushed, his mouth set in a tense line.

'He's here,' Maddy murmured to Sadie, who followed her gaze to see Gregory. He took a glass of champagne, then looked around and spotted Maddy, giving her a strange, unsettled smile as he moved towards them, straightening his tie so that it hung in the centre of his chest again like a pendulum. He was wearing a pocket watch that Maddy hadn't known was going to be part of his costume. Its chain twinkled in the golden light. Maddy saw that his forehead was glazed with sweat.

'I thought you couldn't come. I brought a friend.'

Gregory frowned. 'I said I'd meet you here. I said that I had a feeling there might be a delay in London, but I never said I'd miss it altogether.' He tossed a charming grin at Sadie. 'You know how it is. Agents, trains, crowds. Schedules go right out of the window.'

'But you left your ticket at home.' Maddy's heart was beating a little faster now, fluttering: a pretty little bird in a cage.

'I told you on the phone. I contacted the organisers and they said not to worry. I just had to show identification.'

Maddy took another glass of champagne from a passing waiter and took a large gulp so that the bubbles stung her throat. It was what she'd wanted, wasn't it? Gregory not standing her up, Gregory being where he was meant to be, with Maddy. This way she could compose herself and handle everything with care, work out how to detonate the bomb so that it did not obliterate everything. But she felt no relief, because something was the matter with Gregory, she realised as they stood around awkwardly, Sadie still shifting about to the jazz music, women with cigarette holders and rattling beads bumping into them softly as they made their way to the ballroom. Gregory was radiating some kind of … what was it? Fear? Yes. He was afraid of something. He downed his drink, eyes darting around the room as he sought out more alcohol. This wasn't like Gregory, for a start. He was usually the one who pulled Maddy back from the bar.

'Well,' she said, linking her arm through Sadie's. 'The line was terrible when I spoke to you. I got the wrong end of the stick and thought you weren't coming at all. But it doesn't matter, does it? We can all still have a good time.' Maddy tried to make her words smooth. But Gregory wasn't listening. He was pulling at his collar again, staring across the room.

'Shall we go through to the ballroom?' Sadie asked, and Maddy felt a pop of relief. Yes, the ballroom. What a good idea.

She smiled at Sadie gratefully. 'Let's. We'll see you in there, Gregory.' Maddy pulled Sadie away, not waiting for Gregory's reply and not turning back to see if he would follow.

Huge doors were flung open along the edge of the ballroom, the distance an expanse of grey-blue sea. Glittering chandeliers hung from the ceiling and vases filled with peacock feathers and flowers were placed on each surface at regular intervals. Maddy used to be familiar with the designs of events like this one. She remembered the ache that started from her stilettoed feet, right up through the arch of her back, as she chatted and drank the long evenings away.

It was as she was recalling that particular ache, those particular days, that she saw her.

She was in a black-and-white dress which hung on her skinny frame exactly as it should have done; exactly how it would not hang on Maddy's curves. Maddy felt dizzy, as though she might fall to the ground, or as though the ground itself might crumble beneath her so that she plummeted to the hot core of the earth.

Gregory was beside Maddy then, a hand on her waist, and the girl continued to move towards them with her gloating face, her perfect figure that wasn't even real yet.

He's mine, the girl might say to Maddy. *Everything is mine.*

The girl reached them. A gold bracelet glinted on her slim wrist as she brushed Gregory's arm with her fingers.

'Gregory,' she said, a cat-cream grin on her face. 'I didn't know you were going to be here.'

Gregory's face was calm but the sheen of sweat on his forehead became more pronounced. A small, slow bead began its descent down his temple. Maddy didn't believe it for a minute. They'd probably arrived together. *Come with me*, he'd probably urged the girl. *Stupid, clueless Maddy will never suspect a thing.*

'It's Mr Archer, Pearl. And I certainly didn't know you were going to be here, either.'

Pearl laughed, threw her head back slightly, exposing a delicate neck.

Gregory turned to Maddy and Sadie. 'This is Pearl, one of my students.'

'Not really,' Pearl interjected, still grinning like a doll. 'Not now. My last exam was in June, actually.'

June. Maddy had seen the girl with Gregory in July. It was August now. Maddy felt exhausted thinking about all the days, all the nights and hours and minutes that this had absorbed her for. But for how long had she been oblivious before she saw them?

'I remembered everything you told me to put in it, Mr Archer,' Pearl continued. She rolled his name around in his mouth, saying it slowly.

Maddy tried not to visibly flinch. 'I'm Mrs Archer,' she told Pearl. She did not hold out her hand for Pearl to shake. 'And this is Sadie. My best friend.'

'Best friend?' Pearl gave a little laugh, a tinkling sound that was absorbed by the excited chatter; pianos and saxophones; the clinking of glasses and popping of corks.

'Oh, I'm sorry. Did that sound childish?' Maddy glared at Gregory, her breaths short and jagged in her chest. Pearl *was* a fucking child, and that didn't seem to bother him. She took the final gulp of her drink. Why did the glasses have to be so *small*?

'Well,' Gregory said. 'I have a couple of people I want to say hello to now that I'm finally here. Very nice to see you, Pearl. All the best.' Words as hollow and stiff as wood.

'That's her,' Maddy told Sadie as they watched Gregory and Pearl both move away from them, into the glittering crowd. 'He couldn't stand that. All of us standing together. I've never seen him squirm so much.'

'You need to speak to him.'

Maddy turned to Sadie and looked into her pretty blue eyes. 'Here? Now? I don't think so.' She could absolutely not let people see some kind of tacky showdown. Perhaps Sadie wasn't quite as wise as Maddy had thought. The feeling that Maddy shouldn't have been completely honest with Sadie returned. The whole night had so far been a seesaw of emotions, up and down, despair and joy taking turns to lift Maddy and then slam her against the ground again. Sadie wouldn't understand any of this. How could she? Her husband didn't have hold of her future in his fist, crumpling it like a bank note, tearing it into pieces so that it floated to the ground.

Maddy opened her little gold handbag and felt in the zipped compartment. Yes, there they were: smooth and round against her fingertips, reassuring little tablets of oblivion, there if she needed them. Harper had given them to Maddy some time ago now, before Eliot, before Harper refused to even have a gin and tonic or single glass of wine. The pills distanced you from life in quite a nice way, Harper had told her, but at the time Maddy hadn't really been able to understand what she meant. She wondered now if the pills might do other things too, if they might make people like Sadie drop their guards instead of standing and watching disaster from a faraway utopia.

TEN

Pearl

The day was slowly turning into the evening by the time I arrived back at the flat at my parents' house. When Maddy had swung onto Candice's huge gravel driveway, I'd continued driving straight ahead and turned down a side street lined with bright green trees, so glossy they looked fake. The urge to creep from my car to Candice's, where Maddy was spending the evening, had been visceral, almost painful.

But I'd managed, somehow, to stop myself.

I wasn't great with time these days: my brain liked to skip bits of it, chop it from my memory. But when I was watching Maddy or Sadie, it was even worse. They swamped my life, pulled me from reality without me noticing. They had done since I'd first met them. At the beginning, I suppose I'd wanted to know how they'd managed to get their lives in such perfect order. How Maddy had managed to marry Gregory and build her life of absolute perfection. How she also managed to have an easy friendship with Sadie. Sadie's life was flawless too. How did they *do* it?

It was intense at first, a burning need to know as much as possible about them. The need had faded a little in London, and I'd managed to mainly watch them from a distance on Instagram and the odd website where they might pop up. As time drifted on, they became like my very own celebrities, supplying my harmless addiction of aspiration, escape and a feeling of intimate knowledge that made me feel less alone. Now I was closer, the need to know more had lit up again into something similar to when it had all started with Gregory ten years ago.

When I arrived back at the flat, there was a note stuck to the door.

WHY DO YOU INSIST ON BEING SO DIFFICULT?

The handwriting was huge, haughty and looped, and I could sense Blanche's annoyance radiating from it. Honestly. I could have dropped dead or been kidnapped for all my mother knew. She was no different these days from how she'd been when I was a child. I didn't even know why she'd had a child. My father must have wanted me, because he was the only one who seemed to get the slightest bit of pleasure from talking to me. All I remembered of Blanche when I was really little, before the digs about my looks and my hugely disappointing academic skills began, was being hissed at to go off, to go away, to stop humiliating her. She was forever having people round for impromptu dinner parties. I would smell salmon mingled with perfume and alcohol, and cars would clutter the outside of our house. She never wanted me there then. And she certainly didn't want me around now, apart from when it suited her, or when she wanted to control me like a little puppet.

I ripped the note down and crumpled it up, then threw it onto the scorched ground. I headed straight to my bedroom and ripped off my shorts and vest, then lay naked on the bed. The crisp white sheets were cool and soothing against my skin. I took some more deep breaths. Four, seven, eight. It was Henri who'd told me to do that. My therapist. My parents had always been keen on me *seeing someone*; *talking to someone*. I think my mother saw it like some sort of insurance against my behaviour. She said she feared for me, whatever that meant. I translated that to mean she didn't trust me, even though I'd never really done anything that hurt anyone, even after everything that happened to me. I sometimes wondered if that was why my dad had been so keen for me to move back – so he could stop me from whatever it was he thought I might do, or whatever my mother told him I might do.

Anyway, everyone and their dog in Kings Hill East probably had a therapist, but I'd never wanted one. There was something so ironic and backwards in it all: trying to move on from what had happened by dwelling on it. Henri had liked to tilt his head to the side and look at my disgusting face head-on, as though he was proving a point that he was definitely strong and resilient enough for all this. He used the word *resilient* a lot, like a talking textbook. He was a show-off: not out for me at all, but for my dad's weekly bank transfers. Was there actually anyone who wasn't all about themselves in this world? Doubtful.

I was still terrible at the breathing exercise. I spluttered and gulped in new air as I sat up and pulled my pink cashmere bathrobe around myself. I felt like I was drowning. I'd always hated Henri. He was the kind of man who thought wearing loud, patterned trousers was a personality trait. He always referred to my *mates*, as though I was surrounded by people just like me. Yeah, right. He understood nothing. I'd stopped going to Henri eventually because I'd decided he was making me worse, and wasting my dad's money. I'd told Dad I was fine and didn't need the sessions anymore, and then I'd moved to London.

Now, I took out my phone and turned it on. It had been off for most of the day, to try and silence my mother. She would be furious with me for not being there tonight. As expected, her text messages were repetitive, the level of bossiness increasing with each one.

> I should have reminded you earlier. I knew you'd forget.

> You can still make it if you leave now.

> Come on, darling. Don't make me so disappointed in you.

There was also a message from Dad. He normally defended me but now and again Blanche hammered him so hard with her complaints that he gave in.

> You really are causing your mother a lot of stress, darling.

I thought about calling him. He would do that performance where he told me one thing but would mean another. *I'm sure she will understand if you don't go. And I understand, of course.*

But he didn't, really.

I ached with the need to contact Gregory, but something stopped me. Thinking of him made me feel uneasy. I tried to remember what he'd said to me when I'd been at his house earlier. I couldn't remember the precise words, only his face. He'd been annoyed. Best to leave him for a time. He'd come around.

But my fingers were twitching, my phone ready to connect me with *someone*. I tapped out a message to Trafford and then remembered what he'd said to me last time I tried to reconnect us. I deleted it, feeling a hollow ache. As beautiful as the design of this flat in my parents' grounds was, it seemed so empty. The loneliness that had always hovered over me in London was somehow amplified now that I was back, so aggressive that I felt like it might turn me inside out.

I had worked with an interior designer called Ruby on the restoration of the flat. My parents had never done much with it before: just used it for guests, even though the main house had seven bedrooms. But as soon as I had agreed to come back, Dad had clicked his fingers and Ruby had appeared to make it into the most beautiful flat in Kings

Hill East. Dad knew the best interior designers because Goldman Estates sold the best houses to the richest people.

Before I met Ruby for the first time, I'd wondered if I could get into interior design myself. I'd imagined maybe asking her if she could give me some tips on how to get started. I'd even thought that if I showed a natural ability for designing (which I'd suspected I would – my London flat had been to die for and I'd designed that all by myself), maybe we could join forces. Ruby and Pearl. Precious together and apart. What a brand. Meant to be.

But then I had met Ruby to talk about her plans for my flat and she hadn't been able to stop staring at my scars as we spoke. Her cool green eyes had flickered with things that my stupid, broken memory would typically not let me forget. Disgust. Sadness. Curiosity. All the worst things, certainly not ones that I wanted to see every time I met with clients and business partners.

So interior design was out, and Ruby took my ideas and Pinterest boards and we didn't see each other again. The next time I was back in Kings Hill East, the flat was done.

Despite the sinking way that Ruby had made me feel, her work on the flat had been perfection. It was exactly what I'd asked for: lots of deep green velvet and gold in the living room with a specially designed coffee table and matching drinks cabinet. Every single thing in the bedroom was in crisp, bright white, so that I felt as though I were sleeping in the clouds.

The notes from my mother and the thought of the weekend ahead made me crave someone with me: the warmth of their chest and the subtle beat of their pulse.

Maybe I needed a pet? I could buy a cat to keep me company and call it something witty like Bitch.

But no. I'd had a kitten when I was little. My father had brought it home after that awful dinner party, the one where I'd had the accident. As always, I'd been told to go upstairs and play on my own that night whilst my parents ate dinner with their friends. I'd sneaked downstairs, hoping that my dad would feel sorry for me like he sometimes did, and would let me eat some of their leftover dessert or chat to some of the nicer friends they had. But he'd been deep in conversation with some man, and my mother had told me to go away, her hand waving me from the room. One of her friends had laughed a horrible little laugh. And then I'd tripped on my way upstairs. Someone had discarded a wine glass, and I hadn't seen it. The glass had shattered beneath me. I still had the scars now, three little lines along my forearm: a warning of what was to come.

The visit to Accident and Emergency and the stitches had been traumatic. My mother hadn't even come with us. My dad had obviously felt so guilty about it all that he'd arrived home with the kitten a few days later. But I hadn't liked its little grey features. It had been too beautiful, too symmetrical, and it had irritated me. I'd felt imperfect in comparison, with ugly gauze and the stench of hospitals stuck to my skin. And I didn't want a kitten. I wanted my parents. I wanted to sit with them at their dinner parties and be able to sip some of the wine in pretty glasses and wear nice dresses like all the women did.

Dad had given the kitten to some colleague in the end.

So maybe not a cat.

But someone. A warm chest. The murmur of a heartbeat. Conversation and company. It was all I wanted when I was little and had listened to the hum of other people talking from my lonely bedroom. And it was all I wanted now.

I glanced at the time on my phone and did some slow calculations, my brain clinking as I made it work. I should have been with Blanche at the training about an hour ago and I tried to decide if I should set off now: if doing that would be better than not going at all. Blanche was claiming she wanted me there but I doubted she'd be okay with me appearing halfway through, on my own terms and own time. She had never liked how unpredictable I was: how she'd been unable to control what I might do, even when I was young.

I sighed, then sprung up from the soft white bed, dropped the cashmere robe so that it pooled around my feet and pulled my shorts back on.

ELEVEN

Maddy
___

Ten years earlier

Maddy had never really noticed Gregory putting his hands on her waist or kissing her cheek lightly before. It had been something that she had taken for granted, like everything else: her beautiful home, her *my husband is Gregory Archer, yes, the author of* Watched, and their expanding joint bank account that got fatter and fatter each month. But tonight at the Gatsby Ball, Gregory's lips on her skin jolted electroshock images into her mind: him kissing Pearl, keeping secrets and charging towards success with somebody else, leaving Maddy behind.

Maddy moved away from him eventually, pushing him gently with her elbow so that nobody but him would notice. She turned to Sadie.

'Do you ever want to escape?' she asked Sadie.

Sadie smiled her nice pretty smile and Maddy hoped she would say yes.

Yes, I want to escape sometimes.

Yes. Sometimes it isn't enough.

But of course Sadie didn't answer, just cocked her head to the side like a spaniel as she tried to work out what Maddy was saying. Maddy tried to say it again but her words bumped into one another, blurring at the edges so that Sadie frowned and Maddy gave up and took a slurp of her drink. People were dancing, and the men had discarded their jackets, their braces stark black against crisp white shirts so that the crowd started to look zebra-like, moving so fast that Maddy couldn't tell where one person ended and another began.

'Let's dance!' She pulled at Sadie, but Sadie stayed fixed to the spot. She'd been dancing subtly all night, so why wouldn't she go to the dancefloor with Maddy? What was the point in being at a party and staying in one place the whole night?

A woman in a peacock-blue dress moved to the balcony outside and others followed. Sadie watched them, and said something about the storm. Maddy caught some of her words but not all of them. They wandered around in her mind like lost children. *Lightning. Soon. Inside.*

But whatever Sadie had said had obviously made some kind of sense because a few moments later, the whole sky lit diamond-white with the first fork of lightning. A collective murmur from the crowd floated between the jazz notes.

It was then that Maddy saw Pearl. Pearl glanced in Maddy's direction, but looked straight through her. Then, she was gone and there was Gregory, returning inside from the balcony. Maddy braced herself but he wasn't coming towards her. He was walking towards the doors of the ballroom, in the same direction that Pearl had gone just a moment before. Maddy swiped her bag from the marble shelf next to her.

'They're leaving together.' Her words weren't loud enough and she cleared her throat. 'What should I do?' Maddy asked, turning to Sadie. 'What if he doesn't come back at all? Do you really think that I should—'

But Maddy's words faltered as she saw that Sadie had gone too. The storm had cooled the air suddenly, and Maddy shivered, feeling goosebumps prickle her arms. She looked at her watch, but the ticking golden hands were meaningless because she didn't know what time it had been when she'd stopped talking to Sadie, since the first lightning strike.

It had felt like seconds, but had it been, really? Or had it been much, much longer?

How long had Maddy been standing alone?

She left the ballroom and made her way through the castle. The music quietened as she reached the reception area. She stumbled, her ankle throbbing with a dull ache as she did. She carried on, the pain distant, as though it were happening to somebody else. Then she was outside. The rain had started, single fat drops at first, then more and more until shards of water bounced from the gravel. There were distant shrieks from the people who'd gone out on the balcony. Maddy imagined ruined hair, streaked makeup, damp dresses. Mother Nature doing her wicked and powerful deeds.

Raindrops scored Maddy's cheeks, hammering into her

hair and onto her shoulders. She squinted and pushed her sodden hair from out of her eyes as she stared around her, seeing nobody and hearing nothing but rumbles of thunder and the distant sound of the party. Nobody would be out here, in this. Gregory hated being rained on. He liked being dry and comfortable. She needed to go back inside.

There was what seemed like an insurmountable number of rooms, and after Maddy had been in the first few, they began to all blend into one: statement chairs in bright blues and deep purples, oversized lamps and thick velvet curtains; rows of books the colours of jewels. Maddy roamed from one to the next, seeing nobody. She pushed open huge, intricately carved doors, moved down vast corridors that seemed to take her round in circles, away from the noise of the party and then back towards it.

She pushed open yet another heavy door. Behind it was another short corridor with a downwards staircase at the end. Maddy clung to the thick mahogany banister as she descended, her feet unsteady beneath her. She glanced back. The door had swung shut behind her. She went further and further, and each time she thought the stairs might end, they twisted around and carried further and further on, giving Maddy the feeling of starting something impossible. Her ankle pulsed. The lower she dropped in the castle, the further she felt from reality. Nausea was heavy in her stomach and her legs seemed to tangle beneath her. If she fell here, who on earth would find her?

She stopped for a moment and steadied her breaths. Looking ahead or back was pointless: there was no way of seeing how far she'd come or how much further she had to go.

She pushed away the realisation that she'd have to go back up the stairs again to return to the ball at some point, and carried on, down and down until finally, breathlessly, she reached a scuffed fire door. She hesitated, wondering if opening it might set off alarms and evacuate the whole castle. Her spirits lifted a little at the thought of Gregory, pale and horrified at Maddy going missing as the staff did a headcount. Maybe Sadie would even feel a little guilt for vanishing, leaving Maddy alone.

Or maybe they were both long gone from the ball and would have no idea if everyone was shunted out into the grounds, crawling over the clifftops.

Maddy pushed on the metal bar on the door and forced it open.

She was on the beach then, a dream-like change in setting. She clambered over a low wall and then there were pebbles uneven beneath her heels and threatening to pull her down. The sea roared in the distance, unsettled by the storm.

The rain drove into Maddy's face and she turned from it, looking back up at Falcon Castle, its golden lights moving and blurring as she blinked water from her eyes. The castle seemed so high from here, on top of its gleaming cliff. She didn't know if she could climb that far again. It didn't seem like anyone was up there, or along the shore line. She had probably wasted her time.

She took her phone from her bag, fumbling so that it slipped from her fingers. When she retrieved it, she pressed

Gregory's number. Voicemail. She tried Sadie's, and it rang and rang.

Maybe *they* were together, somewhere else entirely. Maybe she couldn't trust anyone, even Sadie.

The rest of the night loomed: the endless stairs back up to the ball; the sight of herself, drenched and furious, in the many, many gilded mirrors on the castle walls. This was not the person Maddy Archer was meant to be at parties – or anywhere. She should have been next to Gregory tonight, enjoying the champagne and judging the canapés. They'd won best-dressed couple at some themed events before: again, something Maddy had always curated. They'd won so much! Spa days. Luxurious hampers. Once, a flying lesson.

She moved from the shore back into the castle. The lights had turned off and the corridor was black. Maddy put on her phone torch and stumbled up the stairs. The fire door to the beach, which she hadn't closed properly, banged behind her and made her jump. She shivered, suddenly freezing in her soaking dress. Pausing on the stairs, she scrolled through her contacts. Who could she call, now? Her fingers hovered over Candice's number and then moved upwards.

'Maddy? Everything okay?' Aiden's voice was like butter. She rarely spoke to him alone these days. She wondered if she should put down the phone, pretend that she'd called him by mistake.

'Hello?' He was always a little on edge around Maddy, ever since he'd got together with Candice. The final nail in the coffin of her friendship with him. Maybe that's where her friendship issues came from.

'I'm here,' she said eventually. Her words were dull, thudding in the silent pitch-black corridor. The signal was poor and Aiden sounded faraway, underwater.

'Where's Gregory?'

'He's gone. I can't find him. I came with a friend and she's gone too.'

'Maddy, you need to go home. Can you get a cab?'

'Probably not.' She remembered the ticket to the ball, a blurred memory of something about pre-booking cabs, which she had done, but she had no idea if it had been and gone, or wouldn't come for hours. And the cab would arrive upstairs, not down here. A laugh bolted from her mouth unexpectedly at the thought of a cab sprouting legs and lumbering down the staircase.

'Maddy, are you there? Is it not worth trying for a cab? I can call you one.'

'Why did you choose Candice, Aiden? Why wasn't I enough?' She heard a knife-edge in her voice, and a distant horror that she was demanding answers to these questions after so long fluttered around Maddy, too far away to pin down. 'Why didn't you love me?'

'Maddy, you're not making sense.' Oh, come on, Aiden. As if he never knew she loved him. She waited for him to say more, wiping the water from her face, her fingers coming away coal-black with make-up. She imagined Candice in the background, motioning for Aiden to end the call. *Get rid of her.* 'Look, just get a cab, and then let us know you're home safe, okay? Candice will call you in the morning.'

Candice and Aiden, cosy with coffee and world news tomorrow morning. *What a weird phone call from Maddy. She's finally lost it.*

'Forget it,' Maddy told him as a sudden roar of thunder rippled outside. She moved up the stairs one at a time. She still had thousands to climb. She wanted to click her fingers and be at home. Dry, surrounded by the things *she'd* worked for. Maybe she wouldn't even let Gregory back in. Changed locks and fury: she never thought this would be how it all ended.

There was a pause, a crackle on the line, and Maddy opened her bag. There were no pills left, but there was something else in there that made her heart sing.

She pulled it out.

'Look…' Aiden began.

'Honestly,' Maddy said at the same time. 'Forget I called. Forget everything.'

It was six months later when Maddy's world tipped on its axis, when she finally saw what she'd done in such an explicit and enduring way. The news about the hit and run had finally subsided, thank God. The red car. The teenager left for dead. The poor girl's life-changing injuries. The praying for anyone with any information coming forward.

But what would coming forward have achieved? Maddy concluded that the damage had been done, and whose fault had that been? Pearl had been outside because she had been out there with Gregory, making him follow her and taking him away from Maddy and all she had done for him.

Aiden had kept quiet too. No more urgent, desperate pleas for Maddy to be honest. Already, the conversation was covered with a thin veil of time, to be pressed further and further down until, Maddy hoped, she wouldn't remember it at all.

Because the thing was, nobody else really knew what had happened. Even Maddy told herself constantly that there was a chance she'd done absolutely nothing wrong. She wasn't in her right mind that night. She could barely remember it. She might have even imagined Pearl's face in the headlights, a muffled scream ripping through the night. If Maddy tried hard enough, she could even believe the white lie she had told Sadie about them hitting a deer. They had hit something, yes, but it hadn't been a person. They had *not* hit and run.

Someone driving a red car had done the hit and run.

Not Maddy, not Sadie.

After the ball, life had bumped along to a cold, bare January that stretched on and on: bleak and endless days that were grey and damp. One day, when it was finally almost February, Maddy returned home from Vibe, where she'd dropped Eliot off at the dribble-coated creche and forced her way through a Pilates class. Her fingers were stinging with cold as she unlocked their front door. She scooped up the mail from the mat when she got inside, tossing it on the custom-made sideboard in the hallway. Mail still made her feel sick, ever since Gregory's tie had appeared last year in that Manilla envelope. They'd managed quite well since Pearl had been out of the picture and in hospital. It wasn't quite back to normal but they were existing in their marriage, which was more than Maddy had expected six months before.

She put Eliot into the playroom and dumped some blocks in front of him, and then rushed back to the pile of letters. The one on top was addressed to Maddy, her name scored across the top of the envelope in giant letters. Maddy's pulse raced as she picked it up. She leaned against the sideboard and pulled open the envelope. Her eyes skittered across to the door, and the wide windows either side, and she turned away from them.

Two photographs were inside the envelope. There was no letter. It was a moment before Maddy's brain processed what she was looking at. The images were grainy, as though they were photographs of photographs, zoomed in too far so that they'd lost their original shape. But if she stared and held them at an angle, she could just about make them out.

Skin sewn together in one: crusting black-red lines zigzagging across pale flesh.

A mouth in the other: a perfect cupid's bow disrupted by a deep gash that rose up and up.

Realisation prickled at Maddy at first, and then burned through her, in her stomach and her throat. She clutched the photographs to her chest as she moved through the house, into Gregory's study. She pulled out his top drawer, grabbed a new envelope, and then stuffed the photographs inside and sealed it with tape from his brass dispenser. If only taping them in an envelope would stop the images from flashing into Maddy's mind again and again, imprinting themselves sharply on her memory so that she would never forget.

She took a pen and wrote the address that she knew off by heart on the new envelope, and then returned downstairs, crumpling the old envelope in her fist. She could hear Eliot banging his blocks together; a car passing the house outside; the gentle tapping of rain against the windows. Outside, the light was fading and the streetlights were flicking on, golden against the deep blue sky. The hallway smelled of Maddy's favourite peony and violet candle and other familiar scents of the day, of their house: coffee and wine and Gregory's lingering aftershave.

All was as it always was.

And yet everything, suddenly, had changed.

Maddy retched, vomit pushing itself from her, smacking violently onto her polished oak floor and splashing up the cabinet that they'd paid someone to design especially for them, a perfect fit and a perfect colour to complement their perfect lives.

TWELVE

Sadie

Sadie could hear music floating up from beneath her room at Falcon Castle. It sounded like a live band. It was the first time Sadie had heard an instrument being played live in a place other than Kings Hill High assembly hall and she felt another part of herself, one that she'd tried to quiet for so long now, stirring in the depths of her body. She imagined the musicians' evening, instruments under their fingertips and music surrounding them. The longing for who she used to be washed over her and she automatically removed it from her mind.

'It's a bit of a way down from here,' she said to Rob as she stared out of the window of their room. That was an understatement. The drop from this room was deadly: their window seemed to jut out more than all the others, so that Sadie couldn't even see the cliffs beneath them. 'It's as though we're floating.' She could hear the gulls crying over and over again as they soared past the window.

'It's a great place.' Rob's voice was cautious. Sadie

shouldn't have accused Blake of taking her dress. That, and the smashed mirror, had made things all worse. It had all pushed Rob further away than ever. Here, and now, she needed to say less to him about her suspicions.

'It really is.' Anxiety caught at Sadie. *A great place, really?* She took a small breath and carried on. 'It's been ages since the last time we did something like this together.'

Rob seemed to relax a bit and sat down at the desk. There was a huge painting of an eagle over it, swooping down towards them. Downstairs there had been stuffed birds on shelves behind glass: black beady eyes following Sadie and Rob as they found their room. When they'd arrived at reception, Sadie had recognised nothing. She'd stared up at an imposing tapestry depicting a masquerade banquet. Next to that, a floor-to-ceiling window flaunted the crashing sea beyond. Huge masks hung down from the high ceiling; technicolour roses and candelabras filled the surfaces, and the sweet scent of money had stuck in Sadie's throat.

'I logged into Instagram on the way here. I'm following Blake,' Sadie began. Rob looked up at the eagle and closed his eyes, just briefly. She could almost hear his thoughts. *Here we go again. Can't she just leave it, for once?*

'It's a good thing.' Sadie smiled as she spoke. 'I downloaded it ages ago but I've never used it.' She could just use the app to keep up to date with Blake without having to message her constantly. Maybe find out about Blake's boyfriend: the mysterious G. Try and connect with the world that she felt so far from these days. Do something a normal, relaxed mother would do. 'I wondered if seeing her with her friends might reassure me, I mean. Show me that she's safe. I won't need to hound her as much then. I know she finds me suffocating.' There. She'd said something truthful to Rob to try and remove the distance between them. It felt strange, the most surface of her worries, but a true one all the same, circling above them in the stuffy room. She grabbed her phone from the bed and opened up Instagram. As soon as she did, an image of Blake filled the screen. She was alone, grinning, wearing her favourite blue cropped T-shirt. #summer#weekend#happy.

'You okay?' Rob was looking over her shoulder at the photograph, breathing calmly, steadily, smelling of aftershave and goodness.

'Yeah. Good.' Sadie hoped that Rob couldn't hear the tremble in her voice. She brought the screen closer to her face, cold fear running through her body. She zoomed in, trying not to panic, trying to act normal for the sake of Rob.

'You sure?'

Sadie glanced at Rob. Even though she wasn't looking at her phone anymore, the picture she'd just seen was imprinted in her mind.

'I just don't recognise where she is, that's all.' She spoke brightly, trying to be okay. But the background hadn't looked anything like Evie's house. Sadie had seen the house a few times because Evie and Blake had been good friends for years. But it wasn't only that. There had been another person behind Blake, peering at the camera like a ghost. The figure had been tall, blonde. Straight from Sadie's nightmares. A threat.

'They'll be having fun somewhere.' Rob's words were

simple but they meant so much. *Leave it.* He kissed the top of Sadie's head and she felt an old, familiar warmth. She would try her best. For one night, she would make sure that she stayed in the present. She would keep one calm eye on Blake, but she wouldn't let anxiety take over her. She would reclaim what she used to have with Rob.

'I'm going to have a quick shower. Try to cool down.' She could feel his eyes lingering on her as he spoke.

'Cool down?' She made herself give Rob a grin but it felt all wrong, a clown-like grimace rather than anything remotely flirtatious. She laughed in spite of the fear uncurling inside her. 'I think I need to relearn how to flirt.'

Rob laughed too as he pulled open the glass door to the bathroom. There was a free-standing bath in there. Luxury toiletries. Bath petals that smelled of roses.

Everything, *everything* took her back to Blake. Sadie thought about the yellow, headless roses again, and then she pictured Evie's house, where Blake would be sleeping on the floor tonight, golden legs tangled in pink covers. She wondered, not for the first time, what kind of security system Evie's parents had. She pictured her own house too, later on in the dark, someone inside again, smashing up her precious world.

She picked up her phone again as the glass door slid open and Rob disappeared behind it, his figure becoming a blur.

Instagram had refreshed, and the post had gone. Sadie scrolled wildly, trying to find it. Suddenly, she wondered if she'd imagined it, if the figure in the background *had* been blonde, or had been Evie all along, or nobody at all.

Sadie had felt like this when it all first happened, when Maddy had convinced Sadie to meet her at Kings Hill Park a few days after the accident, and they'd walked around the lake, watching swans gliding through the water and children feeding the ducks. The news stories were everywhere by then.

We are asking witnesses to come forward.

'You're probably traumatised from hitting the deer and everything. Honestly, what happened was absolutely nothing to do with us,' Maddy had said. She'd stopped walking and looked head-on at Sadie, her dark brown eyes wide and earnest.

Now, Sadie stopped scrolling as the image of Blake she'd seen before returned to her screen. The sound of the shower turning on, water blasting down onto ceramic, was distant, as though it was on the television or in another room, someone else's life.

Snap back. Go and join him.

Sadie stared down at the picture. Blake was the same as she had been on the last one a few minutes ago: head cocked slightly, her hair in mermaid waves, her arm on her hip. #summer#weekend#happy. But the background was clear of a person, just a blurred scene with nobody in it.

Sadie shook her head, trying to dislodge the image of her mother that floated in her mind, screaming blue murder about something that hadn't ever been there: an intruder, an enemy. She imagined their home again, smashed, things decapitated. She thought again of Blake's headless flowers that Sadie had stuffed in the kitchen bin before she and Rob left for Falcon Castle earlier, squeezed in sideways so that their pretty green bodies were snapped at all angles.

Sadie closed her eyes, trying to ignore the ever-present wails of her mother inside her head that were merging with the cries of the gulls outside and the sound of the shower.

'They're trying to kill me.'

'Help me, Sadie! They're outside. They're waiting.'

But her mother had been drunk, and ill. The smashed mirror, and the flowers, were real: not hallucinations.

She closed her phone and stood up, took a breath. And then there was a knock at the door.

THIRTEEN

Maddy

Maddy dreamed about Sadie the night before the Masquerade Ball, but then that was nothing new. She had dreamed about Sadie ever since they'd first met. Blonde hair, trailing down her tanned back. An open, bright face that made you feel as though the sun was shining directly on you. The woven cotton bracelets that had hung on her wrists the day Maddy had first spoken to her: hot colours like red and amber and brick.

Maddy had managed to get Sadie to meet her in the park a couple of days after the Gatsby Ball. She remembered feeling disappointed in Sadie that night, but it was only because she'd been so sad, drunk and desperate. It didn't mean Maddy didn't want to be friends. That day at the park, she had wanted to be reassured that Sadie wasn't going to back away from Maddy after the accident had been on the news, all over social media and the radio, seeping into everything. But there had been no such reassurance. Sadie had known that Maddy had slipped that little crushed pill into her drink. She'd confronted Maddy about it, her face guarded and furious, framed by the glittering lake beyond. Maddy had denied it, but it was obvious Sadie hadn't believed her.

I wanted to see the real you, Maddy had been tempted to admit. She didn't remember a lot, but she did remember that, because it was something that had clouded the whole evening. *I was sick of everyone else being so perfect when I wasn't.* Maddy had lost all control and she'd opened up her life to Sadie, peeled away the skin for her to see the pulp and the sticky guts. She'd wanted to see another side to Sadie in return. She'd wanted Sadie to drink, dance and cry and be as raw as Maddy felt.

But Sadie wouldn't have understood this, which was the very problem. So Maddy had denied it that day in the park and she had tried to stop Sadie talking about the news appeals for witnesses, because it had been busy, and one of the children tearing past on scooters, or someone walking their dog, or a harassed mother dealing with toddlers and dropped ice creams, might have heard them.

After that day at the park, Sadie had started to avoid Maddy completely. Even sending on those dreadful photographs had been met with a wall of silence. And now, ten years later, Maddy was still trying to chase Sadie in yet another dream. Sadie darting away from Maddy, impossible to catch; Maddy's legs dead, stuck to the ground as Maddy tried to pull herself forwards; Sadie turning back towards Maddy, screaming, black-red blood streaming from her mouth; her face melting, and her features morphing into Aiden's features. He was sobbing, shouting Maddy's name.

Maddy woke up with a horrible jolt.

I know you.

She picked up her phone and opened the message that had come from Sadie yesterday, and her own reply. Sadie's original mobile had been disconnected soon after Maddy had last seen her, so this number was obviously new. Or not Sadie's at all.

She swiped to close the message and opened her tracking app to see Gregory's location. He was in a hotel in London, but that told Maddy nothing, really. He could be there with anyone, doing anything. The thought was old and tired, walking its favourite path around her mind in its worn-out shoes. She moved on to her routine online searching. Although Sadie herself didn't seem to be on any social media platforms, the internet still told tales if you looked for them hard enough.

Sadie Summer Kings Hill West.

Blake Summer Kings Hill High.

Sadie Summer music teacher Kings Hill High.

On it went. 3am darkness and then the first birds singing outside. Five thirty and the slow sunlight burning white behind the blinds.

There was nothing new to see online. Maddy knew all the main things that there were to know. Sadie still lived in the same house as she had done when Maddy had first met her: 4 Radley Drive in Kings Hill West, near to leafy parks and primary schools; florists and coffee shops; nice families and pretty children. Sadie obviously still had the perfect marriage with Rob. Blake looked like some kind of model teenager. But Maddy didn't know what Sadie looked like now, and that bothered her. The Sadie of Maddy's imagination was always exactly the same as the Sadie she'd first met. But that was the brain for you, ignoring everything it knew. It had been ten years: Sadie would look different now. There had been new posts on Blake's Instagram account a couple of nights ago. It had apparently been the final school production of *Into the Woods* and there had been no Sadie in any of the photos. Maybe she hadn't been to watch it, although Maddy wouldn't have thought Sadie would be the type of mother to miss her daughter's performance. Maddy imagined them all going out for a special dinner afterwards to celebrate Blake. The pretty bistro near the school perhaps. Or the Italian on the centre of Kings Hill West main street. Blake luminous with success. Smiling waiters, giant peppermills and lots of laughter.

Maddy spent the final silent hours of the morning zooming in on the screenshots she'd taken of Instagram until Eliot padded into her room like a giant pet and she tried to act like a normal mother, one who was only obsessed with home décor and handmaking winning fancy dress outfits for school events; shopping for organic vegetables and reducing plastic use.

At ten am, once Eliot had been safely dropped off at his friend's house for the day, Maddy pulled on her workout leggings, trying to ignore the electric sting of anxiety she'd had since she'd seen Aiden at the dinner party last night. Maddy needed to speak to Sadie about everything as soon as they arrived. *If* Sadie arrived.

Maddy's phone vibrated on her bedside table, making her jump. She leaned over and answered it, tucking it under her chin as she hitched the Lycra of her leggings over her stomach.

'Aiden is going to take Eliot for a game of tennis later,' Candice said. The name Aiden burned a hole in the very centre of Maddy's chest. 'So make sure he has something to wear. Sport in this heat! I think he's mad, but who am I to comment?' Was that a hint of irritation with Aiden? Candice was chopping as she spoke. The knife tapped in the background like a heartbeat. Maddy thought of Aiden last night, slicing lemons and then slicing Maddy's life.

I know you.

If this was one of Maddy's television dramas that she liked to watch, she'd be frustrated. *Why didn't you finish your conversation?* she'd think, and she would roll her eyes. *You should have asked him what he meant.* These characters always acted like it was impossible, were put off by the slightest barrier.

But it *had* been impossible. There had been too many people there: Eliot, Candice and their mother all ready to listen.

'Don't feed Eliot a load of junk before he arrives,' Candice continued on the phone. 'I'm going to cook him a nice meal later. He didn't eat much paella at all last night. He told me that he'd already had chicken nuggets at school for lunch. Honestly, Maddy, I know you're not into nutrition, but I saw that programme on those factories where they make chicken nuggets, and you wouldn't believe the things that…'

Maddy shut her ears off as she stood up again and rummaged in her drawer for her white gym vest. It had been there the other day, and she hadn't worn it since. This kept happening. She still hadn't dared tell Gregory that she hadn't been able to find the diamond-and-emerald necklace he'd bought her when they got married. He hadn't been happy that she'd put a post on Instagram about it. He'd said something about inviting thieves into their lives. He was one to talk.

A limited edition, he'd said when he'd very first presented her with the necklace. *Like us.* She'd thought it was a sweet thing to say at the time. That all seemed so long ago. What she and Gregory had now was nothing like the marriage they'd started out with.

She opened the box that the necklace should have been in. Empty.

Maybe she had lost her mind as well as her necklace. Perimenopause, wasn't it? The women at Vibe were obsessed with perimenopause. Paranoia, collapsing necks, insomnia. A whole basket of treats: a joint gift from time and biology. Maybe she was being overly anxious and Gregory *was* in London with Tim and signing books in charming little Primrose Hill book shops and playing squash with other tanned, good-looking men who were faithful to their wives. Just because their relationship wasn't the same now as it had been at the very start, it didn't have to mean anything catastrophic. Yes: there had been Pearl. But they had been fine for so long. And it was normal for marriages to change over time, she reassured herself as she stared around her room, wondering if the necklace was there somewhere, silently watching her look for it. Marriages all lost something in the end, like a plump young face eventually losing its collagen. If only you could inject a marriage with filler.

Anyway, Maddy was getting distracted. She needed to focus on the necklace. She knew she'd worn it at the Gatsby Ball and she'd put it back in its box after that. She hadn't been able to bring herself to wear it since, but she had checked on it all the time. The last time she'd seen it in the box was probably only about a month ago, so it should have still been there, safe and sound. The box being empty made no sense, unless someone had stolen it. But then, Maddy was always losing things. Ever since she'd had Eliot, her mind was a mess, like one of those puzzles with an overwhelming tangle of overlapping lines and only one way out. Except there didn't seem to be a way out very often. It was as though part of her brain had been expelled from her body along with Eliot and the accompanying gunk and blood.

'Well, anyway, thanks for having him,' Maddy said now, interrupting whatever Candice was saying about the floor sweepings of frozen food factories. 'Better go. Someone's at the door. I'll see you in a few hours when I drop Eliot off.'

A delivery man actually *was* at the door. It hadn't just been a white lie to get rid of Candice, although who could have blamed Maddy if it had? He put a box on the doorstep before giving Maddy a nod and jumping back in his little blue van.

The box was small, with a heart-shaped sticker and bound by a white taffeta ribbon. It was full of mini blueberry muffins.

I want to talk to you.

I know you.

She picked one up and took a bite.

Moist. Sweet. Heaven. Even better than the one she'd eaten last night, although the nausea she'd had at the dinner party was back again now.

There was a tiny card to go with the tiny muffins. The text was pink. She knew that font. Allegra. Unimaginative but whoever sent them wouldn't have chosen it themselves, just typed the words into some online box. Maddy's breaths became sharp as she read them, each one a potential grenade.

She swallowed and tossed the box of cakes into the bin. She tore up the card, this time into so many pieces that it would be completely impossible to piece it together, even though it didn't really matter today because by the time Gregory came into their bedroom, the cleaner would have been and everything Maddy had tossed away would be somewhere else, unseen, the bin empty and the room smelling of newness and luxury-brand polish.

FOURTEEN

Sadie

Sadie pulled the heavy door to their room at the castle open and came face to face with a teenage boy in a bright blue suit.

'Hi,' he said, handing Sadie a large black package tied with a glittering bow. 'For you both. Happy Masquerade Day.'

She thanked the boy and locked the door behind him, then set the box down on the bed. The masks inside were nestled together: glittering black, studded with tiny, pointed gems. Sadie reached out and touched one. The gems scraped against her skin and she pulled back.

'Thought you might have joined me,' Rob said. He was out of the shower now, beads of water still glistening on his skin and disappointment etched on his face.

'Yes. I was going to but then the door…' the sentence trailed off, too pathetic to finish. She would message Sarah, Evie's mum, to say thank you for having Blake. Sarah would reply and say something mundane about the girls hanging out in the garden or ordering pizza, and then at least Sadie would know that Blake was safe. And then she would relax, and try her best to get through this. No. Not get through it. *Enjoy it.* For Rob, and for their marriage.

She tapped out a message as Rob opened the wardrobe to get out their things. 'They've hung up our outfits for us,' he said. 'Nice place.'

Sadie pressed send and the message swooped away.

> Thanks for having Blake this weekend. Hope they're having a great time together.

Once Sarah had replied, Sadie would put away her phone and concentrate on Rob. She *had* to. Even if this weekend took Sadie from the everyday routine she'd built for herself: her bed, her shower, her classroom, her meetings, her dining table, the supermarket, the hairdresser and lifts for Blake. Even if it made her deviate from her brightly lit, well-known path filled with familiar faces and formulae. She would go downstairs in her mask in a room full of strangers who would all be in masks too. Anonymity, just for one night. The only person who would know who she was, and matter to her tonight, would be Rob. If someone was playing games with her, nobody knew where she was, which surely meant she was safe.

'Is my dress…?' She stopped talking as she joined Rob near the cavernous wardrobe and saw what was hanging there. Today was starting to feel like a disjointed dream, an Alice in Wonderland-type fall through all of her fears.

She turned to look at Rob.

'Did you bring that? Did you find it?' She heard knife-edge tension in her words, but couldn't help it. Fear reared up in the pit of her stomach.

Rob peered into the wardrobe where the dress hung: black, a smatter of sequins on the left shoulder. A pair of strappy black shoes were beneath it.

'You brought it? So you didn't lose it after all.' His words were controlled and careful. Eggshell-thin.

Sadie reached for the dress. 'No. I definitely didn't bring this.' Heat and panic prickled at her skin. She imagined smashing the window and jumping, sailing down past the jagged cliffs and crashing into the water so that this would all be over, forever. She took the dress from its hanger, cradling it in her arm like a corpse. 'I brought a dark green dress. A newer one.'

'You can't have done. Look, my clothes are the ones I brought.' A moment of clarity passed over Rob's face and he brightened. He was taking off his towel, pulling on his clothes. 'They must have mixed up your dress with someone else's.'

'No. The dress in the wardrobe is mine. The exact one that was missing.' Sadie shook her head again and again, her thoughts banging against each other. She caught her reflection in the elaborate full-length mirror to the side of the bed. Her expression was crazed. *Was* this all her? *Was* the dress slightly different from the one she'd lost?

She was losing her mind.

'I don't know what's going on here, Sadie.' Rob moved away from her. 'But I think when we get home, you need to see someone. Have a chat with the doctor.' He'd suggested this before, saying things about anxiety, paranoia, being careful with his tone like he might be with a patient at work: a lonely old person with muddled, frightened thoughts.

'I shouldn't have come here,' Sadie said quietly. She always, always felt like she might go mad – like she might already be mad. But here at Falcon Castle, it was as though insanity had taken hold, eating everything in its path. 'I don't mean with you,' she said to Rob, painting over those horrible words. 'I mean…'

'Maybe you're right. We're obviously way past the point where a night away will fix things. Too much to salvage.' Rob covered his face with his hands and his voice broke. Sadie's heart felt as though something had taken a sharp bite out of it. It was the first time she'd ever heard him say something like that. The words, craved and dreaded all at once, strangled her whole body, tightening her chest.

'We're not past recovering, Rob. I promise, we're not.' The truth about why she was so anxious bubbled up inside her. But the truth was too big to say. How could she do it? And what was she even going to tell him? It wasn't a full story. She knew the beginning was meeting Maddy and she knew the ending was this, but the crucial middle? The bit that changed everything in one stroke?

She couldn't remember.

And why was that?

Bad decisions ruin lives. One second changes everything. Going along with someone you know you shouldn't go along with, or saying yes to something when you know it should be no, or looking at something you shouldn't be looking at instead of the road or your child in the bath or your friend on a night out. Those were the kind of things Rob always said after seeing drowned toddlers or teenagers with limbs torn from them or families hurled from their cars. They were the kinds of things he'd started to say after a man whose brain was hazy with alcohol and cocaine had crashed into his parents' little Fiat and crushed their whole lives into nothing.

'I'm going home.' Rob cleared his throat, pulled himself straight. His eyes drifted around the room, to the masks, the wardrobe, then to Sadie. 'I've tried enough. You stay here. Have a night away. Please, God, try to relax. And on Monday, you need to speak to someone. A professional. Okay?'

She couldn't do that. She would have to tell him. But the words were stuck, sinking further away.

'Rob, don't do this.'

'I'm not doing anything! I tried hard, Sadie. I brought you here but you regret coming.'

Sadie thought of how he'd tried to pull her from her quicksand of anxiety over the last ten years. There had been disagreements about how protective to be with Blake; about how often Sadie woke in the night, especially lately as the noises and shadows had seemed somehow to become more frequent. But even through the disagreements, Rob had fought Sadie's demons alongside her, even though he couldn't see them and didn't understand them. He'd withdrawn from their neighbours, when really, he wanted to be sociable and turn up to their BBQs and drinks on their glossy green lawns. He'd sat inside, night after night, with their curtains drawn, drinking tea and sharing chocolate and laughing at bad films. It hadn't been the way he'd expected things to turn out but he'd gone along with it all the same and because of that, they had still managed a kind of happiness. He'd hugged Sadie tight and looked for intruders in the dark. He'd accepted the strange, strained version of her who thought that there was a monster waiting around every corner for them.

But Rob had a limit and Sadie could feel herself pushing and pushing against it, a door that would soon fly open with nothing but darkness behind it. 'I didn't say that. I don't regret being here with you.'

'You did!' Rob's voice rose high, up to the swirling chandelier above them. The black eyes of the birds watched him, watched Sadie. 'You're blaming some mix-ups with a dress for not wanting to be here with me. I can't understand you anymore. You're always hiding something.'

Sadie felt fear prod at her with long, sharp fingers. At first, when the accident had happened, she'd managed to hide her waves of anxiety and guilt behind Blake's primary-school age: the business of reading books and dolls in prams; endless washing and tidying of toys and brushing of hair and teeth. But now, the waves had become bigger and stronger, pulling them both under more often. The guilt and anxiety, especially recently as things had gone missing and the nighttime noises were louder and closer, were impossible to hide and impossible to ignore. Rob's words made her inside ache. She'd been so unfair to him, expecting him to step closer and closer to her, as she kept backing away.

He was leaving, the door open, his car key in his hand.

'I'll come and pick you up tomorrow,' he said quietly.
And then he was gone.

Sadie went over to the window and pulled hard on the catch until it eventually sprang free. She leaned out into the salty air that she'd avoided for so long until her lungs were full and her head swam. She breathed in time with the distant music, like she used to do when she was playing on stage. It worked a little to calm her, just as it had back then.

She would go after Rob, and they could both go home. Start again somehow. He would expect her to go after him so that they could try to work through this. Sadie wasn't the type to stay at a party on her own and he knew it. She imagined Rob waiting in the car until she arrived, the radio low. Familiar guilt squeezed at her. She was doing it again: expecting him to stretch so that she didn't have to. She shouldn't be making Rob wait. She shouldn't have driven him out.

She picked up the room key and moved towards the door, but as she did, a sharp knock made her drop it.

Sadie used to drop things all the time when she was scared. She dropped an ashtray once when she was trying to tidy the flat she lived in with her mum. It had landed on her mother's foot. *Butterfingers, butterfingers*, her mother had said, over and over again, laughing at Sadie until the laughter turned to tears. The crying was always more frightening than anything else for some reason. Then Sadie had dropped another thing because she had been so on edge but she couldn't remember what now. It was one of those memories that seemed to have been wiped, like her mind was a faulty old radio that needed to be tuned back in.

The knock on the door was obviously Rob. He had come back. And as soon as she heard back that Blake was safe with Evie, Sadie would need to put on the dress and act like a normal person, for Rob and for their marriage. She would try to place herself a million miles from all the fear and chaos she felt inside her, and she'd tell him that she'd realised there were possible explanations for the dress, her dress, being in this cupboard, in the place of all her worst fears. She would let herself, just this once, listen to the music, and she would force herself to speak to the musicians about all the things that made her who she was, that she had stuffed down inside her for all these years. She would be herself again, just for one night, otherwise she might lose her grip and end up somewhere she did not want to go.

She opened the door. She would hug Rob tight and press herself against his quiet strength. They would get through this. They had to.

But behind the door wasn't Rob at all: it was someone else who made Sadie fall through time at a speed that stopped her heart.

FIFTEEN

Maddy

Maddy shifted gear and glanced in the rearview mirror. Falcon Lane was deserted apart from her Range Rover. She never thought she'd drive along this road again. She barely drove at all, if she could help it. The gym, play dates for Eliot and Candice's house. That was her lot, and even that felt like too much sometimes. It was partly why she sometimes let herself have more than the allowed one glass of wine before driving. She knew it was wrong, especially after everything that had happened. But today, she'd had no alcohol at all, and she was definitely a worse driver because of it: over cautious, slamming down on the breaks too often and taking too many glances behind her instead of looking ahead.

Maddy jammed the air-conditioning button with her finger. Nothing. This car was brand new. It shouldn't have broken air con. But the button was doing nothing, and the sweat was rolling down her collarbone, much more than it had done in the cool gym when she'd done her class at Vibe.

So she was preoccupied with the unpleasant dampness blooming beneath her top, the tightness in her chest and the thought of what might happen later, the decision she might make.

And then she thought that she saw something in front of her car: a horrible blur of movement against the grass scorched grey by the heat. She slammed the brakes on yet again, harder this time, her sweating foot sliding forwards slightly in her white wedge heel, her heart lurching through the windscreen.

She closed her eyes for an instant, not wanting to know what was coming next.

But nothing did come. Her car bumped against the hedgerow slightly and a few birds fluttered out in panic. She stopped dead. Her hands shook on the steering wheel and she took a breath. Nobody was hurt. Nobody had even seen. It had probably just been one of the birds, swooping low near her windscreen.

She opened the car door shakily, and stood for a moment, shielding her eyes from the sun. Then she got back in the car. She would have to make it to the castle. She just needed to be more careful. The heat, the raw panic in her blood, it had all made her drive too fast and breathe too little without even realising it. She'd starved her brain of oxygen and sense. *Get there faster, get it over with faster*, her body had been telling her. Flight mode.

Maddy took her bag from the passenger side. She took out her water bottle and gulped, then stopped as the nausea she'd felt over the last few days overtook her. She found her phone then tapped through the numbers and dialled

Sadie's. She'd tried her a few times now but Sadie hadn't answered yet. If she had, then Maddy might have felt better.

Or perhaps worse.

It didn't matter. Sadie's phone rang out and out.

Falcon Castle, which was already a million times more glamorous than it had been at the time of the Gatsby Ball, was dripping with themed decorations. It was no wonder such an incredible amount of money was now made by this event each year for White Feather. An enormous tapestry of masked figures at a banquet table hung along the back wall of the reception area. Commissioned especially, probably. Giant masks were placed around reception on marble pedestals, their ribbons curling to the floor. Maddy imagined with a pang the adrenaline of starting the plans for a new event: pitches and quotes and the delicious feeling of it all coming together. The ball's marketing department was obviously excellent. Perhaps she could ask someone who worked here about any available freelance work. But then, maybe not. They were obviously at the top of their game, using talent, not some washed-up freelancer who had let clients trickle through her fingers like sand. Maddy had let that happen over the last ten years, the brassy confidence she'd once had dulled year after year. She stared up at the tapestry, the masked figures looking back down at her sadly, trapped in their make-believe world.

'Ticket?' A willowy receptionist, mid-forties, dark hair,

nodded as Maddy showed her phone and the email that Gregory had forwarded to her. The receptionist was wearing an elaborate Venetian mask with lavender feathers protruding at all angles. Maddy watched her eyes carefully for the usual impression that Gregory's name gave: a flash of desire, then a smile to try and hide it all. Yes, there it all was.

'I love your husband's books. I prefer them to the TV series, although the series was brilliant too. I know he worked on it. But it's never the same as the book, is it? I have already preordered his next one. It's too long to wait though, still another few months,' the woman added. She reached awkwardly over the tangle of feathers above her forehead and smoothed her cropped black hair. *Gregory doesn't like short hair*, Maddy wanted to tell her. *Or women older than him. So you needn't be so nervy: it will never happen for you.*

Instead, Maddy smiled graciously. 'He'll be so pleased. He might have arrived already, actually?'

'No. Not yet.' *I'd have noticed.* 'Drinks are already being served, and as you can hear, the band has started. The dinner, performance and beneficiary talks begin at eight. There will be prizes too, of course. We'll take your bags to the room for you right now.'

Maddy thought about the last time they'd been here. There had been no dinner or talks, no invitation to stay over at the last ball. The bedroom was huge and decorated in a way that was meant to scream opulence.

What if the ball had included a room last time? Maddy imagined herself barricaded inside, locking Gregory out.

Pearl still on the road, perhaps. But Maddy and Sadie inside with the wild rain lashing against the window, their lives and friendship intact. It wouldn't have saved her marriage though, would it, because that had already started to go wrong before the ball, before the storm and the roads and the puckered scars. She found herself becoming lightheaded and sat down quickly on the bed. It was smaller than the one Maddy and Gregory had at home, Maddy noted with a fleeting feeling of satisfaction that made her feel a bit stronger. There was a box next to her on the bed, tied with a black ribbon and containing two sparkly black masks. They were high-quality: Gregory would be happy about that. Sometimes these places promised more than they could deliver but that didn't seem to be the case here.

Maddy stood up and found the outfit she'd brought already hanging in the wardrobe: the staff here were impressive. In the end she'd settled for a cobalt-blue silk dress that wasn't frumpy, but not so tight that she would die in this relentless heat either. She'd spent weeks agonising over it, before she even knew for sure that she was going to come. She wasn't sure why, but she'd tried a few outfits on and shown Gregory. If she hadn't been suspicious, she would have thought Gregory found her attractive in all of them, that he was happy she was his wife, the one and only he had chosen, and that was that. He'd taken off his glasses and drunk her in. 'Gorgeous,' he'd said. His fingers had crept over the fabric of the silk ones, including this one. In fact, it was still crumpled from when his touch had made her decide to be bold, and she'd taken it off and tossed it across the bedroom in a ball of bright blue.

So, see: they were still good together. Maybe she was being paranoid. Maybe Pearl had been the only one. One mistake and no more, ever.

The gulls circled outside the room, laughing at her. *Ha, ha, ha. You stupid woman.*

She crouched to open her suitcase. All was as it should be which was pleasing: she sometimes had horrors at the thought of staff taking her luggage, at being parted from her possessions. She took out her new curling iron, her gigantic bag of skincare products and new black silk pyjamas.

She was so preoccupied with not rushing through the unpacking, with smoothing out her things and arranging her products on the ornate walnut dressing table that she almost didn't notice it. It was nestled at the bottom, amongst – horrifyingly – her underwear.

She pulled it out and stared at it, drinking in all the details, as everything she thought might have just been a suspicion, something not yet real, changed colours and shape, like an image in a kaleidoscope.

Maddy blinked back her tears, smoothing down her dress as she marched over to the door. The last ten years had been stretched out far too long.

She needed to see Sadie.

SIXTEEN

Sadie

Sadie's stomach twisted and she felt herself take a step backwards: away from Maddy, away from the past and the darkness that threatened to pull her under.

The music was louder now that the door was open, and Sadie wondered if it was a live band after all. Now that she could hear it properly, the lead singer's voice sounded canned. Had she heard people applaud after each number? She tried hard to think, to focus on anything other than the woman standing in front of her.

'Why are you here?' Sadie combed through possible ways that Maddy might know she was here, in this room.

'You told me your room number,' Maddy said, her voice straight from Sadie's nightmares: a little too loud, impossible to not hear even when you didn't want to listen. Sadie's nightmares always had Maddy in them, staring at Sadie in that slightly intense way she'd always had: dark brown eyes wide, lips slightly apart, about to tell everyone the terrible, poisonous secret that she shared with Sadie.

Enough to wake Sadie up with a bang every time she started talking. She looked exactly the same as she had done all that time ago: arched brows that made her look much haughtier and more confident than she actually was, hair the colour of black coffee, impossibly flawless skin.

Maddy held out a black-and-gold bag as she waited for Sadie to speak. 'Your Masquerade gift bag. They left it outside your door.'

'I didn't tell you anything. I had no idea you'd be here.' Sadie's words came out in whispers to overcompensate for Maddy's noise. Oh, so much noise. She took the bag from Maddy and glanced inside at the swathes of black tissue paper. Rob wouldn't wait forever. She needed to go and find him, get in the car and leave this place right now. Sarah, Evie's mum, still hadn't replied to say the girls were fine. Anxiety was going to consume Sadie whole if she stayed here.

Maddy thrust her phone in Sadie's face. 'I still have your messages.'

Horror pooled inside Sadie from top to bottom: every inch of space in her body filled with hot-red fear. 'Those are not from me,' Sadie told Maddy.

> I'm in room 12. Come and see me when you arrive! S Xxx

'I never put kisses to anyone other than my daughter,' Sadie added firmly. She had to be forceful with Maddy this time. If this was some kind of second chance at friendship, she had to have things her way this time and not fail. 'I didn't message you. That's not my number. Those messages are not from me,' she repeated, sounding like she was casting a spell. *Say it three times, spin around and you'll see your future in the mirror.*

Maddy narrowed her eyes at Sadie. Did she think Sadie was lying? A cold sense of uneasiness gripped Sadie. Maddy had always been overfamiliar, but Sadie had dismissed it that summer. She shouldn't have done. She shouldn't ever have ignored what was in her gut, that sense of *knowing* that reached so far deep it was beneath her bones and organs.

'I need to show you something.' Maddy wasn't listening or taking anything that Sadie said seriously. Had she ever?

No. Sadie didn't want Maddy in her room. She didn't want Maddy in her life. She had *never* really wanted Maddy in her life. When Sadie had met Maddy for the very first time at Stay and Play, Sadie had been drawn into her world. She'd seen that Maddy was broken, and had wanted to fix her. But she hadn't managed to fix Maddy. She'd only caused more damage, for everyone. And now, Sadie wasn't in a position to fix anyone, least of all Maddy. She needed to be assertive this time.

Maddy glanced around her and then focused in on Sadie. 'I have to come in.'

Sadie didn't answer or move. She looked down into the gift bag that Maddy had handed to her and pushed some of the tissue paper aside. What she saw in there made her swallow down a sudden rush of bile. For a moment, she felt as though she might be sick right there on the luxurious carpet and Maddy's ridiculously high white satin stilettos. 'Did you bring this gift bag for me?'

Maddy frowned. 'No. It's your freebie bag. I just picked it up from outside your door. It'll be the usual stuff you always get at these events.'

Sadie reached in and took a rose petal from the bag. It was exactly the same buttery yellow as the roses that had been horribly beheaded at her house. The roses she thought she'd be able to ignore if she just crammed them away in the bin and escaped Radley Drive, Kings Hill West and everybody there.

'How did these get in here?'

Maddy was rummaging in her handbag and pulling out a Polaroid photograph. 'Rose petals. Cute. For all the happy couples here, I suppose,' she muttered, rolling her eyes. Her eyes looked red and watery as though she'd been crying.

'But where did they come from? Please, Maddy. Tell me if you put them in there.'

'Forget the gift bag and the rose petals. I need to come in, whether you like it or not. I have something that you really need to see.'

They stared at one another. There were so many things that Sadie wanted to ask Maddy, but she didn't want to hear the answers so the words lay dormant in her mouth.

'I have to go, Maddy. I'm not staying here.' She imagined Rob giving up on her, glancing in his rearview mirror once more before starting the engine and driving along the country lanes, winding in and out carefully, watching calmly for any potential hazard, a professional at dodging danger and hurt.

Maddy moved on the spot in her white high heels like an impatient horse. 'I know we haven't seen each other for a long time. And I know you've been avoiding me. But this is important.' Her voice broke and her eyes filled with tears.

Sadie dropped the leathery rose petal to the floor as Maddy pushed her way into the room. She wanted to squeeze her eyes shut, to somehow force herself out of this situation and into any other one. 'Maddy, I can't do this now. You're right, I have been avoiding you. And I didn't plan on seeing you again tonight.' There. She'd done it. And it hadn't even been that hard. The realisation was dizzying. Was that all she'd needed to do, all that time ago?

'You're honestly saying you had no idea I'd be here?' Maddy asked. She pressed her forefingers underneath her watering eyes.

'I had no idea at all. And why did you want to come if you thought I was here? Surely you've been avoiding me too?' Maddy still only lived in Kings Hill East, but since that day in the park, Sadie had managed to dodge seeing her day after day. Until now.

Maddy glanced down. Her lashes were longer and blacker these days, as thick and artificially glossy as a doll's. Sadie imagined her lying at a salon, her eyes taped shut. The thought made her go cold.

'I did wonder, to be honest. I thought it was quite out of the blue for you to get in touch with me. I wondered if it might not be you. If it might be someone else, messing with us. And it obviously was.'

Sadie couldn't think about that. Not now. 'What do you have to show me? You need to hurry up.' She could see whatever Maddy had brought with her to show Sadie – the thought of what it might be made her light-headed – and then Maddy would go away, forever. The snaking familiarity that Sadie had first felt when she'd met Maddy was back already. It was the feeling that she'd been drawn to in the first place, because it was what she had been so used to dealing with before she met Rob: the feeling of being the one who was always there for someone who had lost their way, holding hair back and making sure they had water by their bed. Maddy had been adrift, and Sadie had been anchored and safe. She'd had everything, then. It had made Sadie want to be generous, like she'd always hoped people would be with her mother. It had made her want to make things okay for people more vulnerable than she was. She'd been a different person.

Sadie moved over to the mask and picked it up, suddenly wanting to wear it. She placed it over her eyes and tied the smooth black ribbon behind her head, her fingers shaking and slipping over the smooth loops. She *had* to—

Her thoughts stopped as Maddy handed her a Polaroid.

'It's Blake. How did you get a photograph of my daughter?' Blake was smiling at the camera with a necklace of emeralds and diamonds hanging around her throat. It made her look like a made-up version of herself, an AI image, a fake. Blake never wore jewellery like that. She wore '90s-style pendants or simple silver chains.

A sheen of sweat made Maddy's chest shimmer. 'I was going to ask if you'd mentioned me to her, if you'd ever told her what had happened, or that I was going to be here.'

'No. I've never breathed a word about you. Or any of it,' Sadie whispered, feeling as though someone might jump from the wardrobes or out from behind the curtains at the mention of her keeping secrets.

'Well, she's obviously here.'

'How do you know that?'

Maddy jabbed at the photograph with her finger. Her nails were painted blood red. 'She's in my hotel room. Wearing my necklace. And the Polaroid was in my suitcase. I just found it.'

'That's your necklace?'

'Yes. Don't you remember? I wore it the last time we were together actually. That night.'

Sadie stared at the necklace, and a memory slowed ebbed its way towards the front of her mind. Maddy, opening her front door and welcoming Sadie into her home the night of the leavers' ball. Maddy had been wearing a red dress that clung to every part of her body, and a glittering statement necklace. She'd looked like something from a film, and her home looked like a film set too, all artistic sculptures and enormous rooms. But something had seemed so sad about it all, as though Maddy was a child alone in a playhouse, all dressed up and deserted by her friends. Sadie had felt glad she'd gone, and had felt the familiar comfort of being the only person to depend on as she followed Maddy through the house. She'd thought of Rob at home, of Blake tucked up in bed, their memories forming a bubble of safety around them somehow. She remembered wondering how many happy memories Maddy had.

'That necklace is limited edition,' Maddy was telling her now. 'There are barely any of them around.' Her voice became strangled. 'Gregory's been spending a lot of time away from home lately and I have had my suspicions but I never thought…'

Sadie took a step away from Maddy, the small stuffed bear she'd seen in Blake's wardrobe looming in her mind, the anger that emanated from Maddy the night of the Gatsby Ball, when Pearl had appeared.

B & G

Blake had been secretive lately, but this absolutely could *not* be the reason for it. How old was Gregory? In his late thirties, at least. Forty, perhaps. No. There had to be some other G, some boy with a football obsession, a breaking voice and the same lessons as Blake.

'Maddy, she's fifteen years old. More than half Gregory's age.' Maddy had to be mistaken: the boys Blake liked would all be at school, with long hair and trousers speckled with mud. The kind of immature boys in surprisingly mature bodies who threw pens or rolled up bits of paper at girls to get their attention during lessons. And even that was hard enough to cope with. Blake and boys. But *Blake and Gregory*? It was absolutely not true.

'I know. It's disgusting for me to even think it. I don't want to. But she's in my room in this photo. The room I'm meant to share with Gregory. With my necklace on. He was weird about coming here together. He insisted that we came separately. Gave me some story about being in London.'

'No. You're wrong. Blake is at her friend's house.' Sadie tried to believe that, willed her phone to ping with a message from Sarah. It was not true and she would not let Maddy become wild with anger about Blake in the same way she had done with Pearl. 'I'm going to find Rob.' If any part of this was real, Rob would kill Gregory. He would take him in his surprisingly strong arms and he would break him like a cheap doll. She grabbed her phone and stepped out of the room. Maddy followed her, still talking endlessly, words bleeding together.

'I thought it was bad enough with Pearl, but she was at least in sixth form. And he was younger then. But this? I can't believe it. I am so hurt that he is willing to risk absolutely everything, again. And you know what? Most of what we have now is because of me! He'll tell you that it was him, his books, his ideas. Eliot. Our house. But it was me! All me.'

'It's not true,' Sadie interrupted. *Be assertive. Be different, this time*, Sadie told herself. *If you step into the lies now, you'll never find your way out.* 'There will be an explanation.' The words made her step faster towards Rob. They were in reception now. A harp was being played in the expansive corner, the harpist wearing a full Pierrot mask with a single black tear running from the left eye. The stuffed birds were perched high on elaborate golden shelves, dead eyes staring down at them.

A message pinged onto Sadie's phone, making her chest contract as they stepped out onto the gravel. Choking heat pounded down and Sadie pressed her hand to her temple, which felt like it might explode into a million tiny fragments of bone. It took a moment for her eyes to adjust to the blinding sun and see the text.

> Hi, Sadie! Blake left our house this morning? Hope she made it home to you? X

Sadie started to run towards where Rob had parked when they'd arrived at the castle. Gravel flicked up and stung her ankles, burrowing into her shoes and her skin. She could hear Maddy running behind her, invisible lines pulling them to each other.

Rob's car was gone.

'When did you get the photo?' Sadie asked as she swung around breathlessly to face Maddy. Sweat stung her eyes and acid rose into her throat.

'About fifteen minutes ago.' Maddy stared at Sadie with her intense brown eyes and Sadie saw a fleeting expression that she remembered seeing in those first days.

It had been a clear blue Saturday morning in July when Sadie had met Maddy for the first time. She'd just been about to set off with Blake to the Stay and Play at the bottom of the hill, when a piece of Bach music that Sadie adored had come on the radio. Sadie used to be incapable of leaving a room, of even engaging in conversation with anyone, when her favourite music came on. She'd put down her oversized handbag full of snacks and crayons, and she'd picked up Blake and spun her around in time to the beautiful notes. Blake liked music too. They shared that: they shared everything, and they were going to be close forever.

They'd been a little late to the Stay and Play because Blake had been dizzy when Sadie finally put her down, and when she picked up her blackcurrant drink, disoriented from the spinning, she'd spilled it down herself. Sadie had helped Blake to redress, helping her get her smooth little limbs into a new outfit, taking the sodden, stained white dress and soaking it in the kitchen sink, humming the tune as she did it.

There had been a vulnerability to Maddy that Sadie had seen straight away when she met her thirty minutes or so later. There had been sadness in the way she talked and moved. Her voice had been loud and her outward appearance flawless but it had been obvious that happiness eluded her. She had gazed at Blake as though she was missing something or someone. Sadie had recognised that expression from when her mum was young, alone and lost. Her mum had sometimes cried to Sadie that she had no friends.

If I just had someone, I wouldn't need to drink like this, Sadie. I'm lonely. These bottles are my friends, aren't they?

Sadie had said yes to the wine at The Cellar with Maddy after Stay and Play, even though she didn't like to drink even then, especially in the daytime, especially when Blake was with her.

Blake. Beautiful, sweet, perfect Blake.

Yet she'd still met Maddy more often, in those endless summer days. The sun had shone down on them as they'd met at the park and at The Cellar, and Sadie had ignored the tiny little twist of doubt about Maddy in her gut because she knew Maddy had needed her. She should have said no to the first glass of wine. No to being friends. No to trying to fix things for someone she didn't even know. No to believing that one friend for her mother would have folded away all her problems and crippling addictions into a neat little box.

And the worst thing was that she'd taken Blake with her and pushed her into the centre of all of this.

Maybe Gregory had kept track of Blake all these years. That was what predators did, wasn't it? They waited and then they stalked unseen, and finally they pounced. And he'd been able to do it all because Blake was everywhere online. Sadie had known it was a bad idea for a fifteen-year-old to be parading herself in the never-ending universe of social media: her name, her school, her performances that anyone could buy tickets to.

Sadie snapped back into the present.

'You can probably fake Polaroids,' she told Maddy, trying not to be swept along in the same way she had been all those years ago. You could fake anything these days, couldn't you? Most of the world and its people were just versions of someone's imagination or AI or who knew what else. Blake watched one TV show where things that looked completely real turned out to be cake. Absolutely nothing was as it seemed these days.

'It's not fake,' Maddy said, exhaling all of her impatience over Sadie so that Sadie caught a momentary scent of her breath: sweet wine and garlic.

'Okay. Let's say it's real.' Sadie snatched the photograph and stared at it again, the hamster wheel of her mind whirring around and around, the seconds disappearing, one after the other where Blake could be in danger or out of her depth, drowning and needing Sadie to wade in and pull her out. 'How did they even meet?'

'I don't know. This is the first I've come across them being together.' Maddy shielded her eyes from the sun and scanned the car park. 'So where's Rob? Weren't you going to find him?'

'Yes. I'm going to reception.' Sadie didn't want Maddy poking into what was happening with Rob, knowing that he had gone. 'I can ask them if Blake has checked in.'

'I'll come with you.' Maddy pulled her own mask out of her bag. It was the same as Sadie's: black and glittering. 'I'm putting this on. I think the ball has started.' She glanced at Sadie's outfit. 'You need to get ready. You'll stand out too much otherwise. You can't wear denim shorts to a ball.'

Sadie watched as Maddy pulled on her mask. There was something unsettling about her covered face. A creeping sensation washed over her, the feeling of something clicking into place. The rose petals in the gift bag. Maddy back now, as Sadie's world wobbled, about to crash on its side. The bitter taste of her drink at the Gatsby Ball, and Maddy's lies.

'It's all you.'

SEVENTEEN

Pearl

I adjusted my mask in the mirror of my mother's room: the most extravagant room of all. The rooms were all enormous; all opulent. But this one was at the very top of the castle, next to Sadie's. It was in a part of the building that jutted out from the rest of so that I couldn't even see the cliffs, just the thrashing sea below. Even though the heat was stifling, the waves looked steely and frozen. I wondered what it would be like to jump from the window and let my body slice right through them.

'See, Pearl,' Blanche said, suddenly at my shoulder like a pretty ghost. 'I told you it was the perfect job for you.'

I smiled into the mirror. I'd gone cold the first time she had mentioned it, even though the day had been warm with white spring sunlight.

'Your face will be covered! The job's made for you, darling!'

But Blanche had been right. I'd forgotten what it was like to look good. The thrill of feeling in control, asleep for so long, stretched inside me, ready to wake. I glanced at my mother. When I was little, there had been no prospect more exciting than growing up to be as beautiful as her. Now, taking in her reflection, I realised that actually, my mother's eyes were quite close together, her nose slightly too long. It turned out that I looked more like my dad. If things had worked out the way they were meant to, I would have grown up to be even more attractive than Blanche.

Maybe she'd known it was on the cards, and that's why she'd shot comments at me like little bullets as I grew up. Maybe she'd wished for my beauty not to blossom, for ugliness to descend on me like something from a gruesome fairy tale. And then my face had been ripped open and she'd realised the whole 'be careful what you wish for' thing was true.

'I used to read about this ball before I'd even started Goldman Events,' Blanche told me now, ready to pursue a full soliloquy. She pressed her long slim fingers to her forehead, absorbing the sheen of sweat that had broken out through her makeup on her skin. Her face looked fresh and plump from her latest round of Botox, like a perfectly ripe piece of fruit. I had a disturbing image of someone biting into my mother's cheek, revealing pulp and blood underneath, and took a breath to help me erase it.

'It seemed so grand and so mysterious, and yet so humble giving all its profits away. Such a combination. I used to think, I want to run that ball, and when I do run it, I will do it even better. And now I have been doing it for ten whole years. It's come so far over the last decade and I am just so proud.' She smiled the smile of someone who had casually achieved all their dreams.

I straightened my shoulders, looking at my reflection in the full-length mirror. Up here, it didn't feel as though we were back at Falcon Castle. The owners obviously thought it was something special, but really, it could be any one of a million boutique hotels that I'd had been to. The ones I'd seen that had been chosen by Gregory all merged into one in my mind. I had tried to keep away from him whilst I was in London, but sometimes, as the years stretched on, temptation was too much to bear. I'd lied to my parents, of course – they tried to stop me from self-destructing but there wasn't that much they could do from Kings Hill East. And when I joined him, the hotels were all like this one: all doing similar things with dark velour and extravagant, sweeping designs and pretentious wildlife framed and stuffed. All different in exactly the same way.

'I just want to emphasise that this is a very big event, Pearl, with a lot of very important people watching, judging what I've done and how I've done it. I know that being back here might feel a little odd for you. But it's a totally different place now. The current owners have made a lot of wonderful changes. And it's such a special venue. Such a brilliant place for a party. The location all adds to the drama, gives it a nice sense of danger. As we know.'

Honestly, I sometimes wondered if my mother was a normal person with a normal heart. Was it any wonder that I'd turned out like this?

'You haven't been to any of these balls since that first one,' she continued. 'But you should know that people take

White Feather very seriously. It does excellent work for those poor bereaved children.'

I said nothing, breathing in my mother's perfume. No subtle scent for Blanche: hers was the type that made you feel like flowers were being shoved down your nose and throat. I was surprised that the beneficiaries of the charity were in my mother's mind at all, that she cared even slightly about children who had lost a parent. Blanche had never exactly seemed to rate parenthood highly. I barely saw her, and when I did, she would tell me to disappear. As a child, I'd sometimes have quite inexplicable fantasies about finding my mother dead: in the bath, perhaps, staring out from a cloud of bubbles; or cold and grey in her bed. I hadn't ever really understood the daydreams of my mother's stiff, staring eyes, the flowers and sympathies from strangers. But I'd indulged in them anyway, enjoying them as I lay in bed at night. And remembering them now made me feel like if something ever had happened to my mother, I wouldn't have needed a charity to help me through it. It would have been me and Dad against the world together. I perhaps would have been quite happy. Maybe that's why I'd had them in the first place. A dream of being someone's number one. *Not that I'd say this at the ball*, I thought with a smirk.

'Expectations will be high,' Blanche went on, an avalanche in full flow. 'I'm still disappointed that you missed the training session last night. All the other waitresses managed to make it here, on time and ready to learn. It was quite unacceptable that you appeared to think you were above it all. I lost count of how many messages I sent you. Even your dad tried to get in touch.'

'All I need to do is pour champagne. I think I'll manage.' I really had considered going to the training session that my mother had wanted me at last night. I'd intended to drive the little Audi to the castle after I'd got in and read her messages and the note she'd left on the door. But when it came to it, the thought of it all was too much. Blanche's annoyance that I was late, so sharp it would graze against my skin, the others watching as she scolded me like a child, an evening of being smothered and neglected all at the same time.

'I also noticed my staffing spreadsheets look a little different since you took over some of the admin.' Annoyance prickled at me. Why did she have to notice every *single* thing? 'If you've changed anything on there or made some kind of careless admin error, then you need to tell me now, before we go downstairs and things get going.'

My mother had asked me to help with the Masquerade Ball in the spring, when I'd been back home for a few months. I had said yes, which had obviously surprised both of my parents because I hadn't worked since I'd first gone to London. Dad had smiled so hard when I'd suggested that I help my mother's staff with the shortlisting of applicants for the ball's waitressing roles: one of the grins that he probably used on his clients to make them feel special as they signed over millions of pounds for Kensington houses and Scottish castles. *Told you she'd come round*, his grin said to Blanche. *I told you she would get used to the idea of going back to Falcon Castle. And look! She's embracing it! Our little shining Pearl has come through, just like I told you she would.*

I'd felt the guilt I always did when I wasn't being who Dad thought I was, as I wrote down Blanche's passwords and found the file of numbers and applications for tickets; as I opened the guestlist document and swiped clear four rows on the spreadsheet and replaced them; as I took over the list of waitressing staff for my mother to interview. I'd met the first two and had been irritated by them at first, by their matching silky blonde hair and pretty white smiles. But then, as I'd interviewed a third, a brunette this time, an idea had formed in my mind and I'd put a red cross against the brunette's name. Then I'd told all the brunettes and redheads, the ones who had been much shorter than her or taller than I'd needed, that they didn't have the level of confidence for such a big event; that someone else had a little more experience; that they wouldn't fit in well enough with the team. They'd all taken my sugary words like children's medicine, gulping them down bravely.

But I didn't need to feel guilty. Dad would understand. If he knew what had happened that night of the Gatsby Ball – the one I'd been dragged to because my mother's events company was planning it just like it was this time, he'd probably support me. He might even help me. And anyway, I'd make it up to him because I always did. I'd make sure that the team of waiting staff was perfect. And although my mother and her team of pompous people who made up Goldman Events would try to take the credit for the ball running like clockwork for at least the first part,

Dad would know. He'd be proud of me. The thought was soothing.

'I haven't done anything with your spreadsheets. And I won't mess up.' Everything would go perfectly. I'd make sure of it. 'What time's Dad arriving?'

'No idea. He's at a new site in the Cotswolds today. A big one. Lakeside.' Blanche gave me a flinty smile as she put on her own mask. 'Come on, you should already be downstairs serving. Wear the mask at all times, no exceptions. And get all the other waitresses to put theirs on too. There's a standard we need to uphold. Uphold it, won't you, darling? People expect luxury, not … well, you know. No faces now, until midnight.' She glanced at me in the mirror for a moment longer than she needed to, probably wishing I could keep my mask on for a lifetime. She wasn't the only one.

The reception desk that I passed on my way to the kitchen, where my shift as head waitress was about to start, was gilded marble, the large square area lit by low-hanging gold chandeliers. I tried to remember what it had looked like last time I'd been here. The same? Demolished and replaced? No, I had no idea.

The receptionist, Marta, a woman that my mother had selected, with a heavy black fringe and a cute lavender-coloured mask, smiled at me as I passed. Was this a normal, non-sympathetic smile, the smile that I would get if my face was always covered up with a mask? A smile that assumed

I was just another pretty blonde? Not a smile that asked a thousand horrified questions?

'My mother is managing the event,' I told Marta, temptation getting the better of me like it always did. 'She's asked me to check on arrivals for her.' In the end, I'd decided to presume that Gregory and Rob would bring Maddy and Sadie as their plus ones. I'd told Gregory in an Instagram message from an account carefully curated over the last few months that he'd been selected because he was an author and we gave free tickets to people in the arts. In Rob's message, I'd said something about an NHS prize draw. One of them could have quite easily been told by someone who knew how Masquerade really worked that something wasn't right. Of course, they'd both emailed Masquerade separately, checking that the invitations had been above board. But I'd set up alerts for the Masquerade email account on my phone so had seen their messages straight away. I'd replied officially and reassured them. It hadn't taken much for them to believe me. It turned out that they were all so desperate to be here; all so convinced by their good, charitable people personas, that they quite happily believed that they deserved to be attending. It was obviously how their lives were, and what they were used to and comfortable with: things they wanted floating gently down into their laps like feathers so often that it was what they had come to expect.

'Let me have a look at the arrivals list,' Marta said, but as she did, I felt a blast of smothering air from the main doors opening behind me. Her eyes wandered to somewhere beyond my left shoulder and I turned, following her gaze. My heart stopped.

His skin was golden from endless summer days. His scent, even from where I was standing, lit something within me. It was deep, musky and expensive. He glanced at me with the carelessness of someone who was surrounded by different people all the time. It meant nothing to him that he had been with me only yesterday. Even though I had my mask on, I would have expected him to recognise me. But he obviously hadn't been thinking about me. I wasn't on his mind at all.

After he'd spoken to Marta (he had no bags he said, because his *wife* had brought everything he needed), he stepped towards me, smiled a wide, charming smile and held out his hand for me to shake. I took it and pressed my fingers against his, feeling the warmth of our skin together.

The reception phone rang again then, a shrill scream that made me jump.

'I'm very much looking forward to the party,' Gregory told me, and I saw him glance over my white *Masquerade-*branded blouse and black skirt. 'I hope you have plenty of champagne on ice.'

He was speaking to me like he might speak to any member of staff at any fancy event. Like I wasn't a real person, just a prop for the big, grand performance of his life. I smiled at him, feeling the corners of the mask jagged against my cheeks. His breath smelled of coffee just like it had done yesterday in his bedroom, and was so close and warm on my skin that I wanted to close my eyes and pool to the floor like ribbon.

'Oh, yes. We have plenty of whiskey, too.' I'd been going to avoid speaking in case he recognised my voice, but I couldn't help myself. Gregory loved whiskey. He collected expensive bottles of it. *Nothing better than a good book and a glass of whiskey.*

'Well,' Gregory said. 'I'm sure you have plenty to do, so I will leave you to it.' He stepped away from me, and I saw his eyes move over my face, over the black mask down to my mouth.

He frowned.

I glanced at Marta, who was still on the phone, tapping away at her keyboard with her acrylic nails, her eyes focused on her computer screen. I took Gregory's hand again, pressing into his skin with my fingernails. He winced, but I wondered if he liked it. Pleasure and pain were sometimes so hard to tell apart.

'It's you.' He didn't sound as shocked as I would have liked. 'What do you want?'

'You know what I want.' I heard a tremble in my voice and hated myself for it.

Gregory sighed with a sad little smile and took his hand from mine. 'Pearl, listen, you're kidding yourself following me around like this. I almost understood it when you first started all those years ago. You were so young. You had a crush. But you're an adult now. You really should be more aware of what you're doing. Just when I think you've lost interest, you're back. It's quite sad really. Whatever this hold is that you think you have on me…' He shrugged, not even bothering to finish his sentence, still smiling as though this was nothing: a child's spoilt drawing or a dropped lollipop.

'Maddy doesn't want you,' I told him. 'She wants Aiden. So you might as well have me.'

Gregory laughed so loudly and suddenly that I felt the rush of hot blood to my face.

'You're an expert on my marriage now? On all the people in my family?'

'I'll tell them,' I said, my voice low because even though Marta looked as though she wasn't listening, she probably was. Everyone was always doing something they were pretending not to do, every second of every day. 'I'll tell them everything.' My stomach flipped. This was all wrong: I was throwing all my most valuable weapons with no measure and no planning and my words were tumbling out at all the wrong angles.

Gregory puffed air from his nose. 'Tell whoever you want whatever you want, Pearl. They won't believe you. They won't believe any of it.'

'You don't mean it,' I said quietly. I thought of that night when everything changed, of the storm and the leaves whipping from the trees around us. He hadn't meant it then and he didn't mean it now. 'Think of everything you have to lose. I can take it all from you.'

He laughed again. 'Well, yes, Pearl. I do have a lot to lose.' His whispered words reminded me of when he had been my teacher. My favourite teacher. He'd always used my name more than any of the other girls'. I'd even counted during one lesson. I couldn't remember now how many more times he said my name but I'm sure it was a lot more. That was probably why they stopped being my friends.

It was so obvious, their jealousy sticking out at angles like unsightly broken bones. 'But,' he continued, 'I won't lose it just because of some story you decide to tell people. That's what you don't seem to be able to understand. What I have, and what I don't have, isn't down to you. Never has been. You were a jealous schoolgirl with a crush. That's all.'

Gregory shook his head as though he felt sorry for me, and then gave a final wide grin. 'Nice catching up with you,' he said loudly, making my insides burn as he walked away from me.

EIGHTEEN

Maddy
___

'It's all you.'

The assertive tone to Sadie's voice was a surprise. It still had a certain kind of music to it like it used to, but there was a trace of something new – impatience, perhaps? She was a teacher now though, so that made sense. Being a teacher had made Gregory more impatient, less tolerant of noise and excuses. Or maybe that had been the stress of having an affair. The first of multiple ones, it seemed. Maddy's stomach lurched.

'You've been in my house, messing with my things.'

Panic flapped its wings inside Maddy's chest. She thought of the hours she'd spent poring over Sadie's life on the internet: the time she'd spent staring at Blake on grainy screenshots, moving her fingers over Blake's mouth and her golden hair and shining white teeth. 'I haven't been anywhere near your house.' Her words sounded empty, even to her own ears.

'I should have known,' Sadie said, clearly not believing a

word Maddy said. 'I thought I was going mad, that I was imagining someone was out to get us. It's been ruining my life. But I thought I deserved it.'

So it wasn't just Maddy who sometimes thought she was losing the plot. She and Sadie were the same. Must be some hangover from the horror of that night. All the more reason to not let things get out of hand this time: to stop avoiding each other and face the past head-on, right now. Together.

'Sadie, I'm not out to get you. I know that things went too far with Pearl. I know those photos we both got were hard to see. I know that…' Maddy faltered. The words had left her lips too soon. It was the first time she'd acknowledged the photographs and the truth and guilt about both were tangled in her words. She could hear it, and she wondered if Sadie could too. She thought of Aiden. Had he told anyone yet? Maybe he was giving her some time to do it herself. Maybe he expected her to do it at the castle.

Sadie looked at her phone and tapped on it to make a call. She still wasn't in her ball outfit yet, and she pulled at her plain white T-shirt as though she was being suffocated by it. 'Don't.'

Maddy heard the faint ringtone, and saw Sadie looking more and more despairing with each one.

'I want to protect Blake. I don't want her to get hurt.' Maddy's heart suddenly felt like it might burst and splatter out onto the beautiful walls. She needed to end this repulsive *thing*. Gregory could not go round like some predator, stripping young girls of their innocence, their crushes on normal teenage boys and God knew what else.

It was incomprehensible: it was police and statements and broken laws and ruined lives. It was all the things Maddy could not bear, that her life could not stand the weight of. That's why she'd gone along with the wrong story in the first place.

The news report flashed in Maddy's mind: *Police are looking for the driver of a red sports car.*

Nobody else in the family had thought anything of it. But it was clear to Maddy that Aiden had come to rescue her, and must have seen Gregory's car. He must have seen Maddy inside it. He could easily have called the police when the reports of the red sports car were released, instead of trying to get her to admit it that day at her mother's house and again last night in Candice's garden. He could have told them what he saw. But instead, he stood back and risked everything for Maddy. So why was he bringing it all up now?

Of course she had thought of telling the truth: of asking Aiden what he'd done, or not done, and why he'd let the police continue looking for a car like his; of telling Sadie that it had been them all along. But Sadie was so good, so pure and right, that if she had thought – really, actually thought – for a second that they were to blame, she would have gone straight to the police and owned up. And that would have meant the end of Gregory's shiny fame, the end of their money, their house and their perfect life. Maddy had not been able to bear the thought of it. And what difference did it make, really? The damage had been done. And it was Pearl and Gregory's damage really. Maddy had just suffered collateral damage, hadn't she?

Sadie tutted, impatient and annoyed. 'I know how angry you were with Pearl for getting involved with Gregory, remember. I know you're probably as angry with Blake.'

'No. This is completely different. I care about Blake, Sadie. I want to help you protect her.'

'You don't even know her,' Sadie said quickly. Maddy had thought Sadie would be happy that Maddy cared about Blake. Didn't everyone want their children to be adored?

'So? I still care about her.' And Sadie was wrong because Maddy did know Blake. She was hurt by Blake, of course. But now she knew that Blake was probably the latest in a line of inappropriate leggy blonde girls that Gregory had taken it upon himself to be involved with. It wasn't Blake's fault. But it had been Pearl's fault, because she had started it all, and she had taunted Maddy whilst she'd been at it. She'd perhaps even started Gregory's wandering eyes, and she'd spun everything out of control.

If Maddy were Sadie, she would take extra special care of Blake and never let her out of her sight. Maddy never thought that about her own child. But Eliot didn't have the things that Blake had. He didn't have the sparkle that might threaten people or drive them to revenge or madness or destruction. He'd probably be playing Lego at Candice's dining table right now, his mouth hanging slightly open, his brow furrowed as he looked for the perfect yellow stick or blue brick. 'It's Gregory I'm furious with,' she said eventually. She thought of when she'd first met Sadie and spent so long wondering about being open with her. But things felt different now. Maddy's feelings spewed from her impulsively.

Sadie looked frightened as she tapped on her phone and held it to her ear again. 'Rob will come back,' she said, and it seemed like she was talking more to herself than Maddy. 'He won't just leave me here.'

Maddy couldn't help herself: she moved towards Sadie quickly and pulled her into another tight hug. Sadie smelled different than she had done all those years ago. Her old scent of sweet lemons always mingled in Maddy's mind with the tang of Miraval from their first meeting. Now, Sadie smelled of musk and vanilla. It had never occurred to Maddy to change her perfume, but now she realised that she could wear any one she wanted. As soon as she got home, she'd go online and buy a new one.

Sadie pulled away from Maddy and put her phone back into her pocket. 'If any of this is true, and Blake is here, then I can't just stand about. I need to find her. But this place is like a maze.' Sadie shook her head. 'How is this happening? How am I with *you*'—Maddy tried not to feel insulted—'searching for Blake and *Gregory*, here of all places? She's been secretive lately but I *never*…'

Sadie started moving again, more quickly and Maddy followed, forging ahead through the hideous heat and the mind-bending corridors that all looked the same.

It crossed Maddy's mind how fast she might run if she thought Eliot was here, in need of rescuing. She would run, of course. But she wondered, as they raced through the corridors, picking up more and more speed, twisting and turning and almost hurling themselves down the enormous staircases; as she wiped sweat from her forehead and out of her eyes, if she would run quite as fast as this. Maddy pushed herself towards Sadie as they rushed through the maze of corridors. Eventually, she took the lead as though Blake was a finish line, wanting to prove to Sadie how much she cared.

She turned yet another corner and slammed into a hard chest.

Gregory.

'Maddy.' He wasn't wearing his mask: not that it would have made a difference. Masks didn't matter when you'd lived with someone for fifteen years. Maddy would have noticed the way he was standing: chest puffed out, head held high, no matter what. It was obviously the same for Gregory because he knew her even though she had her mask on, although it was hard to know what he recognised in Maddy. Probably not the things she'd want him to, so perhaps she was best not knowing. She looked over at Sadie, who was staring at Gregory.

'I've only just arrived,' Gregory told Maddy. He glanced to the right for a split second, down the corridor he'd just come from. Maddy followed his line of vision and saw it just before it was too late: a flash of blonde disappearing around the corner.

'Sadie, was that Blake?'

But Sadie hadn't seen. 'Where?' There was terror in her voice, and Maddy wanted to take her and hug her again, to make things right somehow.

'There was an interesting photograph in our room,' Maddy informed Gregory. 'A little gift. You might have seen it. Or maybe you took it.'

Sadie stepped towards Gregory. 'Is it true? Is my fifteen-year-old daughter here with you?'

Gregory's fan-smile froze on his face. 'I'm sorry, do I know you?' He prided himself on remembering admirers of his writing. His memory was apparently razor sharp. *I never forget people*, he often said with an exquisite smile.

'Go after her,' Maddy told Sadie.

Maddy and Gregory stood staring at one another after Sadie had disappeared down the hallway.

'What on earth was that woman implying? Something about a fifteen-year-old?'

'That was Sadie.'

Gregory was silent for a moment. He turned and stared down the corridor.

'The Sadie from—?'

'Yes. That Sadie.'

Maddy hadn't mentioned Sadie to Gregory for years. He'd never been that interested in her friends, so after the Gatsby Ball she'd never talked about Sadie again as they'd continued round and round on the pretty carousel of their life. Gregory had never asked why Maddy hadn't seen her again, which made her relieved: Sadie obviously had meant nothing to him and wasn't significant in any way.

'But why was she throwing around accusations like that? Me bringing a young girl here?' Gregory's face was pinched with anger and his words small and clipped. 'How on earth could you let her think that I'm remotely capable of something like that? Didn't you set her straight?'

'I told you. There was a photograph in our room.' More photographs causing problems: snapshots of seconds that were now going to last a lifetime. Maddy should have kept the picture, because now Gregory would just try to lie his way out of it, but Sadie had snatched it from her. She thought it was her story; Maddy thought it was her own. 'A photograph of Blake. She was wearing my limited-edition necklace that I thought I'd lost. And I have no idea why she was wearing it, so I'm having to guess why that might be. Just tell me the truth.'

'I don't know who Blake is. And I haven't seen that necklace in months. This is all nonsense. Absolute, utter trash. And you've fallen for it, Maddy.' Gregory scratched his chin as he spoke, and his golden stubble made an unpleasant sandpaper sound that made Maddy want to cover her ears and scream and scream. His defensiveness was doing nothing but confirming all her worst fears. 'I also think, if you're going to make such awful allegations, you'd at least better do it in private.'

He started walking briskly ahead. Maddy followed, dodging people in beautiful dresses and intricate masks. The sounds of music from the harpist in reception and the band melted together, distant and haunting.

Gregory pulled the door closed when he got in their room, and stood guard in front of it as though he expected Maddy to hurl herself back out into the corridor.

'We need to go to the ballroom otherwise we'll miss the dinner.'

'I want to bring something up with you, Maddy, whilst we're in these unchartered waters.'

Oh, God. Here it was. Gregory wrapping up darkness in flowery language straight from his novel. Finally, the confession about him and Blake. And then that would lead to more: questions about Gregory moving out, or having Eliot live with him, or shared money or homes or who knew what else. She took a deep breath, as though she was bracing herself to jump in an icy pool. Maddy thought of an article she'd seen in a magazine about a woman who'd jumped into water so cold that her heart had seized up. Alive one minute, dead the next.

Gregory cleared his throat. 'Is it Aiden you want?'

'What?' The words punched Maddy in the stomach. Her legs felt weak and she held on to the elaborate dresser beside her for support. 'Where did this come from?'

'Aiden. And you. Have I been missing something quite obvious for years?'

'How ridiculous,' Maddy found herself saying. 'Aiden belongs to Candice. And I'm with you. It's simple, isn't it? Why are you trying to turn this all around onto me, when you're the one with secrets?' Maybe he'd seen the card from the flowers after all. Maybe the muffin box was still in her bin. Maybe the cleaner hadn't turned up and Gregory had gone home before coming to the ball, or maybe he had seen the ripped-up card that had come with the flowers or maybe another of a hundred possible things had happened to make Gregory think *he* had something on *her*. One of the exact scenarios she was trying to avoid, although those scenarios seemed to be multiplying.

Gregory pulled Maddy closer to him. He used to do that in the old days, when they were young and her skin was more elastic and her jeans fitted better. She looked away from him, down at the thick velvety carpet the colour of plums.

'Secrets? Maddy, who have you seen today? Who have you been talking to?' Gregory glanced at the door, as though he thought someone was outside it, listening to them, and pulled at the collar of his shirt. 'You know, don't you?' His words were low.

'Yes, I know. Really, Gregory. A teenager? Again? What are you thinking?'

She stared at him, waiting. A glimmer of sweat made him look athletic, glowing even. How did he do it? He looked better with every year that passed. Maddy sometimes felt like she was trying to cling on to her looks as she approached forty, like a drowning man to a raft. Gregory was the opposite: age was chiselling away at him like a charming craftsman. His hair was still thick, with the slightest kink to it, the colour of rich earth. Gregory's looks sold the life she wanted to sell, bathed them both in a special, golden brand of success.

'Maddy, I don't know what she's been telling you, but—'

'You're lying to me. You're always lying to me. Sadie is telling the truth.'

Confusion swept over Gregory's face and Maddy felt a small flash of triumph.

'Look, Maddy,' Gregory said. 'You and Eliot, and the life we've built. It's good, is it not? You can't let her get in the way of it. You can't let her destroy things for us.'

Maddy took her hands from his, wrestling against him to move away but he was stronger than he looked. 'Sadie is not the one doing that.'

Gregory wouldn't let Maddy go. The bones of his fingers pressed into hers and a moment of relief washed over Maddy that they hadn't stayed in the corridor or gone to the dinner. It wouldn't do for anyone to see them like this.

'I'm not talking about Sadie. I'm talking about Pearl.'

NINETEEN

Pearl

I stared after Gregory as he disappeared down the corridor.

What I have, and what I don't have, isn't down to you.

The words had punched me right in the gut.

I'd thought I was so clever planning tonight. I'd even gone to the effort of making friends with some twenty-year-old loser in a pub outside of Kings Hill a few weeks ago. The desperation of closing time, another night wasted, would make anyone agree to anything. His piggy eyes had lit up at the sight of three fifty-pound notes, and the next minute, Maddy's air conditioning in her flashy Range Rover had magically broken. Wi-Fi, cameras and sanity all messed with. It had been like playing God, and had made me feel superior for once. But where had it got me, really? Gregory's words had reminded me that I was so far from God that it was a joke.

I had no control over anything. All I'd been doing was playing pathetic games at a silly little party for rich people. Maddy and Sadie were probably having the time of their lives tonight after my fake text messages had brought them back together again. They were probably enjoying seeing each other. I had treated them to pure luxury, letting them swan around thinking that they were being good patrons of charity, making the world a nicer place just by existing and drinking free drinks.

They knew what they'd done to me, and they were still living their silky, easy lives. Anger roared in my ears, sounding like static and blocking out the world.

'Excuse me?' Marta was calling me from the reception desk. 'Can I give you a message to pass to the head waitress?'

I sighed. I couldn't be bothered telling Marta that I was the head waitress. I moved over to the desk and took the compliments slip that the receptionist held out. It was smooth and thick under my fingers. I looked down at Marta's fat handwriting.

All good wishes tonight, darling Pearl. Caught up at work. Won't be coming. Dad.

I could hear the band playing in the ballroom: a slow, boring tune that made me want to go in there, grab the microphone and sing something that would make the room seem less like someone had died.

All good wishes. As though I was someone he barely knew. Was my father even bothered about me? Had he ever been, or had I got that all wrong too?

He'd always seemed to care. He'd been the one there for me when things had spiralled with Trafford. I'd knocked back too much vodka the night I'd found out about Trafford becoming a dad, and I'd called my own father and wept to him. Then I'd thrown up in my new stone sink. Dad liked to pretend that my near-hysterical phone call a few months ago hadn't happened. To acknowledge it would be to humiliate us both. But he had been there for me at the time, logical as always, as though my life were a tricky game of chess that could still be won if only we could pause for a minute and think strategically.

Have a fresh start.

I didn't know what screamed more of madness: staying in London near Trafford or being back in the place I'd met Gregory Archer. I should have gone somewhere totally new, but I found new places hard. I'd done it once in London and that had been more than enough. Trafford and a few others had helped. But there was always too much explaining, too many lowered gazes and whispers and wonderings. People knew here. Or they *thought* they knew. Same difference: it meant they didn't ask.

What if I'd got it all wrong? My dad wasn't even here. There was nobody to impress or let down anyway.

I stood for a moment, staring at the chaotic patterns of the corridor carpet. What would it be like to be here *with* someone tonight, instead of working with a bunch of people ten years younger than me? Even with a friend? Or a normal mother? I thought again of Gregory yesterday, of Maddy downstairs in her huge house filled with memories, craving nothing. It had taken so much energy for me to leave and go home to the flat, all alone. And for what? What had it achieved?

Loneliness yanked at me.

I straightened my mask, and walked quickly to the kitchen, where the waitresses were hurrying about, working like ants. Even without their masks on, they looked so alike it was kind of creepy, and even in my despair I congratulated myself at the sea of perfect bodies and faces framed by blonde hair. I let my eyes wander over the group and looked to see if the one I wanted was there.

She had a sharp beauty, like I used to have. The same golden glow, as though she'd been lit from within.

'Blake! You come with me.'

TWENTY

Sadie

Memories swarmed in Sadie's mind as she pushed herself forwards in the dry heat of the corridors. There were so many different ways to go, and they all looked the same. Bright pinks and turquoises, oversized gilded frames around strange paintings of birds of prey and gloss-coated dogs and horses. Plush carpets and door after door, numbers jumping from one to another, making no sense.

When Maddy's call had come ten years earlier and she'd asked Sadie to join her at the Gatsby Ball, Sadie had been reading *The Gruffalo* with Blake and put her to bed. She'd just taken her own grey cotton pyjamas from her nightwear drawer and was about to have a long shower when her phone had rung.

'Sorry,' she'd said to Rob when she hung up. 'I feel like she needs someone.'

He'd understood, because Rob always had done, back then.

Sadie had only been at Maddy's giant house for about ten minutes when Maddy came out with it, the words blurting from her lips suddenly and loudly.

'Gregory's having an affair with one of his students.'

When Maddy had called Sadie her best friend at the ball in front of Gregory and Pearl, Sadie had felt a pop of relief. She was doing the right thing, making Maddy feel as though she had someone who was there for her. Sadie hadn't turned her back on her and now Maddy wasn't as lonely. But beyond the relief, there had been a vague unease. The phrase *best friend* wasn't one Sadie had used since her school days. Sadie had friends but none as good as Rob. He was the closest person to her. Her best friend, if such a phrase must be used. She'd decided then to tell him that when she got home. They'd laugh about it, probably. She would suggest buying each other friendship necklaces, the kind where two hearts fitted together and pulled apart.

She'd never told him, though. After that night, her friendship and everything else she'd had before with Rob had been fragmented, delicate as eggshell. Hairline cracks at first, easy enough to try and ignore, followed by full smashes and messes pooled at their feet.

While with Maddy at the Gatsby Ball, Sadie had wondered how she'd feel if she found out Rob was doing something like Gregory – messing around with a younger girl instead of keeping to his vows. If she would cope with that kind of betrayal. The wondering was a kind of self-preservation, probably: the practising of an escape route.

What if, what if, what if.

But she'd never considered what would happen if she was ever the one to betray Rob. She hadn't ever considered that she would be able to, because she knew she would never ever risk losing him. But what she hadn't counted on was betraying him to avoid losing him.

Sadie should have told Rob every single thing that she could remember the day after the ball. They could have worked it out together. They could have tried to make it right. Sadie had woken up in her clean, white bed with no idea how she'd got there. She'd squinted against the bright summer morning light, trying to remember getting home and coming up with only blank spaces. Rob had been downstairs and she had smelled coffee and heard the spitting of eggs frying. She had vomited in the ensuite toilet twice and then flushed it, tossing some toilet cleaner into the bowl to mask the smell with synthetic pine. She had moved downstairs slowly, clinging on to the banister and trying to push the next wave of nausea away.

Now, Sadie glanced down one corridor which stretched for what seemed like miles. The deep, leathery scent of the castle from all those years ago was still here now, even though it had been renovated. It must have run so deep that it was impossible to remove, like smoke or decay. She exhaled, trying to remove it from her body, but it clung on, making her feel nauseous.

The heat and memories pressed down on Sadie as she tried to find her way through the castle. She didn't know how she had lost Maddy on the night of the Gatsby Ball, but she remembered trying to find her, the rain pounding as

Sadie searched the grounds outside the castle. She had a vague, cloudy recollection of seeing Gregory's black Range Rover, its yellow lights glaring, pellets of rain slicing into the beams. The engine was on, but the car wasn't moving. In the dreams, and in her memories, Sadie hammered on the driver's window, but Maddy seemed to be in her own world, and the rain was so loud that Maddy didn't know Sadie was there. Sadie was just about able to make out Maddy talking to herself animatedly in the rearview mirror. Sadie remembered a deep, ominous fear: something inside her spooking, rearing up and away. She should have left then. She should never have gone. But she had stayed, because that was what Sadie did, and she had never known how to do anything else. She always, always stayed and gave people chance after chance, even when they were mad, or drunk, or destroying everything in their path, quick as a bushfire. Sadie was a fixer, and fixers didn't give up on people who needed them.

'I want to find Gregory and Pearl,' Maddy had yelled, her words carried away by the slamming of the rain on the car and into the sea at the back of the castle.

And then the memories became even murkier and darker, and they were in a strange order like a pack of shuffled cards. And why was that? Sadie had barely touched any alcohol that night. She'd felt rude for leaving an almost full glass of what was probably expensive wine at Maddy's, but as soon as Maddy had poured it, Sadie had realised that she didn't want it: she wanted to be alert, the best version of herself. Once she had one glass, Maddy always managed to get her to have another, and she remembered that she hadn't wanted to do that. She had asked Maddy when she'd seen her a few days later at the park and Maddy had waved away the question quickly.

'Oh, my memory's hazy too. Their champagne was probably cheap. Full of sulphites.'

But Sadie had left the champagne at the ball too, except for the odd sip. She'd said this, and Maddy shrugged, her brown eyes fixed on a faraway spot in the distance.

Sadie would have driven to the Gatsby Ball herself if her car hadn't been in the garage for a service. Rob had told Sadie to take his car, but she had said no.

The memory of before she'd left, weighing up risks with Rob like she always did, was clear and bright in her mind. She'd thought of Blake tucked up in her bed with its duvet covered in dancing purple elephants, thumb tightly in her mouth, and she'd said to Rob that she would leave the car and get a cab with Maddy to the ball. Although Sadie was a fairly confident driver, she didn't particularly like the thought of the winding roads after the ball later on, especially in the predicted storm. And also, Rob might need the car for something. You never knew when an emergency might be around the corner, she'd said.

So she could remember everything that happened before. But the memories from later on in the evening were always so much harder to get to. Sadie had spent so long trying to pull at them, but she only ever came away with maddening fragments so sharp that they tore at her from the insides.

Winding roads.

The trees bending and stretching in the storm, their dark green leaves spitting out rainwater onto the roof.

Water soaking through Sadie's dress to her skin and her bones as thunder began to rumble in the yellow-grey sky.

Maddy putting her foot down on the accelerator and the car lurching forwards and then sideways to dodge a fallen branch.

Mascara tracks scoring Maddy's cheeks.

The wind pushing and pulling at the car, threatening to lift it up and toss it like a toy.

The sodden black world spinning and spinning.

Maddy shouting and shouting.

'Clair de Lune' on the radio.

Now, Sadie strained to listen for the sounds of the Masquerade Ball, *tonight's* ball, to try and bring herself back to the present. She could just about hear the gentle tinkling of champagne glasses and conversation, and the lazy tunes of the swing band. She listened hard to the music, to try to calm herself. Her ears searched for the bars and the beats and the tone of the singer's voice: the details she used to live for.

But she couldn't stay in the present. She was feeling for the final memories, the ones that hacked at her conscience in the silent, blue hours of the night, the ones that were in so many of her nightmares that she didn't know if they were real or imagined.

Maddy lurching the car forwards and shouting incomprehensible things, the tyres of Gregory's car spinning and skidding and the rain washing against the windscreen like a tide, making it impossible to see ahead.

Cracks of lightning above.

A nightmarish thud, a sound so final and terrible that Sadie thought it might be the worst sound she had ever heard.

Then 'Clair de Lune' and the drumming of rain on the roof.

TWENTY-ONE

Pearl

Blake grinned as she heard me calling and beckoning her. She put down the bottle of champagne she'd been pouring into a delicate crystal glass and came over to me.

I had seen Blake on Instagram more and more lately. It hadn't been hard to find her on there. I'd just searched through the Kings Hill High posts and scanned the comments for one from Blake. I knew what she looked like because I'd dropped in on her, Sadie and Rob a couple of times at their house when I'd visited my parents over the years. Summer days in their garden. Winter nights before Sadie snapped the curtains shut. I saw her slip from a child to a teenager in the same easy way I'd done. Her hair became longer, her golden limbs stretched out and her voice became louder.

She posted all the time as @takeablake. Close ups of white teeth, flawless skin that was pulled nice and tightly across her perfect bones, and bright young eyes full of plans. In the end, I ended up wanting to know about Blake more than Sadie or Maddy. Nobody had hurt Blake. Nobody had ruined her chances. She was like an alternate version of me: one who had been taken care of and tucked in at night and listened to, one whose life hadn't been so violently shaken that it had exploded into nothing. Why wouldn't I have been fascinated?

'I'm so glad you said yes to this job.'

Blake grinned. 'Same.'

I could bet a million pounds that Blake lived with a reckless streak the way I had always done, like living with a conjoined twin who always told us to do the wrong thing: to stoke an ember and then stand back to watch the fire roar. It hadn't surprised me that Blake had jumped at the chance of waitressing at Masquerade and had gone along with faking her mother's signature. She was no doubt suffocated by boring Sadie and desperate for a breath of real life.

'I just need to borrow you for another promo shoot, okay? Like I said, we're always needing shots of the best team members. I'm creative manager, so I have total control over the images this year.' Creative manager sounded good. I could almost believe it: almost feel what it would be like if it were real. I glanced at Blake, who looked like she'd accepted what I'd told her. It was nice to know I wasn't the only gullible one. Agents, influential people, fame. It was what Trafford had told me so that he could get the photos he thought would catapult him to some kind of elusive fame. 'We'll take the world by storm, Pearl. We'll show them what they need.' He'd thought my disfigured face could make him look like a nice guy, make him stand out from the crowd. And then as soon as he'd realised it wouldn't work, he'd ditched me. I'd felt so bad about myself for believing him.

'Do I need to put this back on?' Blake took the necklace that I'd given her from her apron pocket, and it caught the lights of the corridors, flashing green and white.

'Yeah. Why not.' I took a detour down a narrower corridor. I'd taken the necklace from Maddy's bedroom not long after I'd first arrived back in Kings Hill East. I'd seen Maddy's Instagram post gloating about it, *a limited edition*, she'd written. The words had burned themselves into my mind because they seemed useful ones to remember: Maddy would never expect to see her precious *limited-edition* necklace on somebody else.

Blake turned, frowned for a second. 'I feel like I heard my mum's voice a second ago.' She looked at me. 'Sometimes I hear her when she isn't there. Is that weird?'

'Totally normal. My brain plays tricks on me all the time. But I've seen the guest list, remember? I'd know if she was coming tonight. I would have told you.'

The lies slipped out easily and gave me a shot of calm. I'd always been good at knowing what would make people frightened. I'd called it magic when I was younger. Blanche always used to lock the door of her walk-in wardrobe whilst she dressed. But more than once, she'd turned from selecting a soft cashmere top or tailored skirt to find me standing on the inside of the wardrobe, staring at my mother silently. A strange, new pleasure had bloomed through me on those occasions. My mother, usually so poised, vulnerable instead; her pale flesh on display, her face marred with surprise and displeasure.

Even when she had changed the little silver lock, I had done it again.

Of course, it hadn't been magic at all. It had been another talent. I had found an article about picking locks and read it over and over again until I could have recited it by heart. It'd only taken a few tries to master it completely. But that wasn't all; what I had really been good at was making people feel their safe little patch of ground had moved from underneath them.

'Mum would never be at a party anyway,' Blake said. 'She'd go mad if she saw me here. She's kind of overprotective.'

'Oh, mine was always like that.' I wanted to laugh out loud. Yeah, right. Blanche caring too much – at all. What a joke. The soft thump of approaching footsteps on carpet and muted voices drifted in the air, louder with each second. I stared down the corridor ahead of us, waiting for Sadie to appear and ruin everything. How typical that would be.

I linked Blake's arm, feeling skin on skin. 'Come on, let's go down here.'

TWENTY-TWO

Maddy
___

'So you know who Pearl is, then? You remember her?' Gregory's words were careful, deliberate, as though he was coaxing someone from the end of a ledge. They were still standing in their decadent, boiling room. It seemed like they'd been in there for hours when really it must have only been a few minutes. Sweat bloomed everywhere on Maddy, under her arms and beneath her mask.

'Of course I remember her.'

'I thought I could handle it. That's why I didn't tell you that she was after me.'

Maddy let out a laugh. 'After you? Because you're always the one who's being chased, aren't you?'

Gregory stared at her and Maddy finally pushed past him. 'I'm going to the dinner before we miss it. And you should, too. I'm sure you're safe,' she added, even though terror was racing through her. 'She can hardly try it on with you whilst we're eating.'

When they arrived in the ballroom and took their seats,

the other guests on the table were already exuberant with alcohol and food, excited and loud, the types of people Maddy was normally grateful for to save her from pretending to be bubbly and happy, because they were the kind of people who wouldn't notice if she was preoccupied. But tonight, she wanted nothing but silence.

Pearl was probably somewhere near them right now, watching Maddy, with her messed-up face and messed-up life. Waiting for the right moment to pounce. The thought made Maddy feel like she might pass out right here in the midst of the food and performances. People would probably think she was part of it all: a clever interpretative dance move to represent some kind of symbolic death.

'I did not bring Blake here,' Gregory was saying quietly, so that Maddy read his lips rather than heard the words. 'I've never met her, for God's sake! And she's a child, Maddy. Do you really think…?' He stopped talking abruptly and glanced around him. It seemed like nobody was listening, but Maddy supposed he was right to stop: you never really knew.

Maddy ate her salmon and tried to work out where Sadie might be sitting. Her eyes wandered around the enormous room. It could have been any ballroom: it wasn't at all how it looked on the night of the Gatsby Ball, and yet the broken memories still lived on, playing like a film inside Maddy's mind. Jazz and sequins, golden champagne and a feeling of hurt and anger so forceful it felt like it might crush her.

She forced herself back to the present. Gregory had given up on talking to her, and had become absorbed in a conversation with some other guests. Maddy caught odd fragments of his sentences as she pushed food around with her fork.

'Well, when you're adapting for television—'

'Of course, those final chapters offer a completely—'

'Writing routine, and then you have—'

'New release, and then after the launch, it kind of becomes—'

Gregory was probably talking about writing because he was dying for someone to recognise him, to say, *Oh! Is it you? Is it?* Maddy had always been thrilled when people had treated him like a celebrity, but tonight it inflamed something in her. She sat back in her seat and toyed with her name card as the beneficiaries from White Feather gave their welcome speeches. A vague sense of horror ticked away inside her as they spoke of loss, their sadness spreading like liquid around the room. It was always the same at these events: an undercurrent of darkness threatening the sense of fun. She got it: how else were they meant to get people to donate all their money? Fear was the oldest trick, and the biggest moneymaker in the book. Fear of missing out, of looking old, of dying or not fitting in or not being a good person. Marketing was so easy when you knew the right buttons to press.

She glanced over to the expanse of thick black curtains at the edge of the room. Had they been closed on the night of the Gatsby Ball? Her memory rippled like water, but she could pull nothing from it.

'You haven't opened your table gift,' Gregory said to Maddy, interrupting her attempts to pull fragments of the past towards her. His voice was smothered by the music, cutlery and all the other voices.

Maddy eyed the gold box that Gregory was gesturing to.

'I got a cigar in mine,' he told her. 'George IV-branded. Nice.'

Maddy pulled the box towards her and tugged at it, peering inside, unable to process what she saw. She imagined herself taking it, running and running until she was at the sea, and throwing it in so that it sank to the bottom forever.

'What did you get? Are you going to want my cigar? Is your gift terrible?'

Maddy shook her head and swiped the box from the table. She looked at her watch. The ticking of the slim hands, around and around, dragging closer and closer towards nine o'clock, made her skin feel as though it was made of electric currents. She looked again at Gregory. Perhaps he'd been on Pearl's side this whole time, and maybe he knew what Maddy had done, and that was why he was pushing horrible gifts in front of her. Maybe it was Gregory nurturing her guilt and fright so that they grew and grew, twisting together so closely and tightly that they could strangle her. Maybe he had a whole legion of women and girls behind him, supporting them, them supporting him in return. Maybe Aiden was involved somehow too, and none of them liked her at all, let alone loved her.

Gregory stared back at her. 'Maddy? Are you all right?'

She couldn't tell who Gregory was anymore. Maybe she'd never been able to. He looked like Gregory; like someone who was handsome and would give her a life that suited her and drove people crazy with jealousy. But did she really know him? Had she really ever understood who he was underneath his expensive shirts, literary theory and a charisma that was as sticky and tempting as caramel?

She stood up, pushing her plate away.

TWENTY-THREE

Sadie

Back in the room, Sadie tried to call Rob again and again. It rang out and out. He would probably still be driving. He refused to speak in the car: said it was way too distracting, even on hands-free mode. The thought of that winding road home, trees bent over like witches either side, made Sadie feel ill. She could call a cab and go home. But what if Blake was here at the castle? What if Sadie was leaving her with Gregory and who knew who else?

She needed to stay.

She slipped out of her denim shorts, and then picked up the black dress. She stepped into it, pulling it up over her shoulders. It was definitely hers. And that made her feel like she needed to both stay and run.

The ballroom was dark, even though outside was still covered in bold yellow sunlight. The whole room glittered with what seemed like a thousand candles. The band had picked up tempo a little, and masked dancers twirled through ribbons. Some performers hung suspended from the ceiling, their limbs twisted around spools of black satin so that their bodies looked broken.

'Wine?' A waitress stood poised with a bottle as soon as Sadie stepped inside. There were people everywhere, their masks glinting in the gold candlelight as they moved. Some of the waitresses had chunky instant cameras around their necks, and were snapping photos as they circulated the room.

'No, thank you.'

Sadie looked out over the sea of people, doubled in the mirrored tables, and a wave of anxiety turned over inside her, threatening to spill over. Except for school assemblies and performances, she was never with this many people. She was so close to strangers tonight that she could smell them, taste their perfume, their drinks and their excitement. She scanned the room for anyone who could be Blake. She looked mature for her age, so she wouldn't stand out as a child. She was taller than some of the women in there. Her long blonde hair, so striking to Sadie in everyday life, was everywhere. More than half the people in the room had blonde hair the same as Blake's.

Two people were sitting diagonally across from where Sadie stood: the dark-haired woman in an eye-catching blue satin dress, and the man in an expensive grey tailored suit. A gigantic silver candelabra was in between Sadie and the woman. The man sat quietly as the woman chatted animatedly to people around them, the light shifting on her and playing tricks on Sadie as she tried to work out if she was looking at Maddy, or not. After a few minutes, the man laughed after trying to eat his food and not touch his huge mask. He ripped the mask off, took a mouthful of salmon and a few people cheered. He looked nothing like Gregory.

It wasn't them.

Sadie stared down at the photo again. The dark blue décor behind was easy to make out, but it could surely be any room at the castle. Perhaps Blake wasn't even in Gregory's room in the picture. Sadie had only seen Gregory once before tonight, and that had been at the Gatsby Ball: the night she constantly tried to erase from her memory. Gregory used to be a teacher at Kings Hill High, but he'd left before Sadie had started working there. She grimaced as she thought of him: the slightly pompous way that he stood, as though he owned the castle; his crudely expensive watch poking out from flawless shirt sleeve. If Blake was here, had Gregory paid for her ticket? Tickets, Sadie knew, were hundreds of pounds. There was no way that saved-up birthday and Christmas money, and the odd leftover bit of pocket money from Sadie and Rob, would have been enough for Blake to buy her own ticket. Maybe she had been gifted one, like Rob. The thought floated into her mind and then drifted away. That can't have been what happened. A child wouldn't be given a ticket to an adult's ball.

A female performer had moved over to the table area now and was twisting and twirling between the guests, so close that Sadie could smell her perfume: woody like incense. A violinist was also moving between the tables, her eyes closed as she played a drawn-out tune. Sadie recognised it as a slow version of a song that Blake listened to in her room sometimes. As she watched, Sadie's eyes met those of the violinist. She stopped playing abruptly and smiled at Sadie.

'You should take your seat,' the violinist told Sadie.

'Oh, I can't—' Sadie protested, but the woman took Sadie's hand, her bow tucked neatly beneath her slim arm.

'The speeches are starting. We hold the cause very close to our hearts.' She led Sadie to two empty seats and Sadie stared down at the name cards. Did the violinist only know to put Sadie there because they were the only spare seats?

Rob Summer

Sadie Summer

'Sit,' the violinist said, nodding towards the chair as people started applauding and the first beneficiary of White Feather made her way across the room, her mask a slash of glittering red across her face. Sadie sat down, aware of people watching her. The moment the speeches were over, she'd leave and call Rob again, see if he'd heard from Blake. Maybe he could come back. Maybe she could tell him why. None of this would ever, ever go away unless she stopped hiding like a child.

She imagined the words over the phone, a silence at the other end.

'Life,' the speaker began, 'can end so suddenly. One second can change everything, for so many people. My parents died in an accident when I was ten. I thought I might drown in grief.'

Sadie put her hands to her throat as the woman continued to talk about dark times, the feeling as though her life was over before it had even really started, and then the support from White Feather that was unconditional and unwavering. People sniffed, some reaching beneath their masks to wipe away tears. All good people, saddened by the woman's words, by the tragedy of losing the people who were meant to keep their children safe forever. What would Blake do if something happened to Sadie, if someone decided that Sadie needed to be punished?

Sadie had promised herself, when Blake was born, that she'd excel at motherhood. But it was all so much harder than it looked, like a complicated version of pass-the-parcel: all nicely wrapped to begin with until you ended up with layer upon layer to tear through with everyone watching and nobody knowing how or when it was all going to end.

'Hey, you don't have a table gift.' The man sitting next to Sadie spoke in the brief pause between speeches and clicked his fingers at a nearby waitress.

'Oh, I don't need one.' Sadie started to stand but the man shook his head and took hold of her arm tightly. His mask was white and plain, more horror film than classic masquerade.

'I'm honestly fine without a gift,' Sadie told him, her eyes surveying the discarded wrapping on the tables and pulling away so that the man released her. Designer candles for the women, cigars for the men. She could live without that. She could live without any keepsake of tonight.

'Here you go!' A waitress placed a little gold box onto the table. 'Sadie, is it?'

'Yes. How did you know my name?' Maybe she had read the name cards. Sadie scrambled to open the box, which seemed smaller than all the others that she could see on the table. Perhaps it was from Blake, a message that she was okay or one that confirmed this was all an immature joke. But inside the box, there was a miniature car.

A black SUV.

Dread filled Sadie's body. She hadn't been going mad. Someone here knew what she'd done. Someone knew the red car had been a dead end, a mistake. Someone knew that, and they had Blake. The terror of the last ten years roared up inside her, blocking off all her senses.

The man in the white mask suddenly stood up and hovered above Sadie like a phantom.

'Ah. Strange. Most of the women have candles.' He smiled at Sadie, his teeth shining in the candlelight and grainy images flashed through her mind. A broken smile. A jagged hairline. Puckered, bloodied skin punctured with stitches.

TWENTY-FOUR

Pearl

I glanced at Blake as we moved down the corridor, wondering if she'd find it strange that I was leading her away from the main part of the castle, to an area that wasn't as elaborately decorated as the other parts. But Blake looked quite at ease, because she was probably used to people wanting to take photos of her and single her out.

'I used to be just like you, you know,' I told her. Such a lie. But I could have been like her, if things had been different. I thought of the times I'd seen Blake's dad from afar, in his dark green paramedic uniform, his features like blurred versions of Blake's. He rode a black mountain bike sometimes, emerging from junctions carefully, looking both ways and then both ways again. I'd seen him with Blake in a supermarket a few days ago, chatting easily, their steps in sync. How easy it was to tell from the way someone walked with their daughter, basket of bread and fruit swinging merrily at his side, that he loved her with his whole being, that he would hurl himself into fire or flood for her. I'd stopped and turned around, my hideous face suddenly hot as the question of whether my dad had actually ever felt like that about me, burned inside me.

Now, Blake glanced to the side as we turned a sharp corner. The stale air swam with thick heat.

'You were like me? How?' Was there now uncertainty in Blake's expression as her eyes flickered towards me?

'Yeah. I think so.' We were going down the stairs now. The staircase weaved around and around, corner after corner. 'Pretty, popular. Everything ahead of me. But then everything just changed. Overnight.'

'What happened?' Blake was weirdly straightforward. No games or manipulations, just basic truths that reflected her simple little life. She'd even told me that she was only fifteen. Some other girls had obviously lied to be here, telling me at the interviews that they were sixteen, desperate for some cash to spend on whatever junk TikTok had told them to buy. But not Blake.

'Oh, I was in an accident. Well, an alleged accident.' We continued down, and down.

'Are you sure this leads somewhere?'

'I'm sure.' I felt the tightness of annoyance in my chest. Blake had changed the subject from what had happened to me and obviously didn't care why I looked the way I did. It had absolutely nothing to do with Blake's life, as far as she was concerned.

We finally reached the exit and I pushed open the fire door in front of us. Castle guests were not meant to go on the bay. A thrill rushed through me as I thought of Blanche's obsession with the owners of the castle, her syrupy voice when she spoke to them. *Of course, oh, of course.*

The exit led straight out to a concrete walkway and low wall. Beyond the wall was a pebbled bay, and beyond that, the sea.

'It's gorgeous out here,' Blake said.

I took a deep breath and tried to think of something else other than pain and scarred skin. I followed Blake's gaze out to sea and focused on the beauty of the evening: the soft lines of pastel glowing in the brilliant light. It helped and the flares of anger subsided a little. From above, in the bedrooms of the castle, the waves looked dangerous and thrashing. But here, they seemed calmer, unlikely to ever sweep anything under their current. The water lapped gently on the stones ahead, the golden-blue light of the evening rippling across the waves. I took my camera from where it hung on my shoulder. 'Why don't you pose in there?' I nodded towards a boat that lay on the shore. It was a small, white boat, prop-like: something from a film.

'Cool. I love that we're the only ones here.' Blake flashed a brilliant, symmetrical smile that made my stomach dip with envy.

'I'll just get a few shots and then you can get out of the boat again, and we'll do some more pictures on the beach. These will be gorgeous. We'll need to push you out a bit though. The water's super shallow here. The tide never even comes in beyond a certain point.'

Blake nodded and clambered into the boat, all golden limbs and hair. I pushed it with all my strength and it finally bobbed down the gentle slope into the water. 'Okay.

Let's go. Try a few different poses. Look straight at me.' I found myself babbling like Trafford had done when he'd first taken photos of me a year ago. He hadn't even told me about Samantha. I'd had no idea that he was engaged.

Beautiful. You're perfect. I love this.

Liar.

As I took the photographs, the sun slid further towards the waves.

'I'm going to go up to the cliffs really quickly and take some more,' I told Blake. 'Distance shots, from above. They'll be incredible for the promo. They might even sell as prints! Imagine that. Blake the supermodel!'

Uncertainty passed over Blake's perfect face. 'How do you even get up there? It seems quite far up. Won't you be ages? It took us long enough to get down here. And I've never rowed or anything before.'

'Honestly, you'll be able to see me in, like, five minutes. I know a quick way up to the cliff.' It was so simple that even I could remember it from a few weeks ago when my mother had forced me to come and see the venue in all its refurbished glory. Up, through the ballroom and behind the swathes of velvet curtains, there was a huge flat stone balcony, and, beyond the ornate railings, rough grassy clifftops.

'Don't you want any of the other waitresses out here too?' she asked.

So, Blake was only actually a risk-taker as part of a pack. Typical. I wanted to roll my eyes, tell Blake how pathetic she was being. I'd had to live alone, without a pack, for so long now. Didn't make pretty little friends everywhere I went. Even before everything went so hideously wrong, girls were too jealous to be around me. Could Blake not last mere moments without adoring company? The annoyance tightened around me again.

'Just keep looking up and I'll be there before you know it. You have the oars, and if the boat starts coasting, just paddle back to the shore.' I motioned how to use the oars. I'd been out with my father a couple of times until my mother had, obviously, put a stop to it. 'Okay? Supermodel Blake?' I had already backed away from the boat, onto the stony ground, and pulled the fire door open. I heard Blake shout something as the door banged behind me. I hesitated, and then took a key from my pocket and locked the door. Nobody else could get out that way, and Blake would be kept safe until I got back to her.

'I'm following the rules for once,' I said out loud, to nobody. 'This door is meant to be locked.' My voice was strange and horribly loud, and I picked up my pace as if I could escape it.

TWENTY-FIVE

Sadie

'I wonder why you got a little car?' The man in the white mask was still talking to Sadie, trapping her in the ballroom, when she felt someone tap her on the shoulder. She whipped around, her whole body shaking.

It was Maddy. At least Sadie thought it was. But there was a frightening uncertainty about absolutely everything here.

'I've been looking for you everywhere.' Yes, it definitely was Maddy. Loud voice, the smell of garlic, salmon and wine on her breath.

The room burst into applause again as the next speaker appeared. The man in the white mask sat down again.

'Pearl's here,' Maddy said.

Sadie felt the world around them drop away, like a set on a stage, as though it had never been real. The man tugged on Sadie's arm, trying to get her to sit down, and she yanked herself away from him.

'I need to find Blake.' She moved away from the table,

feeling Maddy beside her, eyes on her. People tutted as she pushed past chairs and the speaker's words about death, trauma and recovery rang in her ears. She would hear the words again and again, forever and ever, ticking clocks that would not be silenced.

Sadie deserved all of this. She'd known it was coming. She'd hidden from Pearl and what she might do for too long. She'd hidden from all of it, even though she'd known, deep down, the truth. Rob's colleagues had told him about the accident on the road leading away from Falcon Castle the day after the Gatsby Ball. He'd come home from work that evening with a pained expression.

'Bad shift?' Sadie had asked him, pouring omelette mixture into a pan. She'd trembled slightly as she'd done it, hadn't stopped trembling since the night before. She'd been sick another three times since Rob had left that morning.

She'd thought of her drink, the lime and soda that Maddy had ordered for her, and its bitter taste.

She'd thought of Maddy knocking back wine and who knew what else. Maddy in the car. The roar of the ignition.

The words, the story with its gaps and horror and the sense that it had happened to someone else, had all stuck in Sadie's throat.

Rob had grimaced. 'My shift wasn't bad. But Cookson was telling me about yesterday and what happened. Have you heard about it?' He'd glanced at Blake, who was sitting at the kitchen table painting. 'Or did you see anything?'

'No, I don't think so. Tea?' She stirred the gloopy egg and then rested the spoon on the pan and turned away as her stomach churned. Rob had cooked eggs that morning too, and the smell and sight of them mingled with the guilt of her silence.

Rob had sighed. 'An accident on the road back from Falcon Castle. Hit and run.'

Sadie took out a mug from the cupboard and her life as she knew it turned to dust. 'Did they get there in time?'

'The victim was a teenage girl who'd been at the ball. She gave a rough description of the car.' Rob had blown on the tea that Sadie had made him, and then he'd put it down on the table, taken Blake from where she sat on her chair and put her on his knee. She'd laughed and wriggled, grinning at Sadie. And that was it: the moment where Sadie was about to turn down the road of honesty. But it hadn't looked like an innocent road should have looked: it was gnarled and full of shadows and terror and loss. She'd opened her mouth to speak, to let the words, the bitter regret and apologies fall out.

But then, a reprieve: 'The car was red. A sports car. They're going to be asking for information on it any minute now. Hopefully someone will have seen something.' Rob had fluffed Blake's shiny golden hair and given Sadie a smile that said, *we're safe*, and Sadie had closed her mouth and smiled back. A part of her was forever changed in that moment. She'd never kept anything from Rob before. But she'd realised there and then, that if she told him the truth, she might lose him. She might lose Blake. It was that simple. Barely even a choice. Only hours after that, Maddy had messaged Sadie about the deer, about how she'd returned to the scene and hauled it to the side of the road.

'I got one of those too,' Maddy hissed in Sadie's ear now,

bringing her back to the present, so close that the warmth of her breath touched Sadie's skin. She was nodding towards the box that Sadie still held on to tightly. 'It has to be from her. Some disgusting little joke to try and frighten us.'

Sadie had known it all this time. Of course she had. The horror of this was that somebody else knew too.

'The car was never red. You always knew it. And Pearl knows as well.' The words, now that they were outside the ballroom, were louder than she'd meant them to be, floating away like balloons lost forever into the vast sky.

TWENTY-SIX

Pearl

My head was down as I made my way through the maze of corridors. I was absorbed in the instant photos I'd just taken of Blake in the boat. They really were beautiful. Blake looked like a better version of Sadie, as though someone had rubbed Sadie out and tried again, tried harder.

The first time I'd ever seen Sadie, it had been by accident. I'd been sitting in the back of a little bar that sold coffee and wine, working on my applications to model agencies. My whole life was about to unravel before me, like a red carpet. I hadn't known Maddy would appear with Sadie that afternoon. I'd seen Maddy's car nearby, but that hadn't really made me go and sit in the bar. I could have chosen any bar, couldn't I? And I'd happened to walk into one that they entered only a few minutes later. I'd felt hot when they'd first turned up, flushed with good fortune. As I'd studied Maddy and her friend, I could see that the friend wasn't perfect like Maddy, but that there was an easy attractiveness to her beachy blonde hair and clear skin. She gave her little girl a lollipop and the girl – Blake! – sucked on it. Sadie stroked her hair a few times as she listened to Maddy and sipped a glass of white wine. Maybe I'd known that what I had with Gregory wasn't going to last, and I was lonely. Or maybe I was just preoccupied with everything related to Gregory – Maddy, and by extension Sadie.

And that's where it really began.

Memories of that time – of all times – were jagged as broken glass, but I did remember the first time I'd been inside Sadie's house, how the key I'd had cut fitted so beautifully into the slot; the meet-ups that Maddy and Sadie had each week that were like clockwork.

Now, deep in the maze of Falcon Castle corridors, I stopped walking and looked up. I'd not really kept track of where I was walking or where I was planning to go. I shook my head. I kept finding myself doing that, as though my more recent memories just needed a gentle jig and then would all fit nicely into place again.

It was happening more and more lately. Some memories seemed to be locked in place, never forgotten. But others slipped around and fell from view as though my mind were made of ice. Faces and places collided with one another, blurring together. The memory loss often came with anger, clouds with a storm. Tonight, with its secrets and masks, had made it all even worse.

I started walking again, but I still couldn't remember where I was going.

Something was in my mind: something big, waiting for me to act it out.

But what was it?

It was moments like these when I wondered if I should have carried on seeing the therapist guy. The one with the trousers and the breathing. I'd managed to muddle my way through so far since the accident. Nobody cared about me enough to notice I forgot things sometimes. But nights like tonight, when the memories were especially elusive, floating away like ghosts, frightened me.

I was becoming like a helpless old person, grey and weak, a shadow of who she once was.

I hated what they had turned me into.

I stopped, the corridor walls crowding in on me. I wanted to push them from me, move away the world until I knew my place in it. I looked down at the photograph again. There was someone who needed to see this. Wherever else I had been going could surely wait. I glanced at the room number I had scrawled on the inside of my wrist, the ink swirling delicately over my skin and veins.

Then I took a breath, and carried on walking.

TWENTY-SEVEN

Sadie
___

Sadie took a step away from Maddy. 'You lied. And I was stupid enough to go along with it. We ruined her life, Maddy.'

Maddy was trembling. 'It was an accident. A horrible, terrible accident. It was her fault. We didn't do anything wrong on purpose. We can't even be sure it was us.'

'Of course it was! And we did do something wrong. We got in Gregory's car when we were barely able to walk! We shouldn't have gone anywhere *near* a car!' Sadie lowered her voice so that it was barely audible. 'You put something in my drink, didn't you? You denied it afterwards, when I saw you. But I know that you did.'

'No. No, I didn't.' Tears were streaming down Maddy's chin, from underneath her mask. 'The trauma will have made you block it out. I don't remember much either.'

'And the photographs that were posted to me months after it happened,' Sadie said, something clicking into place to make a gruesome jigsaw. 'You said before about us both getting them. Those disgusting close-ups.' Sadie closed her eyes but it was as though the images were burned onto the inside of her eyelids. Her eyes sprang open again. 'I never told you I got them. So how did you know?'

Maddy stared at her blankly, lips parted, eyes wide. 'What?'

'How did you know we both got them?'

'I just presumed.' Maddy shrugged, her eyes staring straight back at Sadie through the black glittering mask. 'Because why would it just have been me?'

Sadie's heart banged and banged, a prisoner wanting release. 'I'm going up to my room, and I'm calling the police. They can deal with this.' The police, and then Rob.

Maddy pulled roughly on Sadie's arm. 'No way!' Her words were furious, spat out. She wasn't crying anymore. 'You will absolutely not do that.'

Sadie pulled away and began running. There was too much to lose to listen to another word that Maddy said. The end of things, her life ripped into a thousand pieces: she'd take it all if Blake was safe. She ran and ran and reached her room, throwing herself inside and locking the door behind her. She couldn't have anybody near her. She couldn't trust one single person.

Maddy banged on the door.

'Sadie! Open the door! You have to let me in!'

Sadie sat on the bed, her fingers trembling as she unlocked her phone.

'Please, please don't do this. What will you even say?'

Sadie closed her eyes, Maddy's knocking banging against her brain. It was when she opened her eyes again that she noticed it on the bedside table. Another instant photograph. She picked it up. The picture was of Blake again. Sadie squinted down at it, trying to slow her breaths. Blake was in a little white rowing boat, wearing a Masquerade blouse like she'd seen the waitresses in, the logo blurred on her chest. Her arms were outstretched, holding onto the oars. The smooth silver waves rolled on behind her, glittering with the setting sun.

Maddy banged and banged against the door, louder and louder.

'Come on, Sadie. Open the door and let's find Blake. I'll help you.'

TWENTY-EIGHT

Maddy

Maddy banged and banged against the door until it felt as though her knuckles might bleed. The night was becoming more like a fractured nightmare, the kind that might wake Maddy from sleep in those frightening early hours of the morning. Priorities collided in her mind, jamming up against one another. Finally, the door opened and Sadie came out. A chill ran through Maddy even though the corridor was filled with stale heat.

'Did you do it? Did you call the police?' Maddy whispered, glancing around her.

But Sadie ignored her, and had already started running away, down the corridor. She'd taken off her shoes and they dangled like dead things from her fingers as she moved further and further away from Maddy.

Maddy hesitated and thought of the note that had arrived with the pretty little box of muffins yesterday.

> *Have a great time at the ball. Meet you on the cliffs?*
> *9pm. Ax*

Yesterday seemed like a lifetime ago now. When she'd opened the muffins, Maddy had thought there was at least a chance they were from Aiden. She'd let herself imagine that he might be there tonight, having escaped from Candice and – a small bubble of guilt burst inside Maddy – Eliot, to talk to Maddy about picking the wrong sister, about knowing what she'd done and keeping quiet, letting his own little red sports car be the alibi that they all needed, because he knew Maddy wasn't a bad person really, and knew she'd been driven to it. She'd let herself ignore the dark look of anger she'd seen on his face in the garden when he'd brought it up the night before.

But as soon as Gregory had told her Pearl was at the ball tonight, the truth had clicked into focus. The flowers, the muffins, the note, had all been tricks. Aiden was at home with the wife he'd chosen years ago, thinking terrible things about Maddy, being furious and let down and wanting her to put it right.

I know you.

Pearl thought Maddy was stupid, that she'd fall for all this like a pathetic teenager with a crush. And the worst thing was: Maddy almost had.

Sadie was in the distance now, at the very end of the corridor. Maddy moved away from her, back towards reception. The dipping sun cast a golden glow over everything as Maddy made her way all around the castle to the back, near the cliff tops. She climbed over the low railings and picked her way over the uneven ground that climbed up to a grassy peak. Salt stung her eyes and her lungs burned in her chest. She pushed herself on and on, heat and anger smothering her, making breathing harder and harder as she moved further up the cliff.

TWENTY-NINE

Pearl

I ended up in the ballroom. I could still smell Sadie's perfume that I had sprayed on myself when I'd been in her room a few moments before: musky and adult, not the fresh scent I would have expected. My mind ached with trying to remember where I was meant to be. Tonight was the worst my memory had ever been. I had totally overestimated myself. I should have brought someone with me. Panic darted inside me: a cat trapped in a box. I knew I was meant to be somewhere other than the ballroom, but after Sadie's room, this seemed the natural place to be. I wished now that I'd made sure that Sadie and Maddy had been given the kinds of mask that would make them stand out. Red or purple: anything but black. Seeing them might have kick-started my memory. As it was, I couldn't recognise anyone at all. Waitresses glided between tables, all blonde ponytails and white smiles as they poured liquid-gold champagne and chatted to all the guests like little experts. My mother's precious training session that I had missed the night before had obviously worked wonders. I'd acted as though I hadn't needed it, but actually, I saw as I stood surrounded by them all, there was a knack to it all that I just didn't have.

Someone clicked their fingers at me.

'More champagne over here.'

I turned away and pretended I hadn't heard. I was staring at the black velvet curtains ahead of me. A memory untangled itself. I moved towards them, gently pushing past bodies and noise until I was slipping between the velvet. The glass door was unlocked. It shouldn't have been. I thought of the sharp cliff edges, the drop to death beyond the railings. I should find Blanche, tell her. But if I did that, the memory of where I was going would desert me again.

I slipped outside, the humid air strangling me as I climbed over the metal railings and caught the skin of my wrist on a sharp piece of metal. I sucked at the cut as I moved over the uneven grass. The taste of blood on my tongue, metal and salt, tossed me back into the past, making me feel as though the world might just drop from underneath me all over again.

THIRTY

Sadie

Sadie ran and ran, trying to wrench more memories from her mind about the layout of Falcon Castle. But last time, she'd been nowhere near the water, that she could remember. The reception area and ballroom jutted out high above the sea. If Blake was in a boat, then there must be a way to get from here to the shore. Maybe Sadie should have gone through with calling the police. When she'd seen the photograph of Blake in the boat, she'd decided to try and find Blake herself first. Police took a long time to arrive sometimes: she knew that from Rob, and she hadn't felt like there was a second to waste. She pictured the vast expanse of sea, Blake alone in the centre of it. She'd never even been in a boat before. It wouldn't take much to toss her over, for the little boat to sail so far out it was never seen again, or for it to be tipped upside down. She pictured Blake going under, eyes squeezed shut, mouth clamped against thick, salty water. Then the image of Blake was erased as the past washed over Sadie again.

She slowed as she almost slapped into a sudden wall, a sharp corner that took her shallow breath away.

We hit a deer.

I went back in Gregory's car and dragged it to the side of the road.

Don't feel bad. It was just an accident.

A thud. 'Clair de Lune', becoming louder and darker and then quiet and twinkling. The unthinkably beautiful flow of piano keys that had always, always made Sadie's chest swell with joy and now would make her think of the rotten core inside her. Darkness and a blanket of rain so heavy that it was blinding.

Sadie rested against the wall for a moment, engulfed in her memories.

'Are you lost?'

Her eyes flew open. A woman stood next to her. She was wearing an immaculate white dress and a silver mask.

'There's nothing for guests down there,' the woman continued. 'Please, follow me back to the main ballroom. There are still prizes being given out.'

'I can't. I have to find my daughter. She's working here.'

'Ah! Well then, I can help you with that.' The woman leaned forwards and Sadie could smell meat on her breath. 'I'm running the event. Your daughter's name is?'

Sadie hesitated. Saying Blake's name felt dangerous. Everything felt dangerous. 'Blake Summer.'

'Okay. Let me find Pearl and she'll get your daughter for you.'

The name froze Sadie and she stopped walking.

'Pearl is the head waitress. She's also my daughter,' the

woman explained airily, gesturing for Sadie to continue following her, oblivious. 'She's actually disappeared too. Perhaps they've made friends.' She turned and flashed a smile at Sadie. Was Sadie imagining it, or did Pearl's mother look worried about something? 'My Pearl does become fascinated with people. She's probably taken your daughter under her wing.'

Sadie stared, unable to form a sentence, but the woman didn't seem to notice. 'Let's head to the kitchen. I'm Blanche Goldman. My events company is running the ball. What do you think of it so far?'

'It's great,' Sadie managed. But other words fought to get out. I'm sorry. I didn't mean to leave her. I didn't want her to be hurt. I should have told the truth. I will do anything. Please, please don't let her hurt my daughter. 'Pearl... She—' Sadie began, but couldn't finish. Her mind tried to process what this woman had been through ten years ago. A daughter with a face and body ripped apart to be sewn back together again. Had Blanche even known that Pearl would survive, or had there been a point when she'd had to consider life without her daughter?

Blanche glanced sideways at Sadie as she pushed open the doors to the kitchen, eyes narrowed. But then they were in amongst the steam, the noise smacking them in the face.

'Where's Pearl?' Blanche asked a willowy blonde waitress. The waitresses all looked like Pearl; all looked like Blake. It would make it almost impossible to find them both. The realisation flooded through Sadie like a dragging pain. Someone had done this on purpose.

The identical waitress looked around her and shrugged. 'I haven't seen her much.'

Blanche sighed and frowned at Sadie as the waitress rushed off into the bustle of the kitchen. She put her slim fingers up to her forehead. 'I really could do with knowing where she is. She needs to be where I can keep an eye on her. I worry about her. She's a bit … vulnerable, I suppose.'

Sadie felt guilt engulf her. Of course Pearl was vulnerable. And that meant Blake was vulnerable too if she was with her, didn't it?

Show her the photo. Tell her you're worried.

But then what? Why, Blanche would want to know, of all the waitresses, would Pearl have singled out Blake? What could she possibly want with her? And why was Sadie so consumed with fear?

Sadie took a breath and gripped the glossy photo she was still carrying. The kitchen staff rushed and clattered around them as she held out the photograph for Blanche to see.

THIRTY-ONE

Pearl

I glanced down beside me at the drop to the sea. It wasn't horribly high, not as high as my room. Even so, if someone was to fall and crack against the stones… The thought was unpleasant and I pushed it away as I saw that Maddy was waiting, just as I hoped she'd be. She looked vulnerable in the stretch of rough land, arms wrapped around herself as though it was cold, even though the air was as close and hot as it had been all week.

Maddy pulled her mask off as I reached her, and squinted in the pale orange light of the sunset. She stared and stared at me until something in her seemed to break. She looked around in the distance, but there was no Aiden, no knight in shining armour. But then she laughed, her mouth wide and clown-like.

'I'm not as stupid as you think. I knew he wouldn't be here. I knew it was you. You were listening to us in Candice's garden last night, weren't you? You sent the flowers. You sent the muffins, and the note.' Maddy took an angry step towards me. Predictable. I was drawing her in, just like I wanted. Maddy was easy as a puppet to control.

I thought of last night, my ear pressed to the fence of Candice's sprawling house. Trapped outside of a life I wanted with a flawless little family who made the most of the sunshine. Simple noises of clinking ice, of food and conversation that were so far from the hostile silence of the flat.

'I'm always listening. I know so much about you, Maddy. I know what you keep in all your drawers, and what you look like when you're asleep. I know all about Eliot. I know you drink too much and then drive Eliot about. Do you even care about him?' He'd be better off with me as a stepmother. I wouldn't be the wicked kind. I'd be kind to him. We were the same, after all. Outcasts. Awkward, sad people who'd grasped out for a good life and grabbed something ugly from the lucky dip instead.

'Don't talk about him.' Maddy's voice trembled as she took another step, the words stretched all out of shape by fear. Interesting. I hadn't thought that Maddy cared about Eliot, but it was the mention of him that made a glimpse of terror pass across her perfect face. Beautiful Maddy, just like the kitten my dad had bought me, who everyone fawned over, who could cut deep with beautiful claws and the power of natural, flawless perfection. And she was finally vulnerable. I'd won. Finally, I had got something I wanted. But it didn't feel as good as I'd thought it would. I still felt empty, as though someone had hollowed out my insides like a pumpkin.

I backed further from Maddy, nearer to the cliff,

watching Maddy take another step too. A horrible fall, I would tell people. She was drunk, as always. It was a tragic accident and I wish I hadn't seen it. I wish I'd been able to do more, but I just didn't get there in time.

We were so close to the edge now that I felt as though she was standing on nothing, hovering over the steel-grey waves like a bird. I heard a splash below, and something clicked in my mind, the shard of a broken memory, edging closer to consciousness – and then gone again.

'How did you know I'd been at Candice's? How do you even know where she lives?' Maddy asked again. She seemed to regain some control and took a step away from me so that I followed her lead, stepping away from the edge again.

'Because you put every single thing online for everyone to see! Because you're always, always showing off your perfect life! You said on Instagram that you were going to be at Candice's. Wonderful Candice, your lovely sister. Not that you appreciate her.'

What was it about so many people hating their siblings? Someone made of the same cells and the same memories surely made life more, not less, bearable? I had always, always wanted a sister.

'Pearl, what do you want from us all? Why were you there last night?'

Oh, I'd wanted so many things: to see them all up close; to make them feel unsure of themselves and their lives like I had done for ten years. To maybe even slip inside the house or the garden while they were all distracted and get Gregory for myself, to finally have what Maddy had even if it was just for one night. To make him see that he needed me.

'To be acknowledged by someone would have been a start. I rang the doorbell, you know. But I waited for over five minutes and nobody came.' The evening air had become a darker tone of blue in the minutes that I had stood and waited at Candice's door. I had seen movements and bright lights from behind the glass of the double doors if I squinted hard, which had made me feel more like an outsider than ever. Gregory would lose his mind over the symbolism of that. 'So I went round to the back.'

And then there had been a wonderful breakthrough: Maddy's voice, a little thick with alcohol, from the garden beside me. I had moved towards the high fence, my tread silent on the artificial grass that surrounded the house like a moat. I realised that I could *see* inside the garden if I stood at a particular angle at the corner of the fence. I'd had to squint, and let my gaze fall through the trees, and then there had been Maddy, in the white playsuit that I would never be able to choose and wear with such confidence. As I had continued to stare, I'd seen that Maddy was with Aiden. They'd been standing close together, as though they were the ones married to each other. Watching them had been like being in the audience at one of those arty plays Trafford used to rave about. I'd stayed silent and rapt as Maddy and Aiden talked about blueberry muffins, as I saw Maddy reach over and give Aiden what she obviously thought was acceptable as some kind of sisterly and platonic peck on the cheek. Safe in their bubble of lies.

'I know you sent the presents. But watching us and

seeing a few posts on Instagram doesn't give you any kind of power over any of us. You're nothing,' Maddy said now. But she wasn't even looking at me: she was staring out over the uneven mounds of scorched grass to the water. Something jerked in my memory again, trying to wrench itself free.

The water. A boat.

The therapist guy had always told me to write things down, to carry a little notebook with me, and I had done at first, then I'd stopped, because the little lilac notebook signalled everything that had gone wrong. I'd hated looking at it. I wrote some things on my skin, sometimes. Sadie's room number was still blurred on the inside of my wrist now. But perhaps – it came to me now, his name suddenly appearing in my mind – Henri had been right, and I should write more things, everything, down to stop memories sliding down the grimy plughole in my brain.

I looked down to the water, my stomach lurching as I took a final step towards it. One more step and I'd be too close. The edge of the cliff was no more than half a metre away from where I leaned over to try to see the shore, and there were signs dotted around warning of hazardous edges, the deadly words at odds with comical little stick men who were stuck in eternal falls. The rocks below were black, slick with salty water and glimmering in the sinking sun.

And then I remembered Blake, in the boat, alone, just as I heard the scream.

THIRTY-TWO

Sadie

Blanche stared down at the photograph. The kitchen continued to whir around them. Music played quietly beneath the noise. It was some awful pop song that Blake would probably know the TikTok dance to. Sadie's heart squeezed.

Blanche's eyes flickered from the photograph to the kitchen staff. 'So that's where she is. This has Pearl written all over it. She does these odd little things sometimes.' She took a subtle step away from Sadie that said *don't cause a scene*.

'I'll go and get them. How do I get to the water?'

'Back to where I found you, and you'll see that there is a door that says Staff Only. Through that, down the stairs and out that way to the water. Get them both back inside, to the ball, and tell Pearl to come to me. I need to go back into the ballroom for the prizes.' Blanche looked torn for a moment, as though she might follow Sadie and leave the ball behind her. But then she bit her lip, and gestured for Sadie to go alone. 'Hurry.'

A feeling of dread followed Sadie as she followed Blanche's directions. These corridors were nothing like those in the rest of the castle. The lights were dim and the carpet smelled like wet animals. The staircase was dim and twisted again and again so that Sadie felt dizzy. Eventually, she reached the bottom. There was a door with a window in it, and the blurred glimmer of what had to be the sea beyond. Sadie rushed towards it and pushed against the door.

It was locked.

She banged on the door. 'Blake! Pearl!'

Silence.

She tried to twist the handle, she pushed and pulled but nothing would give so she turned around and flew back down the corridor and up the stairs again, thousands of them, breathless, the notes of 'Clair de Lune' twinkling in her mind like stars.

At reception, Sadie could hear applause and shouts of joy from the ballroom, the thrum of happiness and drunken fun.

'Sadie, is it?'

She spun around. A man was standing there. He pulled his mask down a little, although Sadie knew who it was anyway. Gregory. He took her hand and shook it. It moved limply in his, a dead person's handshake.

'I think I did quite well to spot you,' Gregory said cheerfully. 'I like the idea of a masquerade ball, in theory. But in fact, it's quite frustrating. Don't you think? You don't know where you stand, or who you're talking to half the time.'

'Where's Blake?'

Gregory was quiet for a moment and Sadie wanted to shake him. There wasn't *time* for handshakes and quiet moments and niceties about the merits and flaws of masquerade balls. 'I was going to ask you if you know where Maddy is. I don't know anything about Blake. Sadie, you must absolutely understand that anything you think you know about me and your daughter … I can't even say the words!' He shook his head. 'It's not true. I don't know how many times I need to say that. Is she…?' He stopped talking as they both heard a faraway scream. Sadie's eyes darted from him to beyond reception, the craggy cliffs and the dramatic orange sky.

If Blake was in the water, they'd be able to see her from above.

Sadie glanced at the receptionist, who was talking on the phone about an invoice for flowers. A burst of applause from inside the ballroom punctuated the end of the receptionist's sentence. Sadie tried to catch her eye, but the receptionist was fixed on her screen.

'I need to find her. She was in the sea before, in a boat—'

'In the *sea*? Are you sure?'

'Yes. I'm sure.' Sadie rushed towards the huge, glass

front doors and pushed them open. The stale heat of the evening prickled against her skin.

Gregory followed and they ran together, along the glass front of the hotel, lit by silvery lights in the ground, all the way around the side to the clifftops at the back. The grassy land stretched on, uneven and rocky.

Two figures were in the distance where the land fell away and met the sky.

'That's Maddy!' Gregory moved faster, overtaking Sadie. She scoured the cliff edge. He was right. One figure, tiny against the broad sky lit with orange and gold, was definitely Maddy, and the other – Sadie felt herself stop breathing and had to remind herself to carry on – was either Blake … or it was Pearl.

THIRTY-THREE

Maddy

The scream seemed to have come from below. Even with the waves and the gulls cutting through it, the noise was piercing. Pearl moved closer to the edge of the cliff and Maddy followed her, looking beneath them. A white boat was just about visible, bobbing empty in the endless blue waves. And then there was Blake, swimming forwards and rising from the water where the waves were shallow.

'What are you doing, Blake?' Pearl's voice was shaking ever so slightly as she shouted to Blake below. 'Why did you scream like that?'

'It was just a joke! You left me for ages!' Blake yelled back. She was so far down that it was difficult to hear her properly. Maddy could just about see that she was wearing a Masquerade waitress outfit that was just like Pearl's.

Cold shock washed over Maddy. 'Oh my God, Pearl! You left her out there? She's fifteen years old! And you sent her out alone on a boat in the sea, when nobody at all was around! Were you trying to hurt her?' It was as though the guilt had brought to life the version of Pearl from Maddy's nightmares, trying to cause all the harm she'd been afraid of. She took a breath. 'If you have a problem with someone, then it should not be with her.'

They glanced back down to the edge of the water, where Blake grinned up at them, in the water up to her knees, her uniform sodden and her golden hair plastered to her beautiful head.

'Find a spare uniform,' Pearl yelled down. Blake stared up, not hearing. 'A uniform! One that isn't wet! My mother will kill us otherwise!'

Pearl's mother? Maddy looked across at Pearl.

'My mother has managed the ball tonight. Her company always runs White Feather events. Her first one was…' She smiled hauntingly. 'Well, you know.'

Maddy thought of the Gatsby Ball, of Pearl appearing and making fury bubble up inside Maddy. 'I didn't know, actually.'

Pearl frowned. 'Goldman Events took over these charity balls ten years ago. My mother ran the whole Gatsby Ball. Why else would I have been there that night?' The words were lost in the air, drowned by waves and screeching gulls.

'I thought you'd gone with Gregory.'

Pearl laughed. 'Actually, no. My mother dragged me there. Gregory was a bonus.'

Maddy thought of her life with Gregory since Pearl had entered their lives: a little montage in her mind. Gregory coming home without his favourite green tie and his top button open to reveal his milky coffee skin underneath, and telling Maddy that he'd left the tie in his office, that he'd taken it off because he'd been uncomfortable.

The tie was the one that had been posted to their house a few days later, along with the sparkly ink note that Maddy had torn up into little pieces, wishing she could do the same to whoever had sent it. And then there had been that day when she'd seen Gregory and Pearl leave his office together, holding hands. Then the Gatsby Ball, and Pearl in her tight little dress. And then the accident. Then secrets and lies piling on top of each other.

'If you hadn't been there, it would have been so much better.' If Pearl hadn't been at the ball, if she hadn't ever been in Maddy's life. Fury was rising steadily in Maddy. Everything that had gone wrong, everything that had followed her around for the last ten years, all the guilt and the doubt, was all because of Pearl. She had let Maddy's life loose, untethered it so that it had floated into oblivion.

'Oh, you don't think I know that? Look at me! Look at what you and Sadie did!' Maddy grimaced and looked away as Pearl tore off her mask. The scars had changed since Maddy had seen them in the photographs that had been posted through her door years ago. But they were the same ones. Pearl's skin was gathered along the whole left side of her face, as though someone had taken her head apart and not quite known how to put it back together. 'You ruined everything for me that night. I've been through hell. I'm still there, stuck in hell forever,' Pearl said, and it felt like Maddy's body was turning to liquid.

Fragmented memories of the Gatsby Ball surfaced now, as they sometimes did, like some dreadful sea monster rising from a slumber. Maddy losing Sadie and Gregory in the crowd; wading through people who were all having fun; the first rumblings of thunder in the sky, like a warning from the universe; an anger so overpowering that Maddy thought it might engulf her, burning through her skin and bones until she was nothing but ash; Sadie's screams as the car hit something in the blackness; a scream from outside the car.

The storm had passed by the morning after the ball and the sun was bright again, the world nice and clean. Maddy had pulled on her gym clothes and run down to the car. Rain from the storm twinkled on the paintwork in the morning light, and a dent in the bonnet had made Maddy's stomach twist.

She'd told Gregory that she had hit a deer. And then she'd messaged Sadie too, saying the same thing. She even added to Sadie that she'd gone back and seen the deer, and moved it to the side of the road. She hadn't even expected Sadie to believe her. Maddy, driving all the way back to the road near the castle when she was in that state, hauling a huge beast of an animal to the side of the road, getting covered in its meaty blood, all on her own? But Sadie had seemed to drink it all in at first. It had seemed that easy. And it had made Maddy feel safe: if Sadie was ever asked about it, she'd talk about the deer, and the story would gain strength and ripple further and further out into the world until nobody knew where it had started, or why.

Gregory hadn't questioned her. He'd already lost interest in that car, and had a new one on order that was coming later in the week. The black one stood in the garage for a while, forgotten. Eventually, it had been fixed and sold. Gone forever.

'Aren't you going to say anything to me? Not sorry? Not anything?' Pearl's voice was desperate.

Maddy raised her chin, a faint gesture of battle. 'It's done. There's nothing for me to say.'

THIRTY-FOUR

Pearl
___

I found myself stepping closer to Maddy. 'You can't even say sorry?'

Maddy was refusing to look at me. She looked out to the sea. 'You shouldn't have been out there on those roads,' she said eventually. 'You were asking for trouble! You should have been inside, at the Gatsby Ball. Just like you should be inside now, away from me and away from Blake and Gregory. Why aren't you? Why can't you ever just stay out of things, out of our lives?'

Anger grasped me at the throat now. Who did Maddy think she was, demanding answers from me? This was *my* horror story, not Maddy's. I ached with frustration, wanting to tell her why I had been outside that night before the accident. I knew it was connected to Gregory, but I couldn't remember why I'd left the ball, in the storm. I know I had screamed at Gregory.

You have to want me!

But I didn't know what had happened before that. And I

only had fragments of what had happened after. When the policewoman with the overbite and thin face had visited me in hospital and asked me over and over again if I could remember anything, I had thought I was telling the truth. I really had thought that I remembered a red car speeding towards me just before all the pain. But it was a dream-like memory that sometimes felt as if it was forced out of nowhere. And that was all. The last memory that remained intact was running into the storm.

I'd thought so hard that it ached. I'd been trying so hard to pull at threads of memories, but they all just came loose and snapped into strands of nothing. This was what it had been like since it happened. Whole chunks of time missing, so that I was constantly stepping over gulfs of confusion, trying not to fall into an abyss where I didn't even know who I was. For all these years, I'd managed to get by with nobody caring. Only one memory had returned since it all happened, and it had taken almost ten years to come. I had been in a restaurant in London about three months ago, just before I returned home, waiting for my father to join me. The new memory had suddenly entered my mind, slotting in as though it had always been there and making me feel like I might throw up. I'd gripped the cream linen table cloth, twisting it in my fist so that the cutlery and wine glasses shifted about on the table.

I'd been going to tell my father about the new memory. He was late meeting me for dinner. We did that sometimes when he was around for work. Mineral water in thick, heavy glasses. Leather-bound menus. I would tell him as soon as he arrived.

I remember now, Dad. It was a black SUV that hit me. Two women were in the front. It was them. And I know who they are. Whoever was driving the red sports car saved me. I had it all wrong before. The man driving the red car used my phone to call the ambulance, and he stayed with me until we heard the sirens.

Dad would hit the table with his palm, an expression of his relief and his pride that I'd finally remembered and made sense of it all. He'd tell me 'well done' and order a bottle of champagne.

The man from the red sports car was a blank in my mind: a kind stranger. But I definitely knew who Maddy was, and that she'd been driving the black car. Dad would listen to me, and he'd believe me. He would help me to make things fair, and right. We'd call the police together and tell them about the car and the new memory that had arrived in my mind like a shiny celebrity. The police would reopen their files and find that it had been Gregory's car that hit me. His pretty little life with Maddy would start to be dismantled, piece by piece. Everything would be put right.

But there had been a curl of doubt in the otherwise straight story in my mind. Because I had asked for it, hadn't I? I'd pushed Maddy again and again, closer and closer to the brink of madness. Of course Maddy had snapped. And Maddy might tell my father how I'd goaded her and tried to take her place. Gregory might even support Maddy and her story. He didn't always know what he wanted: wasn't very good at realising that I was the right person for him.

And, of course, Dad hadn't made it to dinner with me

that night. It hadn't even been because of work. He'd gone out with Blanche instead and sent me a text to cancel when I'd already been sitting there waiting for him for fifteen minutes. My mother had apparently had a terrible, terrible day with a client and she *needed* drinks with my father. She understood I didn't like crowded bars so extending her invitation wouldn't be any good, but I could do my little dinner with him another night, couldn't I? He hadn't wanted to cancel, I knew that. But sometimes she gave him no choice.

So I had kept the new memory to myself, cradling it like a dead baby. And then I had moved back to Kings Hill East. I had been going to tell the police myself what I'd remembered, but it had been so long that I didn't think they'd be interested. Plus, I knew from the first time around that the footage from any nearby CCTV was blurred because of the storm. Not one license plate was visible on the nearest main road. *Gaps in surveillance. Poor-quality footage. Remote roads. We're sorry.* Anyway, the research I'd done on sentencing had made it seem like it wouldn't be worth it. Injury by careless driving barely ended up putting people in prison.

It would have been better if I'd been killed.

Community service, points on their licenses, fines. It all seemed so bland. I could surely ruin them more than any of that.

'I was out there with Gregory,' I said now, snatching back control from Maddy. I couldn't remember much, but I had enough to hurt her. The air at the top of the cliff was thick with heat and salt. I could still taste the metallic tang of blood from my cut.

'Exactly. With my husband. Anyway, nobody ever proved that it was us.' Maddy's voice seemed so confident, that I wondered if the memory of the black SUV – if all of the contents of my mind – was even true, or if my brain had been shaken so hard that all my memories were out of any meaningful order, floating down like dropped papers, a story with no spine.

But I'd seen their faces in the car. The memory was real and Maddy was lying.

'I know it was you. I remember.'

'There was a tip about a red car.' Maddy smiled – smiled! Her face glowed with triumph and something clicked on inside me. I stepped closer to Maddy and the roar of the sea below filled my ears.

'I know. I thought the car that had hit me was red. But now I know that was afterwards.' The red car had been there when there was pain and horror and blood. Up until my last days in London, the red car had just been dragged into the muddle of my mind as I'd tried so hard to piece things together. If my head hadn't been dented and broken, smashed in like a car bonnet itself, maybe I would have remembered it all to start with.

Maddy's face paled and she held out her hands as though I were a frightened pony who needed calming. The action reminded me of Gregory. I had noticed this about people. Most were a combination of those who surrounded them, stitched all together with magical thread. Maybe that's why I wasn't normal. Nobody ever surrounded me or let me borrow their cute little mannerisms, their personalities.

'Pearl. It was all so long ago. You can't possibly change what you think you saw now.'

'If I wanted to, I could. I remember.' I reached out for Maddy's hair and yanked her closer to me, bringing her chocolate-brown eyes and fluffed lashes level with my face. I heard movement behind me, running and breathless shouts to leave Maddy alone. But I clung to her, her dark strands of hair wrapping themselves around my skin, sharp as wire. 'You did it. I *know* you did.'

THIRTY-FIVE

Sadie

Fear snaked through Sadie as she ran towards the cliff edge, where Pearl was pulling at Maddy's hair.

'Pearl! Let go of her!' Sadie's words came out in huge, shaking breaths and she reached out to Gregory – anyone – to try to feel something solid, to stop her from falling and never ever reaching the ground.

Pearl let go and Maddy put her hands to her head.

'Where's Blake?' Sadie asked.

'I think Gregory's the one you should be asking about Blake.'

Gregory held his hands up at Pearl's words as though he was at gunpoint. Perhaps he was, in a way. 'She's talking nonsense.' His eyes darted between Sadie and Maddy. 'She's deluded and a compulsive liar. I told you this before, Maddy.'

Their voices whirled around Sadie's head, lies and the truth merging so that she couldn't tell them apart. 'I heard a scream. Do we need to do something? Call someone?

Please, Pearl. Just tell me what happened. You took her out on the water, didn't you?'

'Blake was in a boat on the water, but she jumped out and swam to the shore,' Maddy told Sadie breathlessly. 'She screamed just to mess with us. She was laughing too. She's wet, but fine. I saw it all. She'll be down with the other waitresses by now.'

Sadie thought again of the stuffed bear she'd found in Blake's wardrobe, of Blake's secrecy. She thought of Gregory being involved with Pearl when she was just a teenager too. Nausea floated through her body as she turned to Gregory. He had denied and denied all evening but that meant nothing. Sadie knew better than anyone that lies fell from people's lips as easily as the truth. Did he look guilty? Perhaps Sadie had seen and felt guilt for so long it was impossible to spot it, like trying to see the blood flowing through someone's body. She needed to find Blake but she needed to be here too, to work out the biggest threats and how to swipe them away from her daughter.

'She's fifteen years old, Gregory. If something – anything – has happened, then we need to know.'

'I have had nothing to do with your daughter,' Gregory was yelling now. 'I'm old enough to be her father, for God's sake! I don't know her at all. It is absolutely not true!' He ripped off his mask and charged towards the very edge of the cliff, flinging it over the edge so that it floated down to the water. Then he grabbed Maddy by the arms. He looked no older than he had done all those years ago: it was like they'd stepped back in time. 'Maddy, you have to listen to me. It's all Pearl. She was lying then, and she's lying now.

She has been watching us all. God knows what she's capable of. She's obsessed.'

Sadie looked over at Pearl. 'You've been inside my house.' Sadie felt the sticky remorse of the years move slowly around her body like tar. She'd known, somehow, that this moment would come one day. She'd thought at points that the smashed mirror and the things that had happened over the last few months had been her own paranoia or Blake or a nameless faceless person or Pearl or Maddy. But now she knew for sure, and she was facing it straight on. She wouldn't turn around and she wouldn't try to hide from it. 'Haven't you?'

THIRTY-SIX

Pearl

Sadie took a step towards me. We were all getting closer and closer to the edge, as though we wanted the sea to swallow us whole. A pleasant image of being the only person left up there floated into my mind.

'Come on, Pearl. Be honest for once.' That was Gregory, his voice soft as velvet. He held tightly on to Maddy's bare arms. Those arms that I had studied in photos online: tanned and toned, testament to Maddy's hours at Vibe. I wondered, not for the first time, who had the most strength between us: who might win, if it came to it.

'You all let me in! You wanted me to be a part of your lives.' I took a gulp of air so big I thought it might suffocate me. Could you do that? Drown in air that was too big for your lungs? I reached into the pocket of my black Masquerade apron, the touch of Maddy's satin hair tie smooth at my fingertips, calming me down. I remembered the scent from the first time I'd touched it. Musky, almost sensual. 'I've been in your bedroom, Maddy.' I brought the hair tie from my pocket and held it in front of Maddy's face. 'I have this. It's yours, from your bedroom. I was in there with Gregory. It was only yesterday. I was kissing him.'

Maddy frowned, blinking slowly. She was falling for it all, just like she had done the first time. Just like she always fell for everything.

Gregory let go of Maddy and she stumbled a little as he did. Now she was the closest to the edge. I stepped forwards too. Every second led us closer to an ending to everything that had happened. Something like excitement sparked in my blood. My mask was still in my hands, and I threw it out to follow Gregory's over the cliff. It floated down to nowhere, lifted for a moment by the breeze and then disappearing.

'No. I'm not having that, Pearl. We did not kiss. She tried to kiss me, because she's got a weird obsession with me, with us and our house. There is a clear difference,' Gregory said, waving his arms around at Maddy. I remembered him doing this when he was teaching me. Some of the other people in our class did little impressions of him sometimes, and that had always made me furious. How dare they mock him? I'd wanted to press my fingers around their necks, pull their silver pendants of hearts and moons and stars so tight that they choked.

'She's practically stalked me for the last few months. Sadie, if you've felt as though there's been someone in your house, then you were right.'

Sadie was touching the black fabric of her dress. I'd taken that a couple of weeks ago from its place in her over-organised wardrobe. And then I'd returned and smashed the mirror only a few nights ago. I was always careful to go in through the back, away from their smug little doorbell camera.

'You took this, didn't you? I blamed Blake. How did you get in?' She looked so terrified that a flicker of guilt passed through me. But I needed to ignore that. She didn't feel guilty, did she? She'd got on with her wonderful life and squashed down every thought of me.

'She's probably been at it for years. She's followed us all over, for sure.' Gregory turned to me. 'I've seen you, you know. Don't think I haven't seen you creeping around our house, turning up in hotels that I've booked for my wife and I.' He spat out the word wife. It was all lies, surely, these lines about him not wanting me there. A part of him *wanted* me to follow him around, just like Trafford had wanted me to. He wanted me to know the intricacies of his life. They'd both loved it: how could they turn down adoration?

'So why didn't you tell me? Why didn't you tell the police?' Maddy looked at Gregory just how I wanted her to. She didn't trust him: how could she?

'Because he loved it. He wanted it,' I told her. He could have ended it all, but he never, ever did. Didn't that tell them all everything they needed to know? I turned to Sadie, who was white with shock and fear. Sadie had been the trickiest one when I'd come back. Her guilt had obviously changed her. She was obsessed with checking doors and windows, always watching, like a frightened antelope ready to leap away from a lion. But at first, before everything changed, it had been easy to get to know her.

Nice handbags strewn over chairs in the busy wine bar that they went to every week at exactly the same time. Highchairs and precious children colouring and eating little yellow lollipops. Gym classes at Vibe at predictable times. Sadie and Maddy hadn't even noticed their keys had been gone. The girl in the key cutting place had been bored, happy to do it while I waited both times. She'd handed the shiny silver keys and their duller twins back over to me in minutes. I had tossed Maddy's keys on the ground next to her parked car at the gym, as though she'd dropped them. I'd watched as Maddy had scooped them up when she returned to it, her face flushed with the good fortune of nobody taking them. And I'd slipped Sadie's nicely back in her bag at the wine bar. It had all been that easy.

Sadie looked like she'd seen a ghost. And that was *good*. I needed to let her know real terror. I needed to force her to experience something other than a rich life full of beautiful people who loved her. 'And the photographs that came through the post,' she said. 'Those awful, awful images. Was that you, too? I had thought it was Maddy.'

I shook my head, thoughts clattering. Had I sent photos? Of what?

'Of your... Of you, after the accident,' Sadie added, seeing my confusion.

'That wasn't me.'

'Fine. That was me,' Maddy said. 'But I got them from Pearl. She's lying. Of course she sent them. Who else would have done it?' There was nothing but anger in her voice. No guilt, no shame.

'Did you tell Gregory about these photos?'

Maddy stared at me. *Don't*, her pretty round eyes begged.

'Why don't you fill him in on why you never told the police that strange things were happening in your houses? Why haven't you told your daughter why you're so worried that someone might be out to get her, Sadie? And did you ever tell Rob?' I turned towards Gregory. 'I was pretty when you first met me in your class, wasn't I? I was perfect. Even more perfect than Maddy. Have you never wondered what happened to me that night after we were together at the ball?' As I watched Gregory, I felt like I might choke on air again, as though there was too much of it inside me and I might drown.

'Oh, Pearl.' Gregory's face softened with a sympathy I'd never seen on it before. His tone was his teacher tone, even after years of never stepping foot in a classroom. The years span and fell and I suddenly felt like I was seventeen and beautiful, listening to his silky voice, turning the delicate pages of *Othello* as he read. 'I already know.'

THIRTY-SEVEN

Maddy

Maddy felt her body trembling: a tremor before an avalanche. She could see the grey sea churning beside her and took an uncertain step away from it, feeling as though there wasn't enough space between her and the edge of the world; the edge of the life she'd become so used to.

Gregory already knew about Pearl's accident?

'Hang on,' Sadie was saying to Gregory. Maddy wondered how she could manage to string words together. 'You already know what?'

He cleared his throat and blinked slowly. 'I knew you'd taken the car,' he said to Maddy. 'But you told me that Sadie had driven it home, and that you'd hit a deer.'

Maddy remembered telling Gregory that the morning after, her head pounding and her mouth dry. Lies, hanging over them and glistening like webs.

'And then there were the reports of the hit-and-run car being red.'

Maddy remembered going to check on the car the morning after, its dent in the bonnet gleaming in the sun. She'd ignored the sticky guilt that dripped into her gut. She'd ignored Gregory saying that his brand-new car was about to be delivered, a sporty little yellow thing, and making a joke about an early midlife crisis.

'But then,' Gregory continued, 'there was Aiden.'

Maddy's stomach took another dive and her head felt too full, ready to burst.

'What did Aiden say to you? When?'

I know you.

'He told me it was you, a few months after it had happened. I said it couldn't have been. But he told me that he saw you.'

So Aiden hadn't left Maddy alone after all. He'd betrayed her. And Gregory had known too, for all these years. Was it any wonder he didn't love her anymore? The world suddenly seemed darker, as though someone had scrubbed it blank and then repainted it all black.

'You knew the truth and you let me tell the police the wrong story?' Pearl clutched her stomach as she spoke to Gregory, as though she was in pain. 'I told them the car that hit me was red when I gave my statement. The police kept asking and asking, and I just wanted them to stop. The only memory I had at the time was of a red car. I didn't know who was driving it. I remembered not long ago that it wasn't the red car that hit me. The driver of the red car saved me. He called the ambulance and waited until they came. I never knew who it was. You could have corrected me, if you knew.'

'It was Aiden,' Maddy said, her voice breaking as though someone were treading on her words. 'My brother-in-law. He was coming for me. Everyone else had left me, and I'd spoken to him just before. He saw it happen. He tried to ask me about it but…' But what? She had put him off and tried to snap shut the past. She remembered the photographs arriving through her door, the handwriting on the envelope. Of course. She hadn't registered at the time, or perhaps hadn't wanted to. It had been Aiden's writing, giant letters that she hadn't seen since they were children. She turned to Pearl, who was shaking, her whole body trembling. 'He sent me those awful images of your injuries. I thought it might have been you. But he must have done it. He must have taken them from a newspaper and tried to frighten me into admitting it. I sent them to you,' she added, turning to Sadie.

'He sent them to me, too,' Gregory said. 'He sent them to me via my agent. He didn't want to give evidence because he didn't want to be involved at all, in case they started looking at him too closely, probably. So he was trying to get me to tell you to admit it, Maddy. I didn't know who to trust, but I knew I needed to protect you. I would have done anything for you. I told Aiden that if he did anything else, contacted us about it ever again, I'd come forward as a witness and tell them I'd seen him do it. He'd been there, and the risk was too high for him. He was backed into a corner. So that was that. We were able to carry on with our lives.'

Only they hadn't, had they? Not really. Her head pounded as the reality Maddy had known for so long shook, shattering everything that she'd built so carefully on top of it.

THIRTY-EIGHT

Pearl

I had been silent, my brain wading through the information being tossed at me, crumbs to a sparrow. At some point, my body started to tremble.

Aiden. Of course it had been one of them.

Despite everything, I almost wanted to laugh. Was Maddy for real?

'You really thought for all these years that Aiden would put everything at risk just to protect precious Maddy? And you thought I would send photos of my face? As if I wanted everyone to see more of it! I couldn't even look at myself for a second! I still can't!' I screamed at them, my words dragging across the flesh of my throat. 'Tonight has been the first night in ten years where people have looked at me normally, because I've been wearing my mask and it has made me look like everyone else!' I pictured Aiden, kneeling in the road as we waited for the sound of sirens and then disappearing before the ambulance came. He must not have told them his name, wanting no part in it all, knowing that whatever Maddy was involved in would drag chaos into his life. But I'd inadvertently dropped him in the very middle of it all by telling the police to look for his car. I wondered what had happened to his jeans, sodden with my blood. 'He will have been waiting for you to tell the truth. Every day that's gone by, he's probably been more and more let down by you. And every day, you've thought he was protecting you and keeping your dirty little secret. You're so deluded.'

'Deluded? You want to talk about deluded, Pearl?' Gregory gave a short, cruel laugh.

Gregory had called me deluded before. Trafford had said it too, the word dumped on top of my heart and making it too heavy to carry around inside me. But they'd all been totally wrong. It wasn't me who was deluded. It never had been. I felt light, as though I might float up, up and away from them all, into the golden sky. 'Aiden was probably waiting for you to become a better person. But you never did, did you?' I reached forwards and shoved Maddy in the chest, her flesh soft and warm beneath my fingers. Maddy took a step backwards, her face rigid with fear.

Gregory leaped in front of Maddy and took her hand in his. Defending her. Always, *always* defending her. I felt hot tears rushing behind my eyes, stinging and burning.

'I could never believe you just left me out there to get hurt, Gregory. You wanted me. I know you wanted me.' But even as I said the words and felt the tears fall down my broken face, I knew they weren't true.

I closed my eyes, trying to see nothing but black, instead seeing images from the past swirling into focus. I had turned on Gregory the night of the Gatsby Ball when he'd rejected me. I'd clawed at him, unable to stop the wave of anger from erupting out of me. He'd tried to defend himself, reaching out to try and calm me, and my dress had ripped. The rain had made the torn material cling to my skin. The feeling returned to me now: saturated material sticking to me.

You have to want me!

'You hate me,' I said slowly to Gregory now. 'And you love Maddy.'

Gregory laughed, putting his hands up as though he was hosting a talk show. 'Hallelujah!' He grinned out at them all, the shining celebrity. 'She's finally got it!'

'But—But I saw you together,' Maddy said blinking slowly, trying to wade through everyone's stories. 'Outside your office. It was so long ago, but I saw it.' She was frowning, as though squinting would let her see the past. 'You were holding hands.'

Gregory shook his head. 'Nope. Absolutely not. There were a couple of occasions where Pearl overstepped the mark. She did things like that – taking my hand and stealing things from my office.' I remembered that day. I'd seen Maddy, the first time in real life, as I'd left Gregory's office building with him. I'd been with him for one of my English tutorials and he'd mentioned he was going to the main block afterwards, so I'd waited for him so that we could leave his office together. I'd searched Gregory's wife a few days before on Facebook to know what she looked like, and there she'd been, standing right there on the school grounds, with their baby in a fancy white pushchair. She'd been bending over at that moment, dealing with a dropped toy. I had taken Gregory's hand as we walked. He'd glanced at it, dumb, then up at me. He'd brushed it away almost immediately, but I had looked around and saw that Maddy had already turned back with the pushchair. I'd hoped that Maddy had seen all she needed to, and I imagined her arguing with Gregory later that night, about me. Maybe my name would spring from the beautiful walls of their beautiful home. Maybe it would make Gregory think *what if?*

I had already sent Gregory's tie to their home, to make it all seem a little more real to Maddy, but to myself as well. I'd turned up to Gregory's office the day I took the tie and asked if he had a copy of some play. I hadn't wanted the play. I'd just wanted to see him, to be alone with him. He'd turned to the wall of books and started rooting, and I'd slipped his tie from his desk into my bag.

I smiled, floating on the memories of those days when it all began. But then Gregory's words reached me as he carried on ranting to Maddy about all the things I used to do. 'She was spoken to by the head of year, and I refused to meet her for any more tutorials.'

Yes. I remembered that too. During my last few tutorials, Gregory had seemed on edge and he'd kept his office door wide open. The thought was heavy as iron, a boot on the heart, stamping and stamping.

'So … there was nothing? Absolutely nothing between you both?'

'No! Never! I didn't tell you because Pearl left soon after, and I'd hoped that would be that. God, how wrong I was.

Every time I thought I'd shaken her off, and decided that it wasn't worth telling you and making you suspicious, she'd be back. But I thought I could handle her myself. I didn't want you to have to deal with it all. I didn't want us to have to involve the police, because then what? Maddy, you have to believe me.'

Gregory hated me and he loved Maddy. No matter what I told him or did, no matter what people believed about him, he would never, ever want me or love me. I'd made it all up. Gregory had seen me as a child, and I'd made up a child's story to make the big bad world seem better. The feeling, as though I was stepping off a high ledge into thin air with nothing underneath me, was familiar. I'd felt it before, at this very place, but I'd forgotten it until now. I began to tremble, and I could hear voices saying things, but my brain processed none of it because it was in the past, living the missing pieces of the puzzle again as though it was the first time. Each memory stung like vinegar in a cut.

You have to want me!

Mud had slid between my toes as I ran from the Gatsby Ball. I'd had my hair done especially, asking the stylist to make me look older. The stylist had laughed at me when I'd said it, and I had felt a little dagger in my heart. She'd been right. I'd only been at the ball because my mother's events company had managed it. I was a tag-along, a child at a grown-up party. My hair had ended up limp, soaking and clamped around my skull.

Gregory had told me the night of the Gatsby Ball that he'd never wanted me. He'd called me a child too: the last thing I'd wanted to be, because I wanted to be Maddy.

I wanted friends who drank bitter alcohol with me and a pretty house of my own with a husband and a cute little boy in a highchair. But Gregory's words had pulled all of those things from me. I'd run from him into the thick, green tangle of trees.

'You came out of the castle to look for me. You followed me outside,' I said to him now, trying to press the memory into a shape that didn't hurt so much.

'I followed you because of the storm. It was a terrible night for one of my ex-students – any child – to be out alone.' There was his teacher tone again: patient, ready to explain over and over until the slowest person, the slowest *child* in the class finally understood. 'I shouldn't have left you. I'm aware that it was a terrible thing to do. But you'd already taken things too far, Pearl. I just wanted it all to stop. I wanted nothing more to do with you. I just wanted to protect my family. They were my priority. They are still my priority.'

'Are we?' Maddy was looking at Gregory with crazed, round eyes. 'You're never here! You're always disappearing. London. Days on end. If it's not Pearl, and it never was, is it Blake?'

Gregory shook his head. 'I don't want to do this now, Maddy.'

Maddy stared at him, on and on.

'Maddy.' He looked desperate, different from how I had ever seen him before.

'Go on! Tell me. Because there's something I am missing. I know there is. Why am I sleeping alone so often? Why am I *still* coming to balls by myself?'

'It's the book!' Gregory's words were shouts, launched across the clifftop. 'I haven't written it. I can't write it.' He pushed his hands through his hair and looked back at Maddy. I fought a horrible urge to laugh at them both. Gregory Archer, unable to write? 'I have kept trying different places to try and get somewhere with it. I'm getting nowhere. The words just will not come. I've been to London, booked hotels and had days in libraries. I thought I just needed some quiet time, away from everything. I can't let everyone down, Maddy. I have a release date that's getting closer and closer. I've signed a contract. There are pre-orders and launches planned. And what, I'm just meant to tell them all that I haven't written a word since my last lot of edits, months ago? That I've deleted half the thing?'

'But you've been with Tim. Hasn't he helped you?'

Ah, Tim. I'd seen photos of them together, Gregory and Tim, the dream team. Tim, the esteemed literary agent and his talented, dynamic author.

'I haven't seen him for months.' Gregory was looking downwards now, his face flushing in remorse. Maddy frowned, confused, slow to understand that Gregory had lied to her, that he wasn't who she thought he was.

'So why didn't you just tell me?'

Gregory laughed sadly. 'I know that you're not happy, Maddy. I know that you put your career on hold for mine, that you have to do everything for Eliot so I can be the big author and bring in the money. I've failed you. And I didn't want to tell you that.'

Maddy stared at Gregory, processing a new version of her life.

'I'm going to find Blake,' Sadie said. But it was just then that we all saw Blake, running towards us, breathless and beautiful. Her hair was still wet but she'd found a spare uniform which was a little smaller than her original one and gripped her perfect body.

Sadie ran to her daughter at lightning speed as soon as she saw her. 'You're safe! You're okay!' She rushed at Blake and threw her arms around her. I couldn't imagine that kind of suffocating love.

Careful, I wanted to warn her. Go at her too fast and she'll fall from the edge of the cliff like a feather.

Blake extracted her limbs from Sadie's, staring at them all. 'Mum? Why are you here? And why are you all outside? What's going on?' Her face was pinched with concern. Good.

Sadie was trembling. 'Come on. We need to get down. It's not safe up here.' She held her arm out, but Blake didn't take it. 'You shouldn't be here.'

'I thought you'd be pleased that I was earning money, doing something responsible. I thought you might not let me if I told you, and I wanted to prove to you that I was able to do it. I had no idea you'd be here too. I only knew tonight was happening because Pearl got in touch with me on Insta to offer me the job.'

'It wasn't just a job. Pearl wanted you here to get at me,' Sadie said, still trying to pull at Blake, get her away from me as though I was something poisonous. 'And what about Gregory? Be honest with me, Blake.'

Blake blinked at Maddy. B&G. An offer for personalised gifts had popped up on my phone and I'd ordered it straight away. Presumably Blake had thought it was from a secret admirer. She probably had loads of them.

'Who is Gregory?'

'He bought you a bear,' I said, unable to help myself. I could feel things coming undone. My breaths were jagged and short, my thoughts jumbled.

There was a snatch of recognition on Blake's face. 'How do you know about that bear?'

Sadie tossed a look at me. 'Leave her. Don't speak to her. I'm so, so sorry, Pearl. About it all. I'll make it up to you. I will do anything. But just leave Blake out of this, okay?'

'Mum? What's going on? Why are you all up here? And how do you know Pearl?' Blake looked around at them one by one. Me, she knew, and she gave me an uncertain, small smile. But Maddy and Gregory were given a cool look, the look of a teenager who saw two middle-aged people she didn't know and didn't care about. 'Who are they?'

'Well, what do you know,' Gregory said. He flashed a sorry smile at us all, too wrung out from his earlier admission to be self-satisfied. 'I presume this is Blake, my so-called affair. Only, she has obviously no idea who I am. I wonder why on earth that could be.'

'You really don't know who he is?' Sadie was visibly giddy with relief, stupid with surprise that her perfect daughter wasn't tainted after all. But what was so surprising about it for her? Her golden life was still flawless. She'd messed up and got away with it, and so had Maddy, and then they'd gone back to their pretty little fairy tale houses while I rotted in a tower full of curses.

And Gregory? He'd sneaked around, lied to Maddy in

the end anyway. So why not do it when I met him, when there was something to be gained from it? Why lie to her about a stupid book, and not me?

The embers inside me took hold, and flames of anger began to roar in my ears. The hurt was so hot and red that I couldn't see through it or past it. I wanted to push them all, push them so far that for once, nobody would be able to save them.

THIRTY-NINE

Maddy

It happened so quickly and so slowly, all at once but in a million moments. They all seemed to be in a line: Pearl, Maddy and Gregory, all equally close to the edge of their lives, the end glittering blue beneath them. And in those moments, Maddy saw Gregory as someone else, someone who was vulnerable in a way she'd never, ever expected. She had so many questions for him, which she would ask him later, in the safety of their own room with its strange staring stuffed birds and its bed that was slightly smaller than theirs at home and the view out to the thrashing sea.

Why hadn't he told her?

Had he really, *really* never strayed?

What now? Now that she knew he'd been loyal after all, and he'd only been hiding something about his book and not other women or girls or desires, and now that she realised she was so giddy with relief that she didn't even actually care much about the book, or all the things she thought she cared about, what now?

The thoughts and questions were like drugs, pumping around and around in her body and making her want to dance and scream out.

Gregory and Maddy.

It didn't have to be doomed. It had never been doomed. That love they'd had at the very beginning could be lured back out from under its shell.

But then Pearl lunged towards Gregory, and Gregory retaliated and forced himself towards her, his face surprised by his own reflex, his arms outstretched. And Maddy's body seemed to move of its own accord. She saw Gregory's face as she stumbled backwards. Horror and fear and something so *final*. She wanted to tell him so much, but there wasn't time.

Oh, Gregory. I'm so, so sorry, because I got it all so horribly wrong. But now I believe you.

We could have rebuilt our world in a different shape. I would have wanted that.

She thought of Eliot.

He needs you. He loves you. Find that love and pull it from him. It will save you both.

Perhaps Maddy moved so quickly and saved Pearl to make amends, to reverse what she'd done ten years ago and every day since.

Or perhaps she would have done it anyway, regardless of what had or hadn't happened all those years ago.

Perhaps Maddy was good, at her core.

The thought was smooth and bright, a candle burning in darkness.

FORTY

Sadie

Sadie grabbed Blake and held her tightly as Maddy moved where Pearl should have been, as Maddy fell backwards, kicking, limbs flailing and cracking against the rocks.

She heard herself whisper *Oh no, oh Maddy, oh my God, oh no, no*, over and over again until it made no sense, until her mind could not process the words anymore.

She watched Pearl shaking as she stared at the sea below, at the small patch of sand where Maddy lay. She watched Gregory put his head in his hands and make a noise that didn't even sound human. And then she looked down, at where Maddy had landed, her head at a strange angle, her eyes staring straight ahead.

FORTY-ONE

Pearl

Then somehow, we were back downstairs, in the ballroom, where I couldn't tell who anyone was, where people were drinking champagne and glaring at me for bumping into them, where the guests had no idea what was beyond the endless miles of black velvet curtain beside them. The band somehow still played and the blonde waitresses I'd been so pleased with myself for choosing somehow still moved around, topping up drinks and smiling in a way that I could never have done.

And then we were outside again, which I knew was still scorching hot even though my body was freezing cold and my heart had surely, surely stopped. There was a covered body being pulled from the sand that looked dirty grey, like ash in the darkness. Most people had left the ball early but some still milled around in their masks, glad for a dramatic climax, as though they were extras in a book or a film.

The body was covered, zipped away forever. The police arrived, what seemed like hundreds of them. They were everywhere, crawling all over, trying to piece together yet another accident.

'I wish I hadn't seen her. I wish it had just been washed away and I hadn't been able to look.' I heard the words and I felt them fall from my mouth but I felt detached from them, as though someone else was saying them. Sadie was next to me, still clutching Blake and taking deep, terrified breaths. And my dad was on my other side.

'I didn't think you were coming,' I found myself saying, still shivering so much that my bones rattled and my brain whacked against my skull over and over again, making me think of Maddy's skull that now lay broken in a bag.

'I need to speak to the police,' Sadie said. Her face showed everything I'd wanted it to. Fear, guilt, regret. I'd never expected to feel those things too, to feel like I was staring into a mirror.

'I'm sure you'll all have to,' Dad told her.

I shrugged and my whole body hurt. 'There's nothing to say. Maddy saved my life. And she's gone.' I looked across at Sadie. 'I want to forget everything.' After so long of trying to remember.

Tears streamed down Sadie's cheeks. My dad took my hand, his face flashing blue and red in the police lights.

FORTY-TWO

Sadie

The police questioned them all, of course. How upside-down things were: they'd never questioned Sadie after the Gatsby Ball.

You've done nothing. Not this time, she kept telling herself as she talked to the officer with the hooded eyes and tufts of coarse grey hair.

Her heart banged on and on as she spoke to the officer. It had been an awful accident, lost footing, drunken stupidity close to the edge. They'd been told not to leave the castle. They'd ignored the danger signs.

And then it was over. The officer nodded his sudden thanks, and Sadie was free again.

Rob knew about the accident through his colleagues: a horrible echo of last time. He was at Falcon Castle before Sadie had even contacted him, and drove them home. Blake sat in the back, a grey hoodie pulled up over her loose hair, eyes down, texting furiously. Her phone pinged and pinged even though it was after midnight. Her world never seemed to stop. Sadie wondered what Blake was typing. She'd been facing Sadie when it had happened. She'd seen nothing. Perhaps Blake's imaginings were even worse than the reality. Body bags, ambulances, broken bones and death. Sadie wanted to reach behind her daughter's eyes, into her mind, and pull out the awful images like strings of black tape from a cassette.

As if she'd heard Sadie's thoughts, Blake sniffed and the tapping on her phone screen stopped for a moment. 'I wish I'd never said yes to working there, by the way. I thought it would be really cool. But when I got there, it turned out to be kind of creepy, so…'

Rob slowed the car slightly as Blake's sentence trailed off into the land of things never said. Sadie took a gulp of stale air as the image of Maddy's broken body passed through her mind.

Maddy is gone.

Pearl doesn't want me to admit what I think I did.

The thoughts were sharp and unfamiliar. She'd grown used to Pearl and Maddy moving around in the shadows of her mind, threatening to tip up Sadie's life and empty everything out.

'You know that question…' she asked Rob. 'If a tree falls down in a forest, and nobody is there to hear it?'

He was silent, concentrating on the road.

'What's the answer? Does it make a sound, or not?'

'Course it does,' Blake said quietly from the back, her

fingers tapping again like butterfly wings on the screen of her phone. 'Why?'

Sadie shrugged, and the guilt and the fear wore on.

When they got home, Sadie asked Rob and Blake to sit in the lounge. It was the early hours of the morning. The house was silent.

'Aren't we going to bed?' Blake asked. She still had her hood up and mascara was smeared around her eyes.

Rob stayed standing. 'It's been a long night for everyone, Sadie. Can't we talk in the morning?' Sadie understood: he'd driven for almost four hours altogether, to the castle and home again twice. His voice was the furthest away from her that it had ever been and yet soon, it would be even further.

But that wasn't a reason not to do it. She couldn't keep packaging things up as reasons not to tell him. She took a deep breath and began talking. 'Do you remember the accident on the night I went to the Gatsby Ball at Falcon Castle?'

Rob frowned. Of course he didn't still remember it. He hadn't even seen it himself: his colleagues had described it – the horror of it – to him. But then they'd described more and more accidents, and he'd seen more and more himself and they'd moulded into one giant accident: irresponsible people doing things they shouldn't that ended in damage and torn-up lives.

'It was a hit and run. Ten years ago. Almost to the day,

actually. You asked me if I'd seen something, and I said no,' she reminded him.

'What's this got to do with anything?' Blake asked, stifling a yawn.

'The head waitress, who gave you the job. It was Pearl. The same girl from the hit and run that night. I think she was the one who invited you to the ball tonight. Her mother was running the event.'

Rob squinted at Sadie. 'Okay?'

'Pearl was in a hit and run?' Blake gasped. 'Oh, God. Her face. Is that how it happened? And how do you know about it?' Her words ran on and on, making Rob's pale silence even more pronounced. 'Hang on. You apologised to her on the top of the cliff. I forgot, because of everything that happened afterwards. But why were you sorry? How did you even know her?'

'I've been putting you all in danger,' Sadie said, nausea swirling, the words dizzying. 'I know now that Pearl has been threatening us, trying to get revenge or scare us. I know you thought I was losing my mind. But I wasn't. All the time, I knew that someone was out to get us. I should have told you.'

'What are you saying?' Rob asked eventually.

'I was in the car with Maddy that night. She was so upset. I don't remember a lot. And it was so hard to see anything. There was the storm, and the rain was so heavy.' The agonising traces of realisation passed over Rob's and Blake's faces at the same time, and terror pushed down on Sadie as she continued.

'It was you?' Rob's eyes flickered over Sadie as though

he'd never met her before, as though he was meeting her all over again and everything that had gone before had been erased.

'I don't know. Well, I didn't know, at the time. We hit something. I only remember parts of it.' The truth, the real truth that was even darker than all of this, wormed its way through Sadie, gnawing at her dark insides to get out into the light. 'Maddy needed someone with her. And she was so angry with Pearl. She thought that Gregory was having an affair with her. Pearl had made it look that way. I didn't want to be friends with Maddy, not really – I knew she wasn't my kind of person – but she seemed so lost. I just felt like she needed someone. I know now that I should have said no to her. I should have been stronger.'

How different things would have been if she'd said no to Maddy that very first time: no to the glass of Miravel after Stay and Play; no to the Gatsby Ball and the car and it all. *No. No. No.*

'You can't try to save everyone who seems a bit lost, Sadie. You know that.'

'So it was Maddy?' Blake's voice was bright and hopeful, clear as when she was an eight-year-old who skipped and played and loved Sadie unconditionally. 'You were both in the car together, but Maddy did it?'

The memory of Maddy's shattered body; her staring eyes, appeared in Sadie's mind. 'I don't know. I think so. But I was with her. I do remember hitting something. Afterwards, Maddy sent me a message to tell me it had definitely been a deer, that she'd been and moved it from the side of the road.'

'And you believed her?' Rob asked.

'I wanted to. And then it turned out that the police were looking for the driver of a red car. The one we were in – Gregory's – was black. So it really seemed like it hadn't been us.' She looked at Rob and Blake, the family she had thrown everything at: lies and energy and all her love, to try and glue it together. *What would you have done?* She wanted to ask them both. She wasn't sure what Blake's answer would be. But Rob's was undeniable. He'd have done the right thing.

'Why can't you remember?' He stared at her. 'You remember everything, all the time. Were you drinking? Had Maddy been drinking when she got in the car?'

Sadie thought of Rob's parents, their whole lives crushed by the drunk driver. He'd told her when they'd first met why he'd become a paramedic. About the visit he'd had about his parents' grey Fiat that they'd only collected a few days before being smashed into head-on by a drunk driver. The driver was unharmed. Both of Rob's parents died instantly. There one minute, on their way to Rob's flat actually, which made it all even more unbearably sad and inextricably linked with regret, then gone forever the next. Rob had adored his parents. His mum had been one of the good mums, baking him cakes and playing dinosaurs with him and having his friends round for fish fingers, and then later, making him huge roast dinners to feed his insatiable growing-boy appetite and being nice to his girlfriends. And his dad, quite simply, had been his hero. 'I'm sure that Maddy put something in my drink. She always denied it.

But I barely drank anything, and then everything just became ... blurred. Strange. I don't remember a lot.'

'Sadie!' His voice broke but he ignored it, thundering on. 'You should have called me the moment you started to feel strange! You should have told the police at the time! How could you think this... Withholding all this information about a *child*... How did you think it was the right thing to do?'

'I didn't want to lose you,' Sadie said, knowing how pathetic the words sounded.

'But it shouldn't have been about that. It should have been about doing the right thing!' Rob exploded. His arms flailed about him. The right thing. Always, always the right thing.

'It seemed right at the time. The only right thing was keeping you both. I couldn't bear the thought of anything else!'

'But if you were so sure that you hit a deer and that they weren't looking for the car you were in, then what changed?' Blake asked. 'Why did you feel like you had something to hide?'

'I got some photos through the post.' She'd thrown them away, terrified. She had ripped them into as many pieces as possible and buried them in the bin outside, beneath the detritus of their life: egg shells and apple cores and dust. 'They were quite graphic. I think they showed Pearl's injuries. And then I suppose I knew. She thought it was us. It was Maddy who sent those to me. I don't even know why she did it, and I can't ask her now.'

Staring eyes. A cracked skull and a line of blood as sticky as jam.

Rob stood up and put his hands behind his head. Small circles of sweat bloomed from under each arm. 'When did you get the photos?'

'About six months after it happened.' They hadn't changed anything, really. They'd just brought the cold fear that had been nestling inside Sadie up to the surface. The fear was still as sharp as it had been then, just like the memories. Opening the envelope, pulling the glossy images and taking a moment to process what they were. Vomit spilling between her shaking fingers. Blake telling Rob that Sadie had been poorly when he got home that night and lines of concern on his face. He had run Sadie a bath and she had resolved to tell him everything as she sat in silent bathroom. But then, somehow, her resolve had seemed to fall down the drain with the lukewarm water.

Aiden had sent the images to Maddy, and Maddy had sent them to Sadie.

Domino after domino, crashing to the ground.

'And you didn't tell me? Why now? Why after all this time, and everything that we've…' He sighed. 'Why are you telling us now? Is Pearl going to go to the police?'

'I don't think so.' Sadie thought of Pearl's face earlier that evening. Something in it had changed, and something had clicked inside Sadie, a shift in her life.

'So you could have got away with it.' Blake said, and a flicker of wonder passed over her face. Why, oh why, tell the truth about something you'd already got away with?

'But I wanted to do the right thing, in the end. Even if I

didn't do it at the time. I'm so tired of keeping it all from you. Even though I feel like Pearl won't bother us anymore, that feeling of being someone different from who you thought I was, is still there.' Sadie looked down, the flecks of cream and beige in the carpet blurring in her eyes.

'Why didn't you think you could tell me for all these years?' Rob asked.

The feeling of lightness Sadie had expected every time she'd thought about telling the truth was absent. She felt heavier, in fact, than she had done in years. Laden with worry and sadness, donkey-like. 'I know I ruined everything anyway. But I was trying to protect it. I was trying to keep it safe.'

'You presumed I wouldn't listen, or back you. Your drink was spiked, Sadie. That wasn't your fault. You were part of something terrible. But I would have still loved you. You just didn't trust me enough to tell me. You have could have told me a thousand times. You could have let me help you.'

'I'm telling you now,' Sadie said weakly.

Rob didn't answer, just turned and left the room. Blake put her hands over her eyes. Her nails weren't jagged and chipped with nail polish today. They were clean and round, like they always used to be when she was a child, in those simpler days that Sadie had tried so hard to preserve. But she hadn't been able to, because you couldn't preserve people, or secrets, or time, could you?

They both listened to Rob's soft footsteps as he climbed the stairs. And then Blake stood and left the room too so that Sadie stood alone in the strange, blue quiet of the night.

FORTY-THREE

Pearl

Six months after the Masquerade Ball

It was a frozen January afternoon. Three o'clock on a Tuesday, the same time every week. The view outside the window was colourless, as though someone had thrown a bucket of grey water over the world.

'How are you doing with the affirmations of self-worth?' Heather sat on her red chair, her fingers poised over the keyboard of her little laptop. She was better than the other guy I used to see, I supposed. I felt like she listened a bit more, and she always wore calm, plain clothes, not the kind of self-appreciative colours and patterns that gave me a headache. 'Is your support group helping?'

I thought about the new people I had met through the group I'd set up for people who had suffered facial disfigurements. I'd done it alone. No Goldman money. Just me. Blanche actually seemed pleased with my work, but then she would always be pleased as long as I was acting normally, not showing her up.

'I'm saying the affirmations like you told me to. But I've searched one of the group members on Facebook,' I told Heather. The words slipped out, wire-sharp on my throat. The person I'd looked up was Katy, a burn victim. Her maniac ex-boyfriend had set fire to her flat and locked her inside. She had one eye: the most beautiful green, the colour of first spring leaves. The other eye had melted into her face. Beauty and ugliness smashed together. I was fascinated by how she had looked before and even more obsessed with how she looked now. Two pretty green eyes and then, suddenly, only one.

'Did that give you the feelings you were looking for?'

I stared out of the window. The branches on the trees outside were as bare as bones and frozen still. I'd been to see Katy too, but I wouldn't tell Heather that. Katy was living with her sister now. Her sister, Lisa, had three golden-haired boys who left scooters and footballs in their huge back garden just outside Kings Hill West. I would go the long way round to wherever I was going just to see Katy and her family, to catch a glimpse of her life. Sometimes I forgot the way, and drove for hours until I finally found myself there.

'I think so.'

'And what feelings were you looking for?'

I thought about it, about what Heather would expect me to say. 'Maybe I wanted to feel less alone.'

'And you did, when you looked at Facebook?'

I nodded.

'And what about when you followed the photographer? What feelings do you think you were looking for back then?'

I hesitated. I had liked feeling as though Trafford were mine. He had taken photographs of me only once, in his flat. It'd been a phase he was going through at the time: experimenting with damaged skin. He had been kind, although his motives hadn't been entirely altruistic: he'd thought that my model agency, RAW, would use his shots and throw money at him. He'd made me a cup of scalding peppermint tea and let me sit on his nice sofa and told me that my scars didn't matter.

But then he'd moved on and left me behind. He had started a new project taking photographs of overflowing bins and rats. Then he'd gone on to scenes outside nightclubs. Artsy shots of lost shoes, drunk friends and abandoned kebabs.

I'd sometimes waited for hours outside his building in Soho for someone to let me inside. I'd followed him on the tube and across all of London, stepping where he had, our feet making the same prints on the pavements, until he'd had enough and started threatening me with the police. His baby had arrived not long ago. He'd taken photos of that, too, and put them online. Clear, trusting eyes looking up at a black-and-white Samantha. Her smiling back down at its perfect miniature nose and downy little head. Such fragile happiness.

I remembered Trafford's tone with me, his frustration. 'I liked it when he got angry with me, in a way.'

'We've talked about your childhood before,' Heather

said. 'About your mother being angry with you, and that being a kind of attention that you came to crave.'

Oh, it always ended up here. Such a cliché. Heather's words faded into the distance as I remembered the past. The dinner party where I'd thrown myself down the stairs as a child. I'd put the discarded wine glass on the bottom stair and aimed my little body straight at it. Bullseye. I could still feel the sensation of sliced skin, stinging and smelling of metal. The satisfaction of my parents' fun without me being over, of sitting on my dad's knee on the way to the hospital and the smell of adult dinner and adult words on his breath.

Heather had stopped talking and was waiting for me to respond. I was silent. She waited and waited. The clock ticked.

She crossed her legs in her plain navy-blue trousers, ever-patient. 'How are you getting along with your parents at the moment?'

'They're nervous.'

My parents had moved me from the flat into their house after the Masquerade Ball. They edged around me each day, waiting for me to crack into pieces.

'What do you think they are nervous of?'

'They don't trust me. They think what happened to Maddy has made me lose my mind. They are scared of me showing them up, doing something crazy. Hurting someone. I don't think they believe that Maddy wasn't pushed. That's why I'm seeing you. They made me.'

My parents and I saw more of each other than we had done before the Masquerade Ball, but I knew it wasn't because they actually wanted to spend time with me. If I went missing until late with my phone off, or left articles about Gregory lying around, then they cancelled plans, ate dinner with me and bought me nice things. But then the more I did things like that, the more obsessed they became with me seeing Heather and being miraculously fixed so that they could get back to their lives and their remade plans. My father wouldn't even be convinced that I didn't need therapy like he had been last time. I hated that.

Heather frowned and began typing. The clacking of the keys scraped along my nerves. 'I do think my parents are working on being there for me,' I said, making her look up. 'And it's making me feel good. I think that's why I have the strength to just stick to looking at people on Facebook. I'd never do more than that. Not now.' I smiled brightly.

'That's good, Pearl. That's really positive.' Heather smiled back.

Afterwards, when it was over and Heather had told me to take care of myself like she always did, I got into my car and drove the long way home. Katy was out. But Lisa and her little boys were all there, sitting at the table in the kitchen diner, the warm light from the house burning a hole in the winter darkness of the afternoon. One, two, three golden heads bent over a game.

Perfection.

FORTY-FOUR

Sadie

One year after the Masquerade Ball

'I was passing,' Rob told Sadie as he stood at the front door. He was wearing his orange T-shirt, and his bike was balancing at his side.

'You were passing Cottle? Really?' Cottle wasn't somewhere anyone passed through. It was a nondescript town about twenty minutes from Kings Hill West and Sadie had moved there about nine months ago when they'd sold their house. Living somewhere different was one of the many things that sometimes gave Sadie a terrified feeling that the ground had vanished and she was falling into nothingness. A bit like the very last feeling Maddy must have ever experienced, Sadie realised soon after it started happening.

'Okay. No, I wasn't passing. I just wanted to check in.'

'I'm glad.' Sadie turned around and gestured for him to follow her inside, bike and all. In the kitchen, Sadie busied herself with the kettle and mugs. Rob knowing what Sadie had done, and what she had kept from him, made it difficult to be around him sometimes. Eye contact with him was like staring in a mirror where Sadie saw who she had been and who that made her now. A lot of the time since the night of the Masquerade Ball, she'd found herself avoiding looking at him.

She cleared her throat and stuffed teabags into mugs. 'Blake's still out if it's her you wanted to see. She probably won't be back for a while.' Blake had finished for the summer a few days earlier. She had been out with friends ever since: friends that Sadie remembered starting high school flat-chested and sparrow-legged. Now they all looked as though they were in their early twenties, curves and pouts; iced lattes and bronzer; big decisions and part-time jobs. Adult lives waiting just around the corner to pick them up and whizz them off into the distance.

'That's okay. I came to see you.'

The words prompted a small tilt of Sadie's stomach, as though she'd gone over a hill too fast. Rob's sadness that she hadn't trusted him with what had happened had been something that Sadie thought might break her at various points over the last year. But over time, she'd learned to accept it.

Could you still love someone if they had made you that sad and disappointed? Sometimes, Sadie felt like she might not want to know the answer.

'Blake's been telling me about uni courses. She's so excited about the idea of moving to London in a couple of years,' Rob said next as he took his tea from Sadie. 'How are you feeling about that?' Blake had been looking at different theatre schools and university drama courses for when she finished her A Levels in two years. Blake had been hurt and silent in those early months after the ball, for Rob and for herself, and she'd spent a lot of time at Rob's flat. But slowly, Sadie could sense an unseen broken bond between them repairing. There had been a couple of shopping trips together, and two films with popcorn at home. Soon though, it would be time for Blake to go again, and Sadie would make sure that she let her.

Sadie smiled at Rob. 'Oh, just brilliantly. How about you?'

'The same. No worries at all. I love the idea of her moving far away and hanging around with boys with long hair and a passion for theatre.'

'Oh, me too. And living with strangers.'

And on they went. Darkness fell softly and quietly as they talked. Blake messaged Sadie to say that she was sleeping at her friend Poppy's house, and Poppy's mum messaged to confirm it.

'People are kind,' Sadie told Rob. 'I'm trying not to be as overprotective as I was, but I think they know how much I'm bound to worry about her.' The details of Maddy's death happening so near to Sadie and Blake at the Masquerade Ball had been spilled everywhere, and Sadie had expected people to avoid her and Blake, as though their trauma might be contagious. In fact, she'd found the opposite: sympathy and care.

She didn't deserve it. But Blake did.

'That reminds me. I saw Gregory the other day. He'd been to parents' evening with Eliot.'

All of those names: Maddy, Pearl, Gregory, Eliot had made Rob go pale and tense for a while after Sadie's confession. It had felt strange to utter them at first, to roll them out into the real world instead of keeping them in a locked box inside herself. Now, Rob nodded. 'How's he doing?'

'He's okay. He's been at the school quite a bit working with the pastoral team, actually. Eliot's struggling.' Eliot had started at Kings Hill High in September, only a couple of months after Maddy's death and Sadie saw him in the corridor sometimes, hunched shoulders, face down, shocked and pale, as though he'd just been slapped. Sometimes, she spoke to him. He was one of the youngest boys in the school, only just eleven, and although he was tall, he seemed too young and vulnerable to be there. Sadie had also started a Lego club at the school and encouraged him to join it. He'd met a couple of other boys there. 'Gregory seems to be spending a lot of time with him. I don't think he did before. I think Candice and Aiden are there for him too, although I'm not sure how I feel about that. Aiden tried to scare Maddy. He was involved.' The effects of what had happened were still reaching out, making everything tremble and ripple.

'I sometimes think about Eliot. That feeling of when he found out Maddy was gone.'

'I know that there's a thread…' Sadie paused for a moment and then pushed on. 'There's a thread between what I did with Maddy, and what I kept secret, and that night on the cliff. And the fact that Eliot is now motherless.' Her words wobbled slightly at the end. Although Pearl had moved away and the feeling of being watched had gone, the cold hand of guilt was always, always on Sadie's shoulder. 'I am looking out for Eliot at school. I know it's not much.'

Rob sighed. 'You're doing okay, Sadie. It's just going to take time for everyone to be all right again.'

They sat without speaking for a few minutes, listening to the summer rain beat against the kitchen windows. Sadie stood from her seat at the kitchen table and flicked on the lamp so that the room was filled with soft, golden light.

'I should probably get back to the flat.' Rob stretched.

'It's throwing it down. And pretty late.'

Rob looked at her. 'I could stay. In the spare room.'

Sadie didn't answer straight away. She stood up and picked up a cloth, wiped a crumb from the worktop and then a smear from the sink. Sadie and Rob hadn't stayed in the same house since the night of the Masquerade Ball. Rob had stayed at a colleague's the night after, and then he'd rented his own flat which he still lived in now. She knew that Rob staying for one night didn't mean all was forgiven and they could snap back to where they'd been before all of this. She knew Rob so well: his careful, sure-footed steps towards where he wanted to be, his pauses when he decided he needed to mull something over before carrying on. It would be a slow, difficult process getting back an inch of what they used to have. The thought of laying down the very first blocks and Rob being here all night, in the room next to hers made Sadie wanted to rear and bolt, and pull him closer to her all at once.

Love and fear felt like the same thing sometimes: twins that were impossible to tell apart.

Rob stood up. 'I'll be okay. I'm tough.'

'The rain sounds heavy.' Sadie looked at Rob as she spoke, straight in the eye. She saw her life and herself: all of it, the good and the bad, the past and a possible future shining way in the distance. She felt herself place down an invisible, tentative block. 'Stay.'

FORTY-FIVE

Pearl

Ten years before the Masquerade Ball

'You have to want me!'

'I don't. I never have. You have to stop this, Pearl.'

The rain poured around us and the trees swayed and the world kept turning. But it felt like I wasn't part of it anymore.

Gregory's words scored my heart like knives on meat. It wasn't true. I knew it wasn't.

'But—'

Gregory held up his hand as though he was stopping traffic. 'No. That's it. I was your teacher. Nothing else. You're young and you'll find a new crush soon. Forget this one, please.'

I remembered that first day in Gregory's office. He'd used a gold cafetiere in the corner and made a cup of coffee. I'd asked for one too and he'd laughed and said of course, and then I'd had to force it down: horribly strong and bitter, like liquid earth. We'd talked through my essay on Iago and I hadn't listened to a word Gregory had said because I'd been watching his lips move and his eyes and the way his caramel-coloured hands fluttered like birds as he talked.

But he didn't want me. He wanted his perfect wife Maddy, who was mature and curvy and had dark hair as shiny as glass.

I gulped down sobs and rain as I ran from Gregory, from the awful ball that I only went to because my mother had forced me to. I must have known on some level that I didn't want to be in competition with Maddy. I must have known he'd never fall for me and leave his other life behind.

'Pearl! Come back!'

Why? So he could call my parents? So my dad could look crestfallen at my weird behaviour for the millionth time and my mother could make a comment that would make my insides crumble?

No. I ran and ran, away from them all, my heart breaking.

Gregory caught up to me and reached out, but I pulled away and my dress ripped.

'Pearl, I have a duty of care. I cannot leave you out here.'

'I'll lie,' I told him, and he shook his head as though I was beyond help. I probably was. 'If you tell anyone about any of this, I'll tell them that you attacked me.'

Gregory's expression darkened. He turned and left, and I stood by the side of the road, the rain hammering down on me.

I didn't know how long I'd been there when the car appeared. It could have been minutes or hours: I felt like I had been drained of all energy, and could move nowhere and do nothing. I squinted through the soaked evening at the headlights. I imagined someone stopping and grabbing me, bundling me into the boot, off to a life where I was locked away. It would serve Gregory right if something did happen to me out in the storm. Maybe if it did, then he'd see me in a different way. Maybe he'd feel like he should have helped me and taken care of me.

I stood, drenched, as the sound of the car's engine became louder and the headlights made crooked shadows on the road. Before I'd even thought about it, I was moving towards it, the rain stinging my eyes, my legs unsteady beneath me. I took huge, gulping breaths of air and pushed myself forwards. The air smelled dark and green, as though nature's deepest secrets were being pulled out by the rain.

The headlights were blinding when I reached the car but I could just about make out Maddy and Sadie in the front. It was perfect. Better than I'd even imagined. I pictured myself crumpled like a broken doll, needing to be loved and nursed back to life. Sadie and Maddy repentant, willing to do anything to help me. The roar of the car was louder than I'd expected now that it was so close to me, the front of it bigger than I'd thought it would be, coming at me fast and loud and too quickly for me to change my mind.

I closed my eyes and launched myself forwards in front of the car, waiting for the pain, and the ending, and the new beginning.

Acknowledgments

My thanks must start with any reader who has picked up this book. I still can't believe that you exist.

None of this – readers or books – would be possible without Charlotte Ledger. Thank you for being so brilliant at helping me to shape my characters and their worlds. Thank you for always being fun, for supporting me endlessly and for giving me opportunities to say things like, 'I'm going to London to see my editor.' I'll be forever grateful to you.

Thank you to Sofia and Kara, and everyone else at One More Chapter whose efficiency and patience has been involved in turning my ideas and my need to write into an actual book. I appreciate you all so much.

I get excited about writing because it gives me the chance to justifiably overthink things; to try to capture feelings and moments, and to make sense of life. I get just as excited about talking for the same reasons. Thank you to everyone who shares such amazing talks with me: over video call, over the phone, over wine in Boca and Arcane, over coffee, over barbeques and pub lunches and over messages.

Thank you to my amazing family for everything you do to help me spin all the plates I've chosen, and for making life so much happier as I do it. The characters in this book sometimes wish for different family members who are more fun, more caring, or less critical. I am eternally thankful that this was pure imagining.

Dean, Jessica and Isobel: this book is partly about the dangers of trying to be perfect, so I should perhaps avoid that word. But to me, you all are. Thank you.

A gripping domestic thriller set in the Cotswolds and perfect for fans of *Big Little Lies*!

RESOLUTIONS ARE MADE

MARRIAGES ARE BROKEN

It started with the party…
Frankie, Verity and Alice live in the idyllic Cotswolds community of White Fir Lake, but behind closed doors everyone has a secret they're desperately trying to keep…

And ended with a bang!
Now, as midnight on New Year's Eve approaches, the three women will face the consequences of a long-ago holiday, one which changed their lives forever … and threatens to shatter their perfect worlds into perfect pieces.

AVAILABLE NOW IN PAPERBACK AND EBOOK

The author and One More Chapter would like to thank everyone who contributed to the publication of this story...

Analytics
Imogen Wolstencroft

Audio
Fionnuala Barrett
Ciara Briggs

Contracts
Laura Amos
Inigo Vyvyan

Design
Lucy Bennett
Fiona Greenway
Liane Payne
Dean Russell

Digital Sales
Laura Daley
Lydia Grainge
Hannah Lismore

eCommerce
Laura Carpenter
Madeline ODonovan
Charlotte Stevens
Christina Storey
Jo Surman
Rachel Ward

Editorial
Rosie Best
Kara Daniel
Paris Ferguson
Charlotte Ledger
Federica Leonardis
Jennie Rothwell
Sofia Salazar Studer
Helen Williams

Harper360
Emily Gerbner
Ariana Juarez
Jean Marie Kelly
emma sullivan
Sophia Wilhelm

International Sales
Peter Borcsok
Ruth Burrow
Bethan Moore
Colleen Simpson

Inventory
Sarah Callaghan
Kirsty Norman

Marketing & Publicity
Chloe Cummings
Grace Edwards
Katie Sadler

Operations
Melissa Okusanya
Hannah Stamp

Production
Denis Manson
Simon Moore
Francesca Tuzzeo

Rights
Ashton Mucha
Alisah Saghir
Zoe Shine
Aisling Smyth
Lucy Vanderbilt

Trade Marketing
Ben Hurd
Eleanor Slater

The HarperCollins Distribution Team

The HarperCollins Finance & Royalties Team

The HarperCollins Legal Team

The HarperCollins Technology Team

UK Sales
Isabel Coburn
Jay Cochrane
Sabina Lewis
Holly Martin
Harriet Williams
Leah Woods

And every other essential link in the chain from delivery drivers to booksellers to librarians and beyond!

One More Chapter is an
award-winning global
division of HarperCollins.

Subscribe to our newsletter to get our latest eBook deals and stay up to date with all our new releases!

signup.harpercollins.co.uk/
join/signup-omc

Meet the team at
www.onemorechapter.com

Follow us!

@onemorechapterhc

Do you write unputdownable fiction?
We love to hear from new voices.
Find out how to submit your novel at
www.onemorechapter.com/submissions